my
daughter's
secret

NICOLE TROPE

my daughter's secret

bookouture

Published by Bookouture in 2019

An imprint of StoryFire Ltd.

Carmelite House
50 Victoria Embankment
London EC4Y 0DZ

www.bookouture.com

Copyright © Nicole Trope, 2019

Nicole Trope has asserted her right to be identified as the author of this work.

All rights reserved. No part of this publication may be reproduced, stored in any retrieval system, or transmitted, in any form or by any means, electronic, mechanical, photocopying, recording or otherwise, without the prior written permission of the publishers.

ISBN: 978-1-78681-784-6
eBook ISBN: 978-1-78681-783-9

This book is a work of fiction. Names, characters, businesses, organizations, places and events other than those clearly in the public domain, are either the product of the author's imagination or are used fictitiously. Any resemblance to actual persons, living or dead, events or locales is entirely coincidental.

For D.M.I and J

CHAPTER ONE

Callie stumbles over the uneven pavement. She almost goes down but is rescued by Mia who laughs hysterically as she holds her friend up. 'We are so drunk,' she announces to the silent neighbourhood.

'Shush,' whispers Callie, holding her finger to her lips as she steadies herself against Mia.

'Who's going to hear us?' laughs Mia.

'The ghosts,' says Callie flailing her arms around. 'Whoo, whoo, Mia, the ghosts of drunks past are coming to get you.'

Mia runs her finger across her lips and smiles. Both girls stand still for a moment, each swaying a little. 'I love Hallowe'en parties,' says Mia.

'Me too, and you look so cute.'

Mia looks down at her tight black leggings and matching black top. 'I had wings,' she says. She tips to the side and then plants her feet firmly apart to stop herself from falling. She looks at Callie. 'And you had cat ears and a tail. Where've they gone?'

'Hmm,' answers Callie. 'We lost them. Never mind. Let's just get back to my place so we can sleep or throw up or something. Thank God my parents are away. Dad hates it when I come home pissed.' She shivers in the early morning air. It's the end of October and the Australian summer is only a month away, but the nights are still chilly.

'You're twenty years old, Callie, your dad has no right to… oh shit, I feel so sick, but I also want a burger. Let's go and get a burger.'

'No, Mia, we have to go home. Why do you always make the Uber drop us so far away from where we need to be?'

'My mum told me to do that. In case he's a rapist or something.'

'Your mum thinks everyone is a criminal and I thought you hated her because she's neurotic and crazy.'

'I don't… I don't hate her, she's my mum and sometimes I think…' Mia gazes up into the night sky.

'You think?' prompts Callie.

'I think she could be right. I love my mum so much. I love my mum and my dad and I love you too, Cals. Whoa.' Mia stops and peers hazily over the hedge next to them. 'People in your street really take Hallowe'en seriously. Nearly every house is decorated.'

'Yeah, there are a lot of little kids. Now walk, Mia, keep walking.'

Mia listens to the sound of her heels on the pavement. If she keeps her mouth closed and takes very small steps she'll get to Callie's house without throwing up, she thinks. She focuses on each house they pass, studying grotesque smiles on pumpkins and spotting skeletons hanging from trees and lounging in gardens. Fake spider webs have turned all the post boxes white, and plastic bats dangle from branches. A witch on a broom cackles and moves her head from side to side, flashing her red eyes, startling Mia. She jumps to the side and then looks at the house across the road, where Death sits on a swing.

'Wow, look at that. That wasn't here when we left,' says Callie.

Mia looks over to where Callie is pointing. A life-size doll swings from a covered front porch. There isn't a hint of a breeze but the dummy sways anyway, making the chain around its neck squeak eerily in the silent suburban street.

'Isn't that where Julia lives?'

'Yeah, but she's gone to Melbourne for uni. I haven't seen her for ages.'

'What's she studying?'

'I told you, remember – journalism. Everyone thought she was going to be an actress but then... boom... just like that, she changed her mind.'

'We're supposed to change our minds. My mum says now is the time to experiment.'

'She means with careers, Mia, not how much alcohol you can consume in one night.' Both girls erupt into hysterical laughter, struggling to stay standing. When they finally stop giggling Mia looks at the dummy hanging from the porch of the large house in front of them. The house rises up three storeys, looming over the flat green lawn that leads to the pavement. The white painted shutters on the windows are all closed and Mia thinks it looks like the house has shut its eyes for the night. The wide timber porch is decorated with potted plants and a swing, filled with artfully arranged pillows. A carved timber front door completes the magazine-perfect façade. It's the biggest house in the street.

'Why've they only got a dummy? Why don't they have... like... some pumpkins?'

'I don't know. I didn't think Julia's mum was into Hallowe'en. She's too uptight.'

'Weird that she doesn't have any other decorations. Julia has a little brother, right?'

'Two. But they're not exactly little. They're sixteen and eighteen.'

'Is the eighteen-year-old hot?'

'Mia, you're twenty. But yeah... he is sooo hot, really built, with this gorgeous smile. He's still in school so... maybe in a few years.'

'He's mine,' Mia says, with a giggle.

'You haven't even seen him!' Callie play-swats her friend on the arm. 'You can't call dibs on a boy you haven't seen!'

'Fine, whatever. But why do you reckon she has something up if her kids are big? My mum said that when my sister turned twelve she was "done with Hallowe'en".'

'Maybe she wants to be part of the neighbourhood or something? Cos if you don't have something on your house then none of the kids knock on your door. They might like the kids knocking on their door?' She pauses, considering. 'Damn, now *I* feel like a burger. Let's go and get a burger. Maybe we can order from Uber Eats.'

'Let's go and touch it,' says Mia, nausea forgotten.

'Touch what?'

'The dummy. It's so big. I want to touch it. Maybe it's a boy dummy and we could…' she says with a smirk.

'Just gross, Mia! Do not even say it. Anyway, it's got long hair. It's a girl… maybe it's a witch.'

'I just want to touch it, Cals. I won't do anything to it, I promise.'

'What for? Ten more steps and we'll be home. I can make popcorn and we can watch scary movies.'

'I'll make it move and freak everyone in the house out. Maybe the cute eighteen-year-old will be home and he'll come out to see what's happening and then… true love.' Mia flings her arms apart and turns a slow circle.

'He's probably out at a party. Why do you want to touch that thing? It's creepy.'

'Just because, Callie. Come on.'

Callie sighs. If Mia gets an idea in her head, she knows nothing will stop her. Her friend crashes through the bushes at the front of the house and climbs onto the wooden railing surrounding the porch.

'Why can't you just go up the stairs?' whispers Callie.

'More fun this way,' replies Mia, laughing.

Callie watches her friend's ungainly climb over the railing, thinking that with her short dark hair and pointy chin she looks like a naughty pixie. She takes the stairs, reaching the dummy before Mia. She reaches out a tentative hand and touches the jeaned leg. It's an odd costume for a Hallowe'en dummy. It has long blonde hair and is dressed in jeans and a red jumper. Not a skeleton in sight.

Callie feels her head clear a little. She takes a deep breath and squeezes the leg. It feels solid, heavy. She walks around the front of it and looks up at the dummy's face, squinting in the pale light from the street. Dragging her phone out of her pocket, she turns on the torch, shining it up at the dummy's face just as Mia comes to stand next to her.

In the light the face is clear. The eyes bulge, the lips are blue and swollen.

There is a beat of silence, a moment in time when all sound is drowned out.

Callie makes a strange noise, an animal howl that pierces the night.

Mia screams. Her whole body trembling, she screams and screams and screams.

*

My sweetest, darling Julia,

I haven't been able to get you out of my mind. Every time I close my eyes I see you standing before me. I reach out and trace the curve of your soft lips and touch the silky gold of your hair. I breathe in your smell which reminds me of a fresh spring morning.

Look at what you've done to me, Julia. I have never written a love letter before. I always wondered what kind of a person writes such a letter – how foolish and over the top they must be. But now I know that love letters are written by those who love more than spoken words can explain. I love like that now.

Look what has become of me because of you. Only you. What a wonderful secret I hold now. The secret of you. The secret of us.

Love x

CHAPTER TWO

I've never met a police detective before but Detective Sergeant Amanda Winslow seems the perfect person for such a job. She called an hour ago and asked if she could come over to discuss Julia. I'm sure she chose her words carefully, not wanting to use the past tense when only two days ago my daughter was still alive. I wanted to say, 'There's nothing to discuss any more.' But I held my tongue and said, 'Yes, of course,' to her request.

Julia is in the past now. It's a horrifyingly surreal thought. I am one of those people now, one of those mothers. You read about them. You fear their experiences and yet you never really believe you will become them. I am one of those and I am not sure I know how to be that person, how to survive being that person.

Two days ago Julia was happy. Two days ago Julia was thriving at university. Today Julia is gone and everything is called into question.

It was not her weekend to come up for a visit. I expected her to come home on the third weekend of every month. It was the deal we made when she moved to Melbourne to study. I made sure that she had a plane ticket ready, and Adrian or I picked her up at the airport. She had never driven back to Sydney before because of how long the journey took. If I'd known she was driving home I would have known something was terribly wrong, but I had no idea. No idea she was coming and no idea of what she had planned.

She hung herself while we slept, unaware of her anguish, unaware of her despair. She hung herself. When we took her down, hands trembling, and removed the chain, there was a necklace of link marks across her throat. Across her crushed windpipe. The image haunts me, will haunt me forever, I know, forcing out all the other moments of Julia's life I carry around with me. I don't want to remember her like that but no matter how hard I try the picture refuses to be erased.

'I am so sorry for your loss,' Detective Winslow says as she stands on the doorstep, her clear green eyes clouded with sympathy. She folds my hand in her own and nods at Adrian, standing behind me, as she talks. It seems impolite to pull away. The sharp, citrus smell of her perfume fills the air and I bite down on my lip so I don't wrinkle my nose.

'How old are you?' I blurt out.

'I'm thirty-two.' She smiles. 'I know I seem young, but I've been a detective for a year now.'

'Would you like some tea?' Adrian asks and I stand back, allowing the detective into my home. Adrian has decided that his current role is that of 'tea maker'. Anyone who comes into the house is instantly offered a cup of tea as though the warm beverage will turn our conversations away from Julia's death and on to more pleasant topics. Today he has already made me three cups.

When Julia was three years old she used to invite me to tea parties in her room. I had to bring a plate of biscuits and wear a big hat. We would greet each other with formal, 'good afternoons,' and then giggle as we drank tiny cups of chocolate milk.

'Thanks, but I'm fine. Shall we sit down? I thought we could go through a few things.'

'We told the constables everything already,' says Adrian as he sits down, fidgeting with his mobile phone, clicking the button on the side, turning the screen on and off. He needs something to do with his hands.

Detective Winslow hitches up her slacks, as a man might, and sits down with her legs apart. She has broad shoulders and big hands. I imagine her squatting under a bar of heavy weights. I am comforted by her physicality. She is young but she looks strong and I can see victims of crime taking solace from her presence. Not that she can do much to help me.

'I understand and I do know how hard it is to keep repeating the story, but the quicker we have all the pieces in place the quicker we can release… her, and you can have a funeral.'

'Why do you have to keep her anyway?' huffs Adrian. I grab the phone out of his hand and slam it down onto the coffee table. Adrian doesn't say anything. Detective Winslow looks at her shoes for a moment to grant us some privacy. I take a deep breath and smile gently by way of apology for my behaviour. Adrian sits on his hands.

'I'm sorry, but suicide is a reportable death and that means that there will have to be an autopsy and that the coroner will have to decide whether or not there needs to be an inquest.'

'Why would there need to be an inquest?' asks Adrian.

'If we find anything we can't explain, then it will need to be investigated.'

'Such bullshit,' says Adrian.

'And how long will that take?' I ask.

'I'm hoping no longer than a few weeks,' says the detective. She nods her head, agreeing with herself. Her skin is smooth and perfect. I imagine she is a fan of clean eating and alcohol-free weekends. 'Basically I'm here to determine the manner and cause of Julia's death, as well as the circumstances surrounding it. We have a few questions so we're just looking into things a bit more thoroughly.'

'What questions could you have? You know what happened,' says Adrian.

'Some of it, yes, but I'm sure if there is a reason for what happened you'll want to know it,' says the detective, looking at me.

'I do,' I agree. *Oh I do, I do, I do.*

'Of course... we really want to... to understand what happened,' says Adrian.

'I just wanted to check again that you've definitely found no note of any sort from Julia, explaining her choice.'

Adrian looks at the wall behind the detective as I shake my head. 'No, nothing.' I feel the agony of that truth ripple through my body. Julia, who has always been able to express herself so clearly, didn't know how to explain why she did what she did. I feel cheated of her final words, of her final thoughts. How much pain must she have been in? How confused and unhappy would she have been? What went through her head just before... just before.

'She left us nothing,' I repeat.

Detective Winslow clears her throat, driving the interview on. 'I've already spoken with Callie and Mia, and I have a colleague in Melbourne who will be interviewing people at the university, but I wanted to check with you if there was anything going on in Julia's life that could have made her unhappy. A broken romance, perhaps?'

'She didn't have a boyfriend,' says Adrian.

'How would we have known, Adrian?' I shoot back. I direct my disdain towards him but really it's for myself. I should have known. This is my failure. I'm her mother, and a good mother would have known.

Adrian shakes his head. 'Claire, she would have told us – she always told us stuff like that.'

'There was obviously a lot she wasn't telling us,' I say.

'Both Callie and Mia agree that she didn't have a boyfriend, so that may be the truth.'

'The truth,' I scoff.

I don't mean to be rude. I'm sure I don't mean to be rude.

'Do you want to take me through what happened again?' she asks me.

'I... I just can't.' I feel myself wilt against the sofa. I close my eyes.

'We heard screaming,' says Adrian. 'That Callie girl was screaming and we came outside to check what was going on.'

'You didn't want to check it out,' I say to him, keeping my eyes closed, hearing once again the ear-piercing, blood-curdling screams. 'And it was Mia screaming, not Callie. Callie was making a weird noise. She sounded like a cat, like a cat who was afraid of something.' I open my eyes. Both Adrian and the detective are staring at me.

'I thought it was just kids coming back from a party,' he says. 'I told you that.'

'Just kids,' I repeat. I can't seem to think straight.

'I know how hard this is and I am so sorry for your loss.' The detective shifts a little in her seat. 'If you need anything at all just let me know. Someone will be in contact with you today to discuss counselling and anything else you may need help with.'

'I don't want to talk to anyone,' I say.

'I understand, but at a difficult time like this it can help to speak to someone who knows exactly how this process works.'

'Difficult, yes,' I agree, noting that she keeps using the word. 'No thank you on the counselling,' I say, as I roll the word around in my head. *Diff-i-cult. Diffi-cult. D-ifficult.* 'I would prefer…' I realise that I don't know what I would prefer so my sentence trails off and I stand up to go to the kitchen and make myself another cup of tea since Adrian is not making any. I know as I fill the kettle that it will join all the others growing cold around the house.

'She's not coping very well,' I hear Adrian tell the detective as I refill the kettle.

'I don't imagine it would be possible to cope well with something like this,' she replies.

'I can't seem to say the right thing.'

'There is no right thing to say, Mr Brusso. I'm sorry to have to ask, but can you take me through that night again, please?'

I push the button to start the kettle, letting the whooshing noise drown out Adrian's words. I stand in the kitchen, studying the little rainbows the sun is creating on the counter top as it beams through the fairy wind-chimes hanging just outside the window. Julia begged me for the chimes when she was four and would rush to the kitchen every morning to watch the two dancing fairies move in the breeze. This morning, they tinkled and whirled in the wind, making me shudder at their delicate sound and the memory of Julia dancing along with them. I asked Adrian to take them down but he refused. 'You don't want that, Claire. One day you'll be able to look at them and remember her with joy. Don't take them away now.' He was right, of course. As I look at them now, I realise it would have chipped off another piece from my already broken heart to see an empty space where the fairies used to hang.

'They're waving at me, Mum! They like my dancing.'

Adrian is worried that he can't say the right thing to me. I think about what the right thing to say would be, what I want to hear from Adrian, or my mother, or my sister Emily, or Detective Winslow. I try to imagine what words would give me some comfort and strangely enough I believe I want to hear the detective say, 'This isn't suicide. This is a murder and we will find who did this,' like the character of a hardened cop would on television. I yearn for there to be some conspiracy that I can untangle to find my daughter's killer. If I cannot have her back, if she cannot be saved, then someone must pay for what has happened.

The kettle clicks off. I pour the hot water into a mug and watch the water darken.

But she isn't going to say any of that. I know she isn't. There is no conspiracy. No murder. No assailant who grabbed my daughter in the dark of Hallowe'en night and hung her from the porch.

The only person who can pay for this then, is me.

'You cannot blame yourself for this,' says my mother and my sister and my husband and the endless articles I have read on the internet. I cannot blame myself for this. I looked at myself in the bathroom mirror this morning, stared into my own eyes and thought, *I cannot blame myself for this.* And then, hands shaking, I took my favourite maroon-coloured lipstick out of the bathroom cabinet and scrawled, 'MY FAULT,' on the mirror. The lipstick broke on the last letter, crumbled and squashed against the glass. I tapped my reflection, watching tears spill and my nose run.

When I went back into the bathroom an hour later the mirror was clean, as though erasing the words could change what I'm thinking, could undo the terrible choice Julia made.

'I tried CPR,' I hear Adrian say. 'I kept doing it until the paramedics came. I just kept pushing down on her chest and Claire was breathing into her mouth. I was afraid I was going to hurt her because I was pushing so hard.' I stick my fingers in my ears. I don't want to hear it again. I don't want to relive it. I don't want to discuss it and I don't want to deal with it. I want to stay in the kitchen, staring out of the window at the garden, where the camellias are in bloom with pure white flowers. I want to have nothing more to do today than plan dinner for Adrian and the boys. I want to forget that my daughter is dead and the tragic way that she died.

'I feel like a boring middle-aged woman in a boring middle-of-the-road job. Nothing different ever happens. I wish my life had at least a modicum of excitement,' I whined to Adrian last week.

'Huh, careful what you wish for.' Adrian had smiled. 'Boring is good.'

Careful what you wish for.

'Mrs Brusso,' the detective calls. I reluctantly return to the living room.

'One thing the doctor noticed was the bump on the back of Julia's head,' she says, when I have returned to my seat on the couch – minus the cup of tea, I realise. I had no intention of drinking it, anyway.

'A bump,' I repeat, turning the word over in my mind. *A bump.*

'It was on the back of her head, around here,' she says, touching her head at the back. 'Do you know how it happened?' I note the way she straightens herself in the chair. This then is what she has really come to discuss. A bump. Could it be...? Would it mean...? Is this the question she really came here to ask? I crack my knuckles in the silence.

'A bump?' I repeat when I run out of fingers to push and twist. 'I... I don't know. Adrian, do you know?'

Adrian looks up at the ceiling and then he closes his eyes. He's picturing it and I see him flinch at the memory. There are new lines on his face today. Overnight he has begun to look his age.

'I think maybe it happened when we got her down.'

'Oh, yes... that must be it.' I cover my mouth with my hand, lean forward and grab a tissue from the box on the coffee table.

'Can you tell me what happened when you got her down?' the detective asks gently.

'I pulled the chain,' Adrian replies after a moment. 'I was trying to lift her to get her neck out of the... to get it out and while I was doing that I was pulling the chain as well. It was attached to the beam.'

'Why was it attached to a beam?'

'I was... I had put it up. I was going to hang a punching bag.'

'A punching bag,' repeats the detective. She sits forward, encouraging Adrian to keep talking by nodding along to his words.

'It was for fitness, you know? I put it up about two weeks ago and I was going to hang the bag up but then I kind of... I guess I forgot.'

'You put it up almost a month ago,' I say.

Adrian grabs my hand. 'Okay, a month ago. I'm sorry, Claire, I've said I'm sorry about that. I've said it a hundred times. I should have hung up the bag.'

I pull my hand away from him and fold my arms. 'But you don't finish the things you start at home because someone else will always do it for you.'

'Claire.' He sighs.

'He was going to train every day using the bag,' I tell the detective, rolling my eyes.

In the small hospital room, decorated with a fake leather couch and a wilted green plant, where they take you to tell you your child is dead, he confessed his oversight. Head bowed, he whispered his mistake, his lapse, his small slip-up.

'I meant to hang it up, I just forgot.'

'You just forgot?' I studied the grey carpet, pushing my foot over a dark stain, thinking about another family who were brought in here for their own devastating news and imagining someone – a mother or a father – dropping their coffee in shock and despair. 'You just forgot,' I stated, because Adrian had subsided into silence.

'Yes, Claire, I forgot. I'm sorry but I don't think… it wasn't my fault. She would have… look, I can't take it back. It is what it is, and I'm sorry.'

'Don't use that stupid phrase on me, Adrian,' I hissed, locking eyes with him as we waited for the doctor to arrive. I had nagged him about hanging the bag the first week he put the bolt and its thick metal chain up. I wanted him to start taking his health seriously so I reminded him to do it once or twice or even three times but then I simply stopped seeing the bolt screwed into the wooden beam on the front porch, accessorised with its innocuous-looking chain. I stopped seeing it and in that perfectly square room I wondered what else I had stopped seeing in my life and in my daughter's life.

If the chain hadn't been there she might have made a different choice. If the chain hadn't been there, if I hadn't taken a sleeping pill and had heard her arrive, if I had called her the day before to check on her, if I had never let her go to Melbourne. *If, if, if.*

Adrian picks his phone up again and looks at the black screen. 'It was for the boys as well.'

'The boys go to the gym.'

Adrian shakes his head sadly. I wish I could stop lashing out at him but I seem unable to control myself.

'Okay, I understand about the bag,' says Detective Winslow, and I can hear a shade of frustration in her voice. 'Let's just concentrate on what happened that night. So, you'd attached the chain to the beam and then Julia… used it, but how did she get the bump on her head?'

'Oh, yes, sorry, sorry,' says Adrian. 'I was kind of holding her with one arm and pulling at the chain with the other and the bolt gave way. I guess the weight had loosened the attachment and then I kept pulling and she kind of dropped and she was too heavy to hold so she fell backwards and hit her… She fell back onto the porch and that must have been when she hit her head.'

I hold my tissue to my eyes, hearing the heavy dull thud of her head hitting the timber porch.

'Okay, I see,' says the detective. She nods as she types Adrian's explanation into her phone.

'Why are you asking about that?' asks Adrian. He slides his phone into his pocket.

'Oh, it may be nothing. There was quite a lot of dried blood on the wound. Although head wounds can bleed after death a little, it is unusual for there to be so much blood. We'll know more when we find out how long it was that she died before you took her down.'

'How will you find that out?' asks Adrian.

'That's what the autopsy is for, Mr Brusso.'

Adrian nods and I nod along with him. Two days ago I'd only heard the word 'autopsy' on television, and 'suicide' was a terrible thing that had happened to the friend of a friend of a friend. I had never met a detective before either. *Careful what you wish for.*

'Mrs Brusso?'

'Claire, the detective is talking to you.'

'What? Oh, sorry. I can't seem to…'

'It's okay, I completely understand. Your husband says there was nothing in her pockets, is that correct?'

'I… I didn't check but Adrian checked – you checked, didn't you?' Adrian nods.

'Her phone was in the car… I don't know why she would have left it in the car as she always had it on her… always.'

Detective Winslow taps some more notes into her phone.

'They gave her clothes back to me… afterwards, at the hospital,' I say. 'They, they cut them off her.' My voice catches in my throat and I bite down on my lip. I don't know what I'm going to do with her sliced-up clothing. I have put her watch and her earrings in the musical ballerina jewellery box she's had since she was five, but I don't know what I'm going to do with her clothes. When I got them I put my nose to the red jumper she'd been wearing and inhaled her smell and for a moment she was right there. But behind the fresh smell of her deodorant I could smell something else… I could smell sweat but not the ordinary smell of sweat. As I sit in front of Detective Winslow thinking about her clothes I realise that what I had noticed was the smell of *fear*, and I push my palms hard against my eyes, preventing any more tears. She was terrified of what she was about to do and instead of coming to me she swallowed her fear and ended her life.

I take my hands away from my eyes to see Detective Winslow staring at me. 'I don't have anything more to discuss right now. Is there anything else you wanted to talk about?' she asks.

I take a deep breath, composing myself. I need to concentrate.

'Have you seen her Facebook page?' I ask. 'I called the number Constable Wentworth gave me after I read some of the stuff on there. He said that the police would want to see her social media.'

Julia's Facebook page has 'blown up' as they say. The comments pour in minute by minute.

Forever in my heart. Love x was the first comment I read. The profile picture was of a pink rosebud. I clicked on it immediately but couldn't find out anything from the page. There was nothing on it but the profile picture. It was like it had been made specifically to post the single comment on Julia's page. It could have been anyone.

The next comment was jarring, twisting my stomach and forcing hot fury through my body.

Another poor little princess who didn't like the way her life was turning out. Who cares? The profile picture was a devil sipping a glass of wine. Who were these people? *How dare you*, I raged silently. *How dare you.*

'Look at this,' I had said to Adrian.

'What an arsehole,' he had replied, barely glancing at it. 'It's nothing. Stop reading that crap.'

Julia's friends were outraged by the post. I found some slight comfort in their anger, grateful to them for speaking up for Julia.

How dare you, you fucking troll?!!!!!!

Julia was my friend and I can't believe that anyone would post something so revolting. I really hope you find out one day what it feels like to be lost, desperate and sad, with nowhere else to turn.

People on here are sick. I hope anyone reading this knows that suicide is never the answer. If you are feeling depressed, you need to tell someone who can help you. Talk to your parents or friends. Every life is precious. Lifeline: 13 11 14

Fuck you all you sanctimonious fucks. I bet none of you did anything to help Julia when she was alive. Everyone is so ready to say how sorry they are after it happens but no one really wants to help. I should know. I spend half my life reaching out to people only to be disappointed.

Julia we will miss you forever. You were the most amazing girl. Heaven has a new angel.

I can't believe you're gone and we'll never get coffee together before class. Miss you every day, babe.

I can't believe we are even talking about this. There are children in Syria dying every day and no one is talking about that. It's just because she was some pretty, blonde, white girl that anyone gives a fuck.

Her life had no impact on the world. She was just another spoiled brat who got pissed off that her life didn't turn out the way she wanted it to. Look outside yourselves people. See the world as it really is.

Only those who have posted loving or kind comments use their personal Facebook pages; the other messages come from strange profiles, set up by cowards who want to harangue and harass.

'I have,' says Detective Winslow, dragging my thoughts away from the stream of messages. 'And thank you for allowing us to use your account to access it. It makes the whole process a lot faster. Constable Wentworth was right. In cases like these we like to see any social media posts that may give us a clue as to why someone has made a decision like this.'

'Did you read the… I don't even know what to call them… the nasty one and the one that just said "Forever in my heart"?'

'I did. It's not unusual for people to use fake profiles to post on Facebook pages. I am getting our tech gurus to try and trace the commenters we can't identify, but they can't really dedicate too much time to it. It's perhaps better to try and ignore the ugly comments.'

'Ridiculous,' mutters Adrian. 'People are ridiculous.'

'They can be,' agrees the detective. 'I'll let you know if we find anything out at the autopsy.' She stands and smooths the front of her slacks.

'What exactly are you looking for?' I ask.

'Standard stuff… drugs, alcohol.'

'Oh, Julia didn't do any of that.'

'It's standard procedure, Mrs Brusso.'

'We don't really know what Julia did or did not do,' Adrian says. 'Maybe it was drugs, at least that would... I don't know, explain it or something.'

'Adrian, Julia didn't do drugs. You know that. She thought that people who "messed up their brains didn't deserve to have brains".'

'She said that when she was a lot younger, Claire. I'm sure you're right and that she wasn't doing anything but if she was, don't you want to know?'

I shake my head. I don't want to know. I don't want to think about it at all. I know that she could have been doing anything with her time, anything at all. She was too young to be so far away from me. I shouldn't have accepted her excuses for not coming home as often as I wanted her to. For eighteen months I watched, helplessly, as she became a little more distant, a little more adult, a little more 'not Julia'.

It's inevitable, I told myself. *She has to grow up and take care of herself even if I'm still paying all the bills*, I reasoned. *She'll come back to me when she's ready, when she feels she's tested enough boundaries*, I comforted myself.

'You're trying to over-mother her. Stop asking her so many questions about her life,' Adrian said, when I confessed my fears.

'She's not your daughter, Adrian,' I tossed at him, watching him wince, knowing I was inflicting pain. He'd been in her life for nearly nine years. How many years makes you a father? A lifetime is not enough for some men.

She is not his child. She was not his child but he knew her better than Joel did. He looked after her better than Joel did.

My baby girl. My baby girl is gone. I cannot comprehend this pain. I cannot breathe through it. I cannot speak through it. I cannot be here with it.

'I'm sorry,' I say to Detective Winslow, standing up. 'I just... I can't talk about this any more. I need to rest.'

I don't wait for her to dismiss me. I walk out of the living room and go to Julia's room. It is the only place in the house I feel like I can breathe properly. The air still smells faintly of Julia's coconut shampoo and the jasmine candle she liked to burn as she studied.

There is a box of her things on top of a white painted chest of drawers. It is filled with the stuff that Adrian brought in from her car after the police asked us to check what she had brought back from Melbourne with her. At the top is BB, her first teddy bear. My mother gave it to her in the hospital on the day she was born and it sat on her bookshelf until I felt she was big enough to have it in her cot. It's about the size of a three-month-old child and I was worried she would suffocate. Once I gave it to her at a year old it rarely left her side. BB was one of her favourite soft toys until she was around ten, and even then she didn't want to throw him out. 'He was my first friend,' she told me. 'I'll love him forever.' She took him with her to Melbourne, which was a comforting thought. Despite her age, her maturity, BB remained the silent sentinel to her life.

Before she could speak full sentences she would hold BB out to me every night for a kiss after I had kissed her soft cheek. I obligingly kissed the bear goodnight for years. 'Goodnight, BB, give Julia sweet dreams,' I would say.

I lean down now and rest my lips on his head. 'Goodnight, BB,' I say, tears dropping onto his soft fur. 'Give Julia sweet dreams.'

I curl up on her white sleigh bed, clutching another old friend – a stuffed, pink dog. 'Noodle the Poodle,' she called it, after a favourite children's book. My father bought it for her on one of the many afternoons they spent together.

'You're spoiling her, Dad,' I told him, loving him for it.

'What else are grandfathers for?' he replied.

I squeeze Noodle tightly, thinking about all the other soft toys that she was unwilling to throw away. She wasn't quite finished with being a little girl. She had so much more growing up to do.

I want her back, I want her here. I want none of this to be true.

But it *is* true. She is gone and she is gone because she chose to go. But why? Why did she choose to go?

*

My sweetest, darling Julia,

I watched you walk away from me today and felt my heart break.

I wish we never had to part. I wish we could lie down to sleep together at night and open our eyes in the morning to only see each other. We are out of time, Julia. We cannot be together yet. I know your heart breaks to leave me as well. I know you hate the secrecy and the lies we have to tell. I wish it were different.

If I could I would change the world for you, Julia. I would change it all, for us.

Love x

CHAPTER THREE

I fall asleep on Julia's bed. When I wake an hour later, I stumble out of the room, groggy and dry mouthed. I can hear Adrian making calls in his office in the next room. The world does not stop for anything and there are still houses to be sold and deals to be made.

Smooth real-estate agent Adrian laughs at something someone says to him. The sound cuts through me. How on earth will I ever laugh at anything ever again?

'That's not who you're married to,' I whisper. 'It's just his public persona. He's grieving just as you are. You know he is.'

I wish that I had a public face I could plaster over my private grief. It would mean I could leave the house, something I'm not sure I will ever be able to do again.

The doorbell rings and I stop walking and stand stock-still, hoping that whoever it is will assume we're out, but it rings again, the shrill tones insistent. I open my mouth to call for Adrian so he can answer the door but I can hear him talking to his assistant, telling her how to handle a difficult client. I'm afraid to move and when it rings for a third time, I grow angry at my own childish behaviour and I march over to the door, flinging it open.

Liam stands on the doorstep, a single pink rosebud clutched in his hand which he thrusts towards me. 'I just heard and I'm so sorry, I am just so sorry.' His voice shakes as he speaks.

I stare at the pink rosebud for a moment, thinking of the Facebook post: 'Forever in my heart. Love x.'

Liam lives with his mother three houses away from us. He is the same age as Julia and has had a crush on her for as long as he's known her. When they were little they were great friends, spending hours together exploring their imaginations, playing pretend with a furious dedication to character. But as they got older Julia began to find Liam strange. He became very involved in gaming and was especially attached to a fantasy game, spending hours and hours on the internet and worrying his mother, Kayla, who had to work full-time after her divorce. At fifteen Liam became obsessed with Julia, sending her long, strange poems and referring to her as 'My Lady Julia'.

'He's driving me mad, Mum,' she told me. 'His poetry talks about how we're going to be married and be together forever and he uses such old-fashioned language that he doesn't even sound like a teenage boy. "My Lady Julia, together we will feast on love forever",' she quoted.

'He really likes you. I don't think I've ever had a man or a boy send me poetry.'

'Yeah, I get that, but he's getting to be a bit of a stalker, you know? He's always hovering around outside the house or waiting for me after I come out of every single class.'

I spoke to Kayla about it and she promised to speak to her son but the behaviour persisted.

'I'll go and have a word with him, if you want me to,' Adrian said to Julia.

'That would be great,' she replied, 'but don't upset him, I don't want his feelings to be hurt. I just need him to stop following me around.'

After Adrian went over to see him, Liam stopped following Julia.

'What did you say to him?' I asked.

'I just told him that I understand how hard it is to be a young man in love and that he is entitled to feel that way, but that he is making her unhappy and that I knew he wouldn't want to make someone he cared for so deeply unhappy.'

Kayla called to apologise for Liam again. 'I think Adrian got through to him. He was so lovely with him, so gentle and kind and Liam understood. He told me he's going to give Julia some space. You've lucked-out with Adrian, Claire… I wish I could be as lucky in my own life.'

Liam thrusts the rose towards me again and blushes. He has become a beautiful young man with silky black hair and deep blue eyes. I'm sure he has no trouble finding a girl to be with. He's studying game design, as we all knew he would.

I want to ask him about the Facebook post, to push him to confess it was him, but I can see his hand trembling and I remember how sweet he was as a little boy. I know how difficult this is for him.

I take the rose. 'Thank you, Liam.' He nods and steps back before turning around and practically running down the front path. *Poor kid*, I think. It was a sweet gesture.

I will put the rose in a small vase and put it in Julia's room.

I make my way to the kitchen, desperate for some water. I pass a picture of Julia on the living-room wall and stop to stare at it as I have done over and over again in the two days since it happened. She is two years old. Her blonde hair sits in perfect ringlets around her face. Her lips are blush pink and her eyes so wide and so blue I was stopped often in the street. 'What an extraordinarily beautiful child,' a woman once said to me in the shopping centre. 'The world will be her oyster.'

That beauty didn't disappear as she grew older. There was an awkward phase at around fifteen when her skin erupted and her nose seemed too big for her face but it was such a short-lived period that I don't even think we have any pictures of her at that stage. In a few months we found the right creams and her skin was, once again, flawless. She grew two inches and everything fell into place. She was too short to model and had little desire to do such a thing, anyway. Her beauty sat lightly on her, only occurring to her when she was dressing up to go out or when she needed to use it on stage. Otherwise she would shove her hair up in a clip to get it out of her face and slouch around in pyjama bottoms all day.

'Why are you staring at me like that?' she would spit at me at twelve and fifteen and eighteen.

'I'm not,' I would protest, but I was. How could I not? Every mother stares, marvelling at the beauty of their own creations.

'She looks so much like you,' Adrian has always said.

'Many years and one bad marriage ago,' I reply. I didn't appreciate my own beauty, either. Does any woman really ever believe in her own attractiveness? Movie stars and models, perhaps. The rest of us squint in the mirror for flaws and as we age they are easier and easier to find.

Once again, I stare at the photo of my daughter. This time she isn't here to tell me to stop. 'Were you taking drugs?' I ask the picture.

I walk away from the photograph, my question hanging in the air unanswered. I have no idea what to do with myself. I can't eat and I have just slept for an hour. I know that I could respond to some of the messages on my phone but I also know that's not going to happen.

There is a voicemail from Barbara on my phone. Her voice is thick with tears and she shudders through her words. I can picture her face and see the anguish written there, see how she would be running a hand through her thick, curly hair which she always does when she's distressed.

'Oh, Claire. I am so terribly sorry, so terribly, terribly sorry. I couldn't believe it when I heard. Not Julia, not darling, beautiful Julia. Lee and I are so devastated for you and Adrian and the boys, and Joel, of course. I know that you won't be able to speak to me now but I wanted to let you know that I am here for you, day or night. Call me whenever you want. Please know that we are thinking about you and mourning with you.'

We have been friends for twenty-five years, can talk for hours about nothing, have been through every life experience at each other's sides but I can't return her call.

'Barbara, what do I do if the baby won't sleep? Barbara, when is the best time to start solids? Barbara, should I send Julia to school this year or hold her back? Barbara, when did Sasha develop an interest in boys? Barbara, what do you do when your daughter kills herself? What do you do, Barbara?

I go to the computer instead and open my email. There are at least fifty sympathy emails. 'Sorry' is written in every single subject line.

I click on one at random. It's from Eric Peters. 'Eric Peters, Eric Peters,' I repeat to myself, trying to summon a face for the name.

Dear Claire,

I am so deeply sorry for your loss. Julia was a wonderful, bright young woman with the world at her feet. I will never forget her beauty and grace on stage. Her loveliness and poise made her a star presence and she was a joy to watch.

She was one of the most talented students I have ever had the privilege of teaching and I know that I will always miss her. She touched the hearts of all who knew her.

I was deeply shocked to hear about her decision since I know she was really happy in Melbourne and enjoying her new friends and courses. I hope that you are surrounded by loved ones and taking strength from all the people who adored and admired her. The world has, indeed, lost a special human being.

Eric Peters

Of course. I am surprised that I could have forgotten him. He's the drama teacher at the high school Julia attended, where Nicholas and Cooper both are now. He began teaching there in the same year Julia entered high school. It was the same year I finally told Joel to leave.

'Let's see how you manage without me,' he had snarled as he bumped his suitcases against the walls, leaving marks that would have to be painted over.

'Just go,' I replied, terrified that he would land one final, fatal blow. My mother and sister were waiting to hear from me because I wanted to do it alone when the children were safely at school. My mobile phone was clutched in my hand, the number for emergency services already keyed in.

I shiver as that day returns to me. I didn't think I would survive it.

I glance through the email again. Julia thought Eric Peters was the best teacher she'd ever had. 'He's what every teacher should be, Mum, really passionate and dedicated.' I close my eyes and conjure up his image. He's a ridiculously good-looking man with blond hair and chocolate-brown eyes. He has the kind of full lips that most women envy and I know that when I first met him I had to suppress a giggle at his beauty. I always thought Julia had a bit of a crush on him – as most of the girls at school did. He managed to get his students excited about Shakespeare and I remember that, despite the rules at the school against it, most of them called him by his first name.

If Eric Peters knows about Julia's death then everyone knows. How quickly the news has spread across the world. Our grief, broadcasted. I look through some more emails, seeing if any of Julia's other former teachers have sent anything, but only Eric has. It makes sense. They were very close. I go to shut down the computer but something niggles at me. I open the email from Eric Peters again. How did he know she was in Melbourne and that she was loving her life? I wouldn't have thought they would have spoken after Julia left school two years ago. Were they still in contact? Julia never mentioned him. And if they were in contact – exactly how close were they? Did he know something about her that I didn't? Would he be able to explain this better than I can?

No, I decide. He says he's shocked, just like everyone else is. Still, I would like to talk to him if he was still speaking to her. I would like to talk to everyone who ever knew Julia. I am starving for information about my child.

I click the star next to the email. I want to remember to thank him for his message. Perhaps he will tell me something new about her, something that will help me understand what I'm finding impossible to understand.

For no particular reason, I google 'Eric Peters' and find him mentioned on the staff page of the school.

> Eric Peters has been the Head of Drama for eight years. He has vast experience as both an actor and a teacher of drama, having lived and worked in New York. He has a Bachelor of Performance from the University of Queensland, a Bachelor's Degree from The American Academy of Dramatic Arts and a post-graduate degree in education from Sydney University.

Next to his bio is a picture of him. He *is* very good-looking, more so since he's aged a little. His face has a more rugged look that suits him. I don't blame all the girls for having a crush on him. I open my email again and think about replying to him, but after five minutes of staring at my computer screen I realise that I have no idea how to ask a man I don't know very well if he knew my daughter better than I did.

My mobile rings and because I am thinking about Eric Peters I make the mistake of answering it.

'Claire,' says Joel, his relief at finally getting hold of me evident in his voice.

Shit. I don't want to talk to him. I don't want him to point out that he has had very little to do with Julia for the last eight years and that therefore her desperate act must somehow be my fault.

'Joel,' I reply, through clenched teeth.

'I... uh... I—' he begins, but then he is quiet and I can hear him taking deep breaths. I know what he's doing because sometimes, if you take a deep enough breath, your body finds a way to prevent you from being so overwhelmed by your thoughts that you lose the ability to speak. Joel doesn't want to cry on the phone with his ex-wife and I don't know that I can bear to hear something from him I've never heard before.

I have managed to avoid speaking to Joel for the last two days. Adrian was the one who called him to tell him.

'It should really be you or one of the boys,' he said, when we arrived home from the hospital.

'The boys are sleep-deprived and don't even know what to think yet, and there's no way I can give him the news. I can't say the words, Adrian, I can't say it.' My voice broke as I thought about Joel hearing his daughter was no longer alive. 'Please, Adrian, I can't tell her father that she's gone. Please call him, or the police will have to do it, and that would be too cruel.'

'Okay, okay, I'll call.' Adrian is afraid of Joel, of his size and his charisma, but I watched him pull out his public face as the sun rose in the sky, mustering the strength to call my ex-husband. 'Joel, mate,' he said when Joel answered, and then I left the room.

'How did he take it?' I asked, heart hammering, when he joined me in Julia's room five minutes later. He lay down on her single bed next to me and put his hand over his eyes. 'He was shocked obviously and then he started crying.'

'Crying... really crying?' I asked, feeling a sharp pain in my chest. Adrian nodded. 'I've never heard him cry before,' I whispered. I was torn, for a moment, between the need to call and comfort Julia's father and my residual anger at him that is always lurking just under my unending, conflicting and complicated love for him.

'Do you think it was everything she witnessed as a child?' I asked, my throat hoarse.

'Claire, I'm sure Joel's violence had an effect on all the kids,' said Adrian, 'but Julia was fine. She was happy. I don't think it was that. All of that was a long time ago.'

It *was* a long time ago. A lifetime and a very different Joel ago.

'I'm coming,' Joel says finally, dragging me back to the present. 'I'm getting on a plane tomorrow morning. I just had to sort out some leave.'

'Joel, we can't have a funeral right now. They won't release her body until they've done an autopsy. Maybe you should wait.'

'I'm coming to see my sons, Claire. I've been on the phone with both of them already, but I need to be there for them.'

'Please don't get aggressive with me,' I say, unnecessarily. He's not being aggressive, I'm simply anticipating aggression. I am used to Joel's aggression, Joel's anger. Or at least, I used to be. I was a clumsy wife to him, always tripping or walking into doors. Clumsy but expert at concealing the bruises. Genius at loving him beyond all reason in between the blows.

I let the silence ride, listening to the mingling of our breaths through the phone.

People say it takes a village to raise a child and that's true, but I know that it also takes an entire village to keep an abusive marriage in existence.

I was the head of the village, of course. The one who got up every morning, covered the bruises, pasted a smile on my face and thumbed through my list of excuses, trying to find which one would do as an answer to any curious questions. 'I walked into a door.' 'I bent down to get something and knocked my head on the table.' 'Nicholas threw a tennis ball at me and I didn't catch it, silly me.'

My children were reluctant residents in that village. Silent and watchful, sometimes patting a bruise or offering a hug. They kept quiet because they were afraid. Joel never hit them but they understood on some deep, fundamental level that he could, and I believe they also understood that I wouldn't be able to protect them. I couldn't protect myself, so what use was I?

My mother was also a resident, who saw what was happening. She saw it and asked questions but then accepted my excuses. 'Clumsy Claire, she was always in the wars as a child.' My parents never pressed, never pushed. Perhaps they were protecting me, perhaps they were protecting themselves from the ugliness that would infiltrate their ordered lives if everyone knew the truth.

Women I have coffee with visited the village and smiled sideways at each new bruise, nodding and agreeing that they too were sometimes too tired to look where they were going. No one ever sat me down and said, 'I know what's happening to you. I know and I want to help so tell me everything.'

It's unfair of me to say this now, I know it is. If someone had sat me down I would have taken offence. I would have denied and denied and then I would have ceased speaking to them. Barbara once tried to give me a book, a memoir written by a woman who had escaped an abusive relationship with nothing but her children and the clothes they were wearing.

'She owns her own recruitment firm now, she's making millions,' Barbara told me, handing me the book with a glowing woman smiling on the cover. 'It's a brilliant read. I think you'll really enjoy it.'

'I can't abide stories like that,' I told her, handing the book back. 'Mostly women just end up trapped in poverty if they leave.'

'Not if they have help and support,' Barbara said quietly, not daring to meet my gaze as she stirred her nearly finished cup of coffee.

'Oh, please,' I said, shutting down the conversation. We moved on to discussing our children.

Joel had me well trained. In between the violent outbursts I was tightly wrapped in the love bubble that included flowers and gifts and weekends away and amazing sex. The kind of sex that you get turned on thinking about the next day, that sends a shiver right through you. Six foot five Joel with arms the size of tree trunks and an incongruous tattoo of an owl with open wings on his back. Joel who worked in security, keeping everyone safe but me. Joel, with his near black eyes and grey-black hair, that somehow managed to look sexy as it whitened, had me very well trained.

I ached for his kind touch and did everything I could to have him throw me a few words of praise. I was completely, devotedly, in love with him. I think perhaps I still am, despite being married to Adrian. I think I still am although I have never wanted to examine this possibility in myself.

But despite this, I did tell him to go. Finally, eventually, after too much time. Was it too late for Julia? Did she see too much?

I know Joel's right about the boys needing him. Neither of them have gone to school today but this morning Nicholas asked Cooper if he wanted to go for a drive and they both left shortly after that. They've been gone all day and I have no idea where they are. I understand their need to flee this house and their grieving shadow of a mother, but I simply don't have the energy for anyone else right now.

'I'm sorry, I didn't mean… I'm sorry, okay?' Joel says, his tone softening into despair. I know he's berating himself. He doesn't allow himself to lose control, not now, not for a long time. But his epiphany came too late for us. He has redeemed himself by becoming someone else entirely but I still cannot completely trust the change, even after all these years. Sometimes I push just to see what will happen. Nothing ever does.

'I know they need you, I'm just saying that maybe you should wait a few days until we know when the funeral will be,' I say softly.

'It doesn't matter. Do you… did you know? Did you have any idea?'

'No,' I say, getting up to go and find a tissue. 'I didn't… if I had, don't you think I would have done something to help her?'

'Of course you would have, of course. I'm not accusing you of anything, Claire. I just don't know what to think.'

'Neither do I,' I say, the words barely making it out of my mouth I'm crying so hard, my body convulsing as the sobs consume me.

'Please, Claire, please just take a deep breath. We'll get through this together, okay? I'll be there soon.'

'Okay,' I sniff. I don't say goodbye and neither does he.

It takes a few minutes but finally my tears subside and I am once again left staring at the computer screen. Eric Peters' picture stares back at me until I shut everything down. I return to Julia's bedroom, to Julia's bed, and close my eyes.

If I'm asleep she's still in Melbourne, still just a phone call away, still thinking about what to eat for lunch and planning a night out clubbing. If I'm asleep Julia is still alive. I would like to stay forever asleep so that she may be forever alive.

*

My sweetest, darling Julia,

Shakespeare said that 'Love is like a child,' in his play Two Gentlemen of Verona. *I confess I haven't read that play – most of the others, but not that one. I saw that quote on the internet today and thought of you. You make me feel like a child who doesn't understand why he can't have everything he desires right now. I am greedy for your touch, for the smell of spring you bring with you, for the way you look at me.*

I wonder if you find me writing you letters strange or if you wait eagerly for them to arrive. I like to think of you waiting for them to arrive. They are so different to an email or a text and I hope you are enjoying the anticipation as much as I know you enjoy my words. I don't imagine anyone else you know gets love letters. I wonder what you think about when you lie in bed at night. I wonder how you sit as you study or read. I imagine your knees curled under you, a hand twirling a lock of hair.

I wonder if you know how powerful you are and how much you've changed my life. You have made the world new for me, Julia. Everything is different now. My morning cup of coffee is no longer just a cup of coffee, but the rich memory of a cup I shared with you. You have allowed me to see the possibility of starting my life again. A life with you.

Love x

CHAPTER FOUR

'This is not just about you,' Adrian said to me last night. 'We're all grieving.' He was angry with me because I wouldn't come out of Julia's room. He doesn't think it's good for me to close myself in there all night and day. I know it's not just about me. I know that Nicholas and Cooper and Adrian are devastated but it feels like it is just about me. I am her mother. I *was* her mother.

I want to be there for my sons and my husband. I have always been so grateful that I was able to dedicate my life to my family, but I just don't feel capable of that right now. The strength it would take to comfort others eludes me. I am being selfish, I know I am, and I am angry at myself for not being able to find a way to explain this to my sons so they understand and accept what's happened. I am lost in trying to find a way to explain it to myself.

Both my sons are grappling with the awful truth of what their sister chose to do.

'But why?' Nicholas keeps asking. 'I would have helped her, you and Adrian would have helped her. She used to tell Cooper everything. Dad would have done anything to save her. She had us and she knew we all loved her. We could have sorted anything out. Why didn't she just say something?' But I couldn't give him the answer.

I have a list on my computer of all the possible reasons. 'Why are you doing this to yourself?' Adrian fumes at me. 'It's like you feel you have to punish yourself for what she did and that's not the truth. You were a good mother, you're a great mother. Let the guilt go and just mourn her, mourn the loss but don't chew yourself up about it.'

Adrian has a way with words. It does feel like I am eating myself up from the inside. I put food in my mouth and try to swallow but end up choking. My grief, my guilt, my pain is sustaining me.

Was she being bullied at university?

Did she get dumped by a boy she truly loved?

Was it because she was living away from home?

Was it drugs?

Was it alcohol?

Was she failing her course?

'I'm glad your father isn't here for this,' my mother said, when I told her about my list. My father adored Julia. Everyone adored Julia. It wasn't just because she was beautiful, it was something else – some light she seemed to carry with her, bathing us all in its glow.

I, too, am glad my father wasn't here to go through this. I believe my divorce, and the reasons for my divorce – a reason no father or mother ever wants to face up to – were the stressors that led to his final heart attack. It killed him. He was a slight man, skinny to the point of skeletal but cursed with sky-high cholesterol and high blood pressure, regardless of what he ate or the pills he took. He had his first heart attack at forty when he was heavier and a smoker, but despite reforming his behaviour he never really recovered. He died a year after I got divorced and my mother copes with his death by constantly pointing out the dreadful things he's missed. Julia's suicide is just one more awful thing to add to a list that includes terrorist attacks, my cousin's car accident that took her life, the rise in crime, and internet pornography, among many other things. It would be funny if it weren't so sad. But I suppose she is grieving for him in her own way and I don't think she'll ever be done. They were married for forty years, something neither I nor my twice-divorced brother and unmarried sister can even possibly imagine.

I still miss my father every day, sometimes speaking to him out loud when I'm worried about something. 'How am I going to survive this, Dad?' I whispered last night, when the ache in my heart spread to my whole body. I tried to feel his soft touch on my shoulder. 'One step at a time, sweet girl,' I think he would have said, but I can't be sure. He's been gone for a long time now and sometimes it's hard to hear his voice. Will that happen with Julia, too? Will I lose the ability to conjure her out of thin air? It's a horrifying thought.

I understand the futility of the list, of trying to find a reason for why she did it, but that's not going to stop me. I need a tangible reason and I know I won't stop looking until I find it.

Today Callie and Mia are coming over to visit me, as though I am infirm or elderly and incapable of leaving the house. It's true. I am. I suppose I have been weakened by death. Aged by grief.

I force myself into the shower and brush my teeth. My hair feels greasy and my mouth tastes sour. I need to at least try to pretend that I am functioning.

Once I'm dressed I go into Julia's room, determined to look through the whole place again in case I have missed a clue, some clue, any clue as to what she was thinking. I stroke BB's head. 'What am I missing, BB?' I ask the silent bear.

I find her stack of year books and begin paging through them. There are lots of pictures of Julia because she was a popular girl, in every drama production the school ever did.

There are many photos of Julia and Eric Peters together. There they are in the middle of rehearsal, or standing and handing out flyers for the latest production, or looking at costumes for an upcoming play. I find myself going back to one picture in particular.

It's from her last year at school when she was Ophelia in the school production of *Hamlet*. The photograph was taken at the final dress rehearsal and the whole cast is on stage. Eric Peters has his back to the camera. His arms are wide and his head tilted and I can see he is explaining something or, probably more accurately, giving the cast a final pep talk before their first performance. The stage is filled with students and I have to go searching for a magnifying glass in the kitchen so I can see the photo more clearly.

I peer through it, studying each of the faces on the stage. A lot of them are covertly looking at their phones, a few are looking directly at the camera and some are looking at Eric Peters. Julia is not just looking at him. She is gazing at him, completely focused on him. The picture makes me uncomfortable and I shuffle my position on the bed before I examine it again. I have never seen Julia look at anyone the way she is looking at him. It's not just a student regarding a teacher I see in that picture, but a young woman adoring a man. I try to talk myself out of this idea, telling myself that I am placing too much emphasis on this one moment captured when Julia may have been tired, or looking to her teacher for inspiration, or thinking about something else entirely. I am seeing things that aren't there. But I keep coming back to the way she is gazing at him.

What if I *am* seeing what I think I'm seeing?

What if there was something between them? Is that why they were still in contact? Was Julia in love with Eric Peters when she was at school? Had she still been in love with him when she died?

And, more frightening than that, was he in love with her?

I close the year book and push it away from me.

'Rubbish,' I say aloud, conscious that I am not just jumping, but vaulting, to conclusions. I leave her room and sit stiffly on the sofa, waiting for the girls to arrive.

Callie's mother, Susan, called to arrange it. 'The girls would like to see you, just to say… how sorry they are.' I knew she had rehearsed her sentence in her head before she spoke it, not wanting to offend me with the wrong words. I only answered Susan's call because her daughter found mine. Her daughter was the first person to howl her distress for Julia. I felt I owed her that after she left two other messages that I didn't return.

'It wasn't their fault,' I stated.

'Of course not, I mean no, of course not but Callie wishes she could have... could have handled it better.'

'She found my daughter's dead body hanging on my front porch, Susan. I think hysterical screaming was probably the best way to handle it.' I bent over as I said the words, feeling them like a punch to the stomach. How could I have said such a thing to her? How could I have thought such a thing? What was wrong with me?

I could hear Susan start to cry on the other end of the phone. I believe I am in the anger stage of grief. I believe I will live here forever. I lash out at well-meaning acquaintances, direct my rage at those who love me. I never knew it was possible to be this furious with the world. Even after Joel left, disappearing for two months leaving me with no money and no idea if he would ever give me another cent towards raising our children, I still managed to acknowledge that there were people worse off than me. I had the support of my parents, whereas some people had nothing. I tried, in between going through the survival sums in my head, to maintain a belief that things would get better. But this is different. I know there is no better from this and I am livid with the unfairness of it all.

Last night I woke up on Julia's bed at two in the morning and couldn't get back to sleep. I made myself a cup of tea and turned the television on with the volume low. A show about modelling hopefuls was on and I watched a young girl gesture and roll her eyes at the camera. 'No one understands how hard this is for me,' she drawled. *How dare you*, I thought. *How dare you still be breathing when my daughter isn't?* It was stupid of me and it's stupid to strike out at people who are trying to be kind.

'I would love to see them.' I sighed as Susan tried to regain her composure.

I have made tea and put out a cake that someone left on my doorstep. We cannot have a funeral, because of the autopsy, but people are still leaving food at my door. What else are they supposed to do?

I have tried to make some sort of an effort to get dressed but I can't go as far as putting on make-up. What would be the point of decorating myself to disguise my grief? It would feel like too much of a lie.

The doorbell rings at exactly eleven, the time Susan said they would be by. I imagine the two of them standing outside, counting down the minutes, wanting to get it right. They are twenty-year-old women but they are still children. My daughter was still a child.

'Up, Mum, up, up, pick me up. See there, Mum, see that, it hurts. Kiss it better, Mum, make it better.'

I open the door quickly. I want this over with as much as they do.

Callie and Julia have been friends since they were little girls of three years old. The day after we moved into our house, Susan arrived with the ubiquitous gift of a welcome cake and I invited her and her ginger-haired daughter in for tea. 'Roy has red hair,' Susan explained, as I looked at Callie.

'It's gorgeous,' I said.

Callie stood with her fingers in her mouth, staring at Julia, who crossed her arms and stared back.

'I have this many ponies,' Julia said eventually, holding up both hands, fingers splayed.

'You have ponies?' gushed Callie and, twenty minutes later, Susan had to threaten her with the loss of television privileges because she refused to leave. The girls were close through primary school, less so through high school, as Callie dedicated herself to her studies and sports and Julia became immersed in the drama club, but they have always maintained a friendship. Although Julia didn't take to Mia, who Callie introduced her to one weekend when she was home from Melbourne. 'She's completely up herself,' Julia declared. 'She doesn't stop talking about her father and all the famous people he knows, like I care about any of that shit. He's a promoter, that's all. Callie just loves all the free tickets Mia gets.'

'She's very pretty,' I said by way of conversation.

'And doesn't she know it.'

'I… we…' begins Callie, as my memory of Julia dissipates, and then she stops as though she has forgotten the words.

'We just wanted to say how sorry we are about Julia, about everything. We could have handled it better and we want you to know that. She was a lovely girl. I didn't know her as well as Callie did but she was really great.' Mia's speech emerges in a rush.

I can see that she is the leader in this little group of two. Perhaps that's why Julia didn't like her. Julia was used to being the one in charge. It's possible she felt threatened by how much Callie adores Mia. I can see the admiration in her eyes as she listens to Mia speak.

'She was so beautiful,' Mia says, 'really just beautiful.' I nod because I hunger to hear people say kind things about her. She *was* beautiful. *Was, was, was.*

Quietly I usher them into the living room where they perch awkwardly on the sofa.

'She looked just like you,' says Mia, and I manage a smile for her. She is trying, poor thing.

'Maybe a visit to the hairdresser would do you some good,' Adrian said tentatively last night as he studied me, no doubt noticing the strip of grey that has appeared.

'That won't be possible,' I replied, because it's not. It's just impossible for me to leave this house right now. It's only been a few days. I don't know why I am even required to get out of bed, but I smile again at Callie and Mia and cut the chocolate cake, watching the knife slide through the thick dark frosting as I swallow to control my nausea.

There is an awkward silence as the girls each take a bite.

'Did she… did she say anything to you in the weeks before?' I ask Callie. I know the police have already spoken to her but I have to question her again. 'Anything at all that made you think something was wrong?'

'No, no, not at all, but we weren't really having long talks because she was in Melbourne – just Instagram and Snapchat, but she seemed okay. She really seemed okay – happy, even.'

I nod because this is the same reply that has come back from everyone the police have interviewed.

'Did she have a boyfriend,' I ask, 'that you know of?' I know what the answer is because the question has already been asked and I sip my tea, letting my mind drift a little. I have dismissed the idea of Julia and Eric Peters being involved as a 'grasping at straws' notion.

It takes a moment for me to realise that Callie has not answered me.

I look straight at her, trying to read her green-eyed stare. 'Callie?' I prompt.

Callie looks at Mia. 'Tell her,' she whispers theatrically.

'Callie…? You told the police she didn't have anyone. Her friends in Melbourne said the same thing. Are you saying you lied?' I realise I sound harsh, but I am unable to stop myself.

She shifts on the couch and laces her fingers together. 'No, no I didn't, we didn't lie. It wasn't a lie. It was…'

'It was what?' I sit forward, legs apart, fists clenched. I hear the strident tone in my voice and see both Callie and Mia flinch a little.

'It wasn't a lie,' Callie repeats.

'Then what was it?'

'I didn't actually know anything for sure, not really… but she did say, she did say that there was someone.'

'Who?' I demand.

'We don't know,' Mia says. She leans over and covers Callie's hand with her own. 'We would have said something if we actually knew anything, but it could all have been a joke.'

'I don't understand.'

Mia sighs. 'In the last few months she started kind of hinting that she had someone, someone special. She said he was… different to any of the other guys she'd dated. I mean, that's what Callie told me.' She looks at Callie, who nods energetically.

'Was he in Melbourne? Was he at university with her?' I direct my question at Callie, wanting her to answer me about the girl who was her friend. Mia was not Julia's friend. I don't want her telling me things about my daughter. It just doesn't seem right.

'We don't know, she just said he was different. She didn't tell us anything about him.' Callie looks down when she speaks and then she reaches her finger out and swipes some frosting off the top of her piece of cake. She sucks it quickly as she looks up at me and flushes.

'But surely someone knew something about him? Isn't there anyone in Melbourne who may have met him?'

Callie shrugs and I resist the urge to shake her.

'This is important, Callie.'

'I know and I'm so… so sorry. I didn't really know her friends in Melbourne all that well. I'm just friends with them on Facebook. I accepted friend requests from everyone who knew her. There's a girl… I think her name is Esther, yes, Esther. She lives next door, sorry… lived next door to Julia. I could ask her if there was a guy, I could ask everyone. I know that she was good friends with a guy named Brian and also another girl… um… Ara, I think. I mean, everyone is really sad and I can ask.' Callie looks down at her feet and I see her cheeks flush with the effort she's making.

'Do you have their numbers? I have Esther's number but not the other two.'

'I don't but I'll get them for you,' she says, so eager to help it's heartbreaking. 'I can contact them for you, if you like.'

'No,' I say firmly. 'No, I'll talk to the police about them but if you could find me their numbers that would be great.' I don't need all of Callie's Facebook friends discussing my daughter. I've had enough of people talking about her all over social media. I know who Esther is and I'm certain the police would have spoken to her already, but what if she also didn't think to mention a possible relationship?

'Can I get you more tea?' I offer.

'Uh, no, thank you,' Mia says and I watch as she looks down at her still full cup. 'We should be going,' she says, standing up and looking meaningfully at Callie, who immediately stands up as well.

'Thank you for coming,' I say. I usher them both out of the house. Relief at having done what I'm sure Susan told them to do is expressed in their bodies. Their shoulders have fallen down from around their ears and Mia almost seems to be smiling. I know they will leave here and dissect the conversation for a short while but then they will get on with their day.

I can't wait for them to be gone. I think about the words, 'different to any of the other guys she'd dated,' and Liam's face appears before me. Could it be Liam? Is that why he brought me the rose and wrote the Facebook post? He's certainly different. It's possible that Julia and he met up again on one of the weekends she was here and grew closer.

'Do you think it was Liam?' I blurt out, just as they step out into the warm November day. Mia looks confused. She's probably never met Liam but Callie has known him for most of her life, just as Julia did.

'I don't… I mean, I don't know but I don't think so,' Callie says. 'I think he's dating someone but I'm not sure who. I can check with him, if you want.'

'No, it's fine. It was just a thought. I'm sure they weren't involved at all.' Callie shrugs her shoulders. She doesn't know what to say to me. I smile to let them know they're released.

I call Adrian on his mobile as I shut the door on the two girls. He's had to go into work today to sign a contract. 'I need to go to

Melbourne. I'm going to try and get on a flight tonight so I have time to pack.' Whoever the person was, there will be more clues to his existence in Melbourne than there are here.

'Melbourne? What? Why? I don't think that's a good idea at all.'

'I need to talk to Esther. She was in the room next to Julia and I need to talk to some of her friends from uni. I know there was a boy she had class with a lot of the time, Brian, I think. One of them may know something.'

'Or maybe they know nothing. She never mentioned Esther to me, and Brian was just someone she sat next to in class. I'm sure they weren't even friends.'

'How would you know?' I shout.

'Claire, Jesus! I'm just saying that these people probably won't know any more than we do. You're so fragile right now, Claire. You're grieving and I'm worried about you. I don't want you to be far away from me and the boys in case you need us. I want to be there for you, Claire. Please let me be there – don't shut me out.'

'I'm not shutting you out, Adrian,' I yell, because I am shutting him out, I know I am. 'I'm sorry,' I say quickly, 'but I have to go. Callie and Mia were just here. They talked about Esther and Brian and another girl, Ara. Julia gave me Esther's number in case I couldn't get hold of her. Esther lived right next door to Julia. If Julia was seeing someone she would have known, would have seen him coming and going.'

'Seeing someone? As in a boy? But the police said there was no one in her life.'

'They said she mentioned someone, that she said he was different to any guy she knew.'

'Different how?'

'I don't know, Adrian. Just different. I have to find out who it was. I have to talk to him. If she had a boyfriend he would have been one of the closest people to her and he might know something, some reason for why she did what she did.'

'Oh, sweetheart. I understand. But do you think having the reasons will make this any easier? No reason could ever be good enough. No reason could ever make sense. I think it would be better if you let this go. Let this go and start planning her funeral.'

'I can't plan her funeral, Adrian, because I don't know when we will be allowed to bury her.'

'Okay, I need you to calm down and think this through. The police have probably already interviewed Esther so if there was something to know they would have told us. I really don't think you're in the best state to get on a plane and go to Melbourne. If you wait a couple of weeks, I can get some time off work and we can go together. I want to be there for you.' He pauses. 'We'll need to sort through her stuff anyway, to decide what to bring home.'

'I can do that now, Adrian. It's not like she's going to be any more dead in two weeks.'

'Claire!'

'I'm sorry,' I say, sinking to the floor in the living room. My legs feel too weak to hold me up. 'I'm sorry. I just can't sit here waiting for them to tell me we can bury her. I need to be where she was for most of this year. I need to see her room and talk to Esther.'

'I don't think you can go alone, Claire. I don't want you to go alone. I want to help you.'

'I know you do but I think I need to go alone. To do this for myself. Please, Adrian. I don't want to fight about this. I'm going whatever you say, but I'd like to know I can call you without you telling me that you told me not to go.' I stand up quickly, purpose flooding through me. I go to my desk and open my laptop.

'Oh, sweetheart, of course you can call me. And maybe take Nick or Cooper?'

'No, no, I *need* to do this alone. I'm sure it will be easier for them in the house without me for a day or so. I want Nick to concentrate on his studying, and I know Cooper needs to knuckle down as well.'

'They've both just lost their sister, Claire. They need their mother.'

While we've been speaking I've found a flight to Melbourne. 'I've got one leaving in four hours, Adrian. That'll give me enough time to pack a few things and get to the airport. All I need to know is that you will tell the boys and hold down the fort for a few days.'

'Isn't that what I've been doing?' Adrian sighs.

It's true. While I have lain in Julia's room, smelling her sheets, immobilised by my tears, or googling, 'suicide', and 'why would someone commit suicide' and 'how to recover after your child commits suicide', Adrian has called everyone who needed to be called, accepted food from those who came to the door. He has been dealing with the police, reporting to me every time Detective Winslow calls. Today he encouraged the boys to go back to school and I have heard him check on both of them every night, something he stopped doing a while ago, when they grew too old for it.

'I'll call you when I get there,' I say. 'I love you.'

'I love you, too.'

※

My sweetest, darling Julia,

I know you think I don't understand or maybe even think that I don't care but I do, my darling, I do. I know that what we're doing is not something we can be proud of. I understand your worries and your fears. But we have to be together. We have to be together the same way the sun has to rise tomorrow, the same way that the seasons follow each other. We have no choice, Julia. Throughout history there have been lovers who have had to fight against great odds to be with each other. Think of us like that. We have great obstacles in front of us and many people who will want to keep us apart but our love is bigger than that. You have become a real-life Juliet and I am your Romeo. Nothing can stop us because we both know the truth. You love me and I love you and we will love each other forever, my sweetest, darling girl. Rejoice in that. Believe in that. Think about that and leave the rest of the world to me.

Love x

CHAPTER FIVE

I open my eyes in the dark. It takes me a moment to adjust, to remember, and then another five shocked, distraught minutes to deal with what comes with my morning realisation that Julia is gone. I close my eyes and sink down into the crushing grief. In the five days since it has happened I have stayed in Julia's bed safely away from Adrian and the boys, not wanting to let them see me adjust to Julia's death over and over again. I barely sleep at night, tossing and turning, but even the few hours or so I do get erase the truth momentarily and I open my eyes, hovering between what I want to be true and what I know to be true. I would like to be able to live forever in those few seconds in between the two.

I allow myself to curl up and cry until I can't breathe, knowing that my family cannot stand to see me like this. At home the boys are quiet as they move about the house. I hear them whispering to each other in the hallway, afraid to draw my attention.

'Can I get you some tea?' Nicholas, my gentle giant, asks me whenever he sees me. He has heard Adrian doing the same thing and perhaps thinks this is the only way to approach a grieving mother. He has always been more concerned about me than either Julia or Cooper have been, but then I think he is more concerned about the whole world than either his brother or sister. After Joel left I would wake most mornings to find him in the bed next to me, by my side, not for his comfort but for mine. He would always have a hand on my shoulder.

'Today's going to be a good day, Mum,' he would say, giving my shoulder a squeeze, before bouncing out of bed and waking up his sister and brother for school. He is the middle child and still so young, but he has an old soul, with the striking ability to feel empathy for others.

When Adrian and I got married, Nicholas insisted on walking me down the very short aisle of our living room. Cooper wasn't interested and Julia was my maid of honour. It felt fitting that my eleven-year-old son gave me away to a man he thought would be able to tell me every morning, 'Today's going to be a good day.'

Once my tears have run their course I realise that today, for the first time since my daughter died, I have a reason to get out of bed. I turn my head and note the sliver of light slipping in through the side of the black-out curtains.

The hotel I chose is the closest one to the university I could find. I was relieved they had a room when I arrived here at eight last night. The room and bathroom are clean and square, clinical and unobtrusive, asking nothing from their occupant. I breathe in, finding the stale smell of filtered air somewhat comforting. Right at this moment, I am simply a woman in an anonymous hotel in the middle of a large city. I could stay here forever, suspended in time, separated from my life. Perhaps it would hurt less.

Hunger gets me out of bed. I have no idea why. I haven't felt hungry for days but perhaps my body is aware it has a job to do today. It needs fuel. Downstairs in the hotel they are serving breakfast. I grab pancakes and bacon and toast and smother everything with syrup, longing for some sweetness.

I have already spoken to Esther. She will have seen something, noticed something. She must have. Once Callie sent me their numbers, I texted Brian and Ara, asking if they could meet me at Julia's room. Neither of them have answered and I prepare myself for the fact that they may not show up.

I remember when Julia texted me Esther's number because I pestered her for it over and over again.

'Why do you need the number of someone else in the hall?' she had asked.

'Just in case I can't get hold of you. In case I'm worried about you.'

'In case you want to check up on me, you mean?'

'Is that so terrible, Julia? You're going to be a two-hour plane ride away.'

'You're neurotic. You need to let go a little and, anyway, it's only an hour and like ten minutes.'

'One day you'll have daughter and then you'll know.'

'Er, yuck. I am never having bloody children. They turn you into a lunatic.'

'Just get me her number please, Julia.' I had sighed, worn down by yet another acrimonious exchange with my daughter.

'Fine.'

She hung up on me, a minute later texting Esther's number. In her last year of high school and the two years since, my attention was very much unwanted. I bothered her, I got in her space, I asked too many questions.

Esther has agreed to meet me, along with the director of the halls of residence, in Julia's room at noon. It's only 10 a.m. but I know that I will go to the campus and wander around until it is time. I was robbed of this chance when Julia started university, as she insisted on driving herself down here. 'I need some time alone, Mum, can't you just let me have that? I'm eighteen.'

'Even in America parents drive their kids to college, Julia.'

'I'm sure that some kids want to drive themselves, Mum.'

I agreed finally because of course I had no choice. Once your child turns eighteen you no longer have the luxury of choice and they know that. How quickly we go from being everything to being nothing.

'At least you're taking BB with you,' I said.

Julia giggled. 'Well, he's my best friend.' She clutched her ratty old bear in her arms, hugging him close to her, reminding me that baby Julia was such a short time ago.

I know it changes, that things shift and suddenly your older child needs your help as they navigate the adult world, but Julia and I were just on the cusp of that, just beginning to enjoy each other's company again. I miss what I almost had. That's what I miss the most.

I know that these memories paint a picture of a fractured relationship. But in truth we got along very well as long as I gave her the space she needed. When she came to Sydney for a visit she would always make sure to put aside one day for just us and even though we rarely discussed anything deeper than her daily life, the everyday stuff, we did enjoy being together. We shopped and had lunch, choosing a different cuisine each time. We giggled over her brothers' quirks and poked fun at Adrian's need for the dishwasher to be stacked a certain way and his socks to be in colour-coordinated rows. We didn't discuss Joel, or at least she didn't want to discuss him. I tried as the years went by to encourage her to give her father another chance but she remained firm on this.

She was only twelve when he left but I let her watch as I shed frustrated, angry tears. She had gone from being Daddy's girl to being ignored by her father. She saw the abuse but I believe, at the time, that she found a way to separate her and Joel's relationship from that. He adored her and she him. Her animosity towards him came after he left, when she struggled with being dismissed along with the rest of us. It was only then that she began going over the incidents of abuse – perhaps as a way of saving herself from missing him, loving him, being rejected by him. I know how difficult that juxtaposition between the man who hurt her mother and her adoring father was for her.

Years later, she still hadn't forgiven him. 'I'm doing what I can, Mum. A text once a week is more than he deserves.'

'At first yes, but not now. Not for many years now. He's not that man any more, Julia, as your brothers have explained. I don't want you to regret not getting to know him as he is now.'

'I don't care who he is now. I text him and I let him buy me stuff. That's all I can do. If I can ever forget some of those times… those hideous, horrible times, then maybe it will be different.'

'I wish you could. Not forget them, but perhaps forgive them. Therapy would help, darling, it really would.'

'Nah, I'm not interested in that. It won't make what he did to you, to us, any easier to live with and besides, I don't want it to be something that doesn't bother me. I want to remember so I never choose a man like him.'

'A man like he is now would be a good man to choose,' I said, the words hurting as I said them, because I would never be with the good man he had become.

The juxtaposition between the Joel I loved and the Joel who hurt me is still something I'm trying to come to terms with, so I know how difficult it was for her. He was a good, if sometimes scary, father to the children. And then he was gone.

I forced him out but only to get him away from me. Not to get him away from his children. Instead he walked out of the door and disappeared for two months.

I texted *You cannot simply pretend we don't exist* every day for weeks, hoping to provoke a reply.

We protected her brothers, she and I together, even turning one terrible night when there was no money and little food in the house into an adventure.

On the day I told him to leave, I had $100 left in my account. Like many women in my situation, I had no access to the other accounts that were filled with money.

'We have to invent a new dish with all this,' Julia had told the boys, throwing everything we had left in the pantry and the fridge onto the counter.

'I don't like rice,' Cooper whined.

'If we put it with soy sauce it's Chinese food,' said Julia, 'and this capsicum is still good if we cut this bit away.'

'I like Chinese food,' smiled Cooper obligingly. I stepped in then, taking over and making a dish that filled us all up.

'You should have just come here, Claire,' my mother scolded the next day. 'Why on earth would you allow the children to suffer through something like that? I would have filled up your fridge. Why won't you let me help you more?'

'Mum, you're helping with the lawyer and I can't ask you to do more than that. You know I'm full-time at the English language college now and I got paid today so I filled the fridge. We'll be okay, it was just one bad night.'

'Rubbish, you should have called. Why didn't you? Please don't tell your father that you didn't come to us. It will absolutely kill him.'

It was the humiliation, I suppose.

Forgive me. Forgive me for everything, were the first words Joel texted me after seven weeks, five days and three hours. He had moved to Queensland where his brother lived.

By then I had only weeks left before the bank was going to force me to go ahead with the sale of the house. My salary didn't stretch to cover the enormous mortgage payments. By the time Joel made contact I was hanging on by a thread, propelled forward each day by my acrimony and contempt for my absent husband. I berated myself for ever trusting him, for ever trusting a man. I cursed myself for allowing the abuse to go on for so long, for letting my children witness what happened, for being a complete failure as a mother and a human being. Few people can hate themselves as much as a woman who has been told over and over again that the physical and emotional abuse she endures is all her own fault.

I lost five kilos. I drank too much and I took up smoking. I was so utterly furious with myself and the world that I could only taste bitterness in my mouth.

And then he made contact.

After two months, he called, he wrote, he texted, he sent gifts for the kids. He paid off the months of missed mortgage payments and sent maintenance money so that I didn't have to sell the house. One night I looked at my bank balance and it had gone from $45 to $10,000. I thought it was a mistake but it was Joel. He sent apologies over and over again. He was trying to fix his mess.

Nicholas and Cooper fell back easily into their adoration of their father after he contacted us.

'He's just different, he's changed,' Nicholas told me, after spending two weeks with Joel at his Queensland beachside apartment in the school holidays. I hadn't wanted to let them go, telling them a simple 'No' when Joel made the request, but the boys asked and then begged and then pleaded.

How do I know they will be safe with you? I finally texted Joel when I began worrying that I was keeping his sons away to punish him, but was ending up actually punishing them. I was worried about his behaviour with them, yes, but mostly I was furious that he thought he could simply waltz back into their lives. He didn't deserve the uncomplicated love of his young children. Not after everything he'd done.

I would kill myself before I hurt my children, he replied. He had never said anything like that before, never even acknowledged that he understood he hurt me. I let them go, putting them on a plane with my heart in my throat.

'We will take good care of them,' the flight attendant smiled at me, watching me swipe away my tears. I wanted to grab him and tell him that he had no idea who I was sending my boys to. Joel had never lifted a hand to his children but what could happen if I wasn't there, if I wasn't available to act as the punching bag between them?

He made them call me every day. As I listened to breathless chatter about surfing lessons and 'the best burgers ever', I tried to hear any hidden truth behind the words. But I couldn't hear anything except two little boys being spoilt rotten by their father. Pictures popped up on Facebook and I examined their skinny, shirtless torsos for tell-tale bruises but there was nothing. He wasn't hurting them. He was loving them.

'Maybe you should have agreed to go,' I said to Julia.

'No way,' she replied. 'Don't even go there.'

Eight years later, I still don't quite know what to believe. He is different, very different. He is no longer that man, but Julia never forgave him. And now she will never have the chance to. If she had managed to forgive him would she be here today? She had Adrian, but was he enough? Did I push a reconciliation between the two of them as much as I could have? What more should I have done?

I shake myself out of my thoughts. I will go to her university and continue my search for the answers I desperately need. It's the only way forward for me, the only way through. It's not enough, nowhere near, because what could ever be enough to take away this unimaginable hurt? But right now, it's all I have.

✢

My sweetest, darling Julia,

Oh, how I hate to see you cry. Your tears wound me more than I can say. I only wish for your happiness, Julia. It's not true that I manage to pretend that what we're doing is fine. I don't pretend and I don't forget. I just put a bubble around us, cocooning our time together. I imagine it like a giant soap bubble, shining with reflected rainbows from the sun and inside it we are safe. It's just you and I. No one else and nothing else matters. Please join me in the bubble, Julia. Put something between us and the world so we can just be together. You and I, without the guilt and the drama.

We have so little time together. Every minute is precious. You are precious. Let us make the most of it.

Love x

CHAPTER SIX

I wander the campus for as long as I can bear it, ostensibly admiring the slick angled steel and glass new buildings that rise out of the ground contrasting with older, squat brick buildings that sit tiredly beside them. I amble across the rich, green lawns, turning my face to the spring sunshine and breathing in the light floral smell that permeates the air. What I'm really doing is watching all the young women sitting under trees, shrieking with laughter with their friends and rushing to their next class, or queuing for coffee at little kiosks that seem to be everywhere. As I look at them all, fresh-faced and bursting with energy, the only thing I can think is, *Julia should be here.*

How do you make such a decision? I think. *How do you decide that the taste of your favourite chocolate, the smell of a summer's day, the feel of your mother's hug, the sound of your friend's laughter, the way a rapt audience watched you perform, are all worth nothing? How do you give up a future that you wanted to fill with travel and experience and life and love?*

How could she do that – and why? Why? Why?

I think about the last serious conversation we had. I had tried to convince Julia, once again, to forgive Joel on her last visit up to Sydney. I don't know why I kept making vague attempts to reunite her and her father. Perhaps it was driven by my own relationship with my father, who was a gentle, strong presence in my life. I don't remember him ever raising his voice to me or my brother and sister. It was my mother who was in charge of discipline, using a harsh tone to keep us in line. My father would sit quietly and listen to her yell at whichever child had broken a rule or behaved badly and when she was done he would say, 'Your mother and I only do this so you can see that you are making the wrong choices. She yells out of love. Don't ever forget that.' The night I told Joel to leave, my father came over and sat next to me on the couch, taking my hand in his. 'You should not have suffered as you did, Claire, and I'm proud of you for taking this step now. Your mother and I are here for you, no matter how hard it gets.'

When Joel came back into our lives and I allowed him to see the boys as much as he wanted, I thought my father would judge me for that choice. But although my mother shook her head and clicked her tongue when I spoke of forgiving Joel for the terrible things he had done, my father just said, 'If you are sure the children are safe and you believe he's changed, then that's enough for me.'

I never showed my parents the email Joel wrote to me after the first time the boys went to visit him in Queensland. I explained it to them, but his words were only for me. *How is it possible for him to have changed?* I had asked myself, wondering if I had been the problem all along. If a different woman would have been married to a different Joel. I tortured myself with that thought. *How terrible a human being must I be to have turned him into a monster?* So I asked. I had to ask. I didn't call because I couldn't bear to hear his voice, aware that even though we separated and even though he had tried to break me physically, emotionally and spiritually, there was still something. Call it infatuation, call it sex, call it love. I didn't know what it was but I wasn't strong enough to hear his voice, so I protected myself in a text: *Was it me? Was I the one who drove you to be that man, the man you say you no longer are?*

He didn't reply for two days. I took that to be my answer. But then the email arrived.

It was never you, Claire. It was never the kids. It was never work or money or a bad day or a good day. It was me. I fucked up. I fucked up beyond what any man could ever be expected to be forgiven for. I deserved to lose you and our children. I know that now. I should have sent money from the beginning but I was… I guess you could call it in shock. The night you told me to go I flew to Queensland. I had intended to go to Leo and stay with him but then I thought about how Amy would look at me when I got there and I just couldn't. I checked into a hotel and I stayed there for four days. I drank in the hotel bar until they closed and then I went up to my room and emptied the mini bar. When I woke up I picked up the phone to call room service to order up more alcohol, more bottles to stop myself thinking and, as I did, it hit me. It just hit me.

It felt like someone had slammed a plank of wood into the side of my head. I couldn't breathe or think straight. I couldn't make my hands work to call room service. I had lost everything and I knew that I was entirely, completely to blame. I knew that I had hurt the woman I loved more than anything in the world. I know you tried to tell me this, tried to tell me what I was doing to you, to us and our family. I used to watch your mouth move, saying the words, but hear nothing. In the darkness of my silent hotel room I finally heard you. I got it and it shattered me. I didn't move for three days after that until security came to check on me. I lay in the bed and I relived every moment of pain I caused you and the kids. I forced myself to remember each incident, each fucking time I hurt you. And while I was doing that I saw the awful parallel with my father and my childhood. I knew the psychology behind it because I'm not an idiot, but I had never connected the dots of my own abuse with those of me when I was the abuser. In my head the reasons for my behaviour had always been justified. It was ridiculous that I couldn't explain away my father's abuse but I could explain away my own.

I kept seeing that day when we all went to the park together for a picnic. I don't know if you remember it but it was about two months before you told me to leave. I remember how you had packed so carefully, making sure there were peanut-butter sandwiches for Cooper and a chicken sandwich for Nick and vegetarian for Julia. I know that you packed three different kinds of sandwich for me so that I could choose and I knew, even as I watched you, that you were doing it so I wouldn't have a reason to get pissed off, to lash out. But I found one anyway. In my head there's an image that I don't know will ever go away. It's me holding onto your wrist, twisting it so hard that you bend your knees in agony. We are standing behind our car which I had demanded everyone get back into because I was so angry that we couldn't find a spot in the park I liked. I can see all three kids looking out of the car windows at us, eyes wide in fear. No one could see us but them. I know when I let go of your wrist I thumped the car hard to get them away from the windows, causing them to jump and avert their gaze in terror. I know by the time we got home all three of them were crying and your face was the colour it goes when you are hiding your physical pain. You were cradling your wrist, keeping it from jarring and an hour later you said you were just getting some stuff from the grocery store. I let you go alone even though I knew you were heading to the emergency room. I couldn't face what I'd done. I never wanted to face it, until I couldn't look away any more.

That day is one of the ones that tortured me the most in that hotel room. I know it was only one incident of many but it was so similar to an afternoon in my own childhood. My mother asked my father to take us all to the park because she didn't drive. I remember her filling the cooler bag with enough beer to keep him happy, taking out one and then putting it back in as she counted because she knew exactly how many it took to tip him over the edge. She must have miscalculated because he too shoved Leo and me into the car and then he too grabbed my mother's wrist. He too was clever enough to be hidden from view. Clarity drowned me. It filled up my lungs and almost suffocated me.

I cried, Claire. I know you've never seen me do that but I couldn't stop. I was like a fucking baby. I wasn't just like him, I was *him, and that meant that I was exactly the same monster. I had convinced myself that my anger and abuse was always justified because of one thing or another – but that was a lie.*

When they found me, in that hotel room, they sent me to hospital. They called Leo. Housekeeping had raised the alarm after three days. I know you asked him where I was and I know he kept telling you he didn't know, but he's my brother, Claire. He was just trying to protect me.

I was told I'd had a breakdown and that's exactly what it felt like – like I was broken down. I didn't know if I could get fixed again. I didn't even know if I wanted to. I stayed in the hospital for three weeks. Talking, doing group therapy, all that shit I've laughed at my whole life.

It took another month for me to recover fully. I stayed with Leo and I saw a therapist every single day. When I was ready I started looking for jobs. I knew it wouldn't take me long. I told everyone I had taken a few months off to get myself right after my marriage broke down.

'You're a giant in this industry,' Stuart, the owner of my new company told me. I didn't tell him how small of a man I felt. I could control a team of a thousand security guards and protect stadiums and rock stars and celebrities, but I couldn't control myself or protect the people I cared about the most.

I still go to therapy every week. I don't know when I will stop or if I will ever stop. I don't think I should ever stop. There is no point in me apologising any more. I've said it enough. The only way I can prove to you that I'm different and changed is to just be *different. Thank you for letting me see Nicholas and Cooper. It means more to me than I could ever explain. I promise I will not let them down again. And if Julia ever agrees to see me I won't stop working until she understands that I know what I did was wrong. That all the fault lay with me.*

I wish we could go back. I wish I was a better man for you and our children. But all I can do is move forward. All I can do is make up for my mistakes.
All my Love
Joel

I couldn't comprehend what to make of the email, of the things he said. Everything I had wanted him to acknowledge, he had acknowledged. All the things I had dreamed of him saying over the years and the realisations I was desperate for him to come to were right there in his words. And yet I didn't know if I could trust him. I questioned myself and everything that he had put me through, viciously rotating my wrist so that the old ache would remind me of the truth. But there was no question he was changed. He is changed.

Julia never accepted that. When I tried to, once again, encourage her to give her father more of her time, we were sitting in an Ethiopian restaurant eating a beef dish simmered with butter, herbs and chilli. We were eating with our hands, using the rice to help lift the beef, mirroring an Ethiopian family at the table next to us. We licked our fingers as we talked.

'Your father loves Ethiopian food,' I said.

'So?'

'So maybe you could, I don't know, give him a call and let him know you have something in common.'

Julia stopped eating, staring at me as I wiped my hands.

'Do you remember the day of my tenth birthday party?'

I kept wiping my clean hands, intent on looking anywhere but at her. 'I do,' I whispered, hoping, praying that she would not detail what happened. I knew what happened, I was there. I didn't want to hear it again. But I kept silent, aware that my therapist had long ago instructed me to allow the children to discuss what they remembered, to never stop them from speaking.

'Me, too,' she said, finishing her diet cola in one large gulp. 'I remember that you wanted the sofas moved so there would be more room to set up the tables so we could do our beading. The lady who was coming said she needed two trestle tables. I know that a week before the party you asked Dad to do it and then again a few days before and then an hour before the party you asked once more, when everything else was set up already. I know I was starting to whine about it because I was worried that he wouldn't do it in time. Do you remember what he said to you?'

'He said, "I'll get to it when I'm good and ready."' Flushed with the heat of the chilli in the dish we were eating, I grew cold in the restaurant as that ugly day reared its head again.

'Yup, and then he went into the garden and got out the lawn-mower, ignoring us. I remember how heavy those couches were to shift, Mum. I remember all of us pushing together, sweating and puffing, and finally getting them out of the way so we could set up. Then he came back inside, about five minutes before my friends arrived. And the lady was already there sorting everything out. She wouldn't have had it all set up otherwise.'

'And then he came back inside,' I repeated, as the picture formed. Joel with his fists clenched and his eyes scrunched. His lips set in a line. In that moment he looked bigger, darker, more ferocious. 'Go to your rooms until the guests get here,' I had told my three children. There were no protests. They just ran. They knew what was coming.

'I just thought we would get it done for you.' I had trembled as I spoke, hoping that the woman in charge of the beading, Lou, I think her name was, would not come back inside the house. She had gone to her car to get some more twine to use for threading the beads. Joel's eyes had swept the room quickly, noting that the woman wasn't there. He growled as he spoke, keeping his voice low.

'And now you've scratched the fucking floor because you dragged them, rather than put them up on their side.'

'We couldn't lift them, Joel.'

'I know. And that's why I was going to do it. I told you I would do it. I'm here in time, aren't I? There are no guests here now, are there? Hello, hello, are any of Julia's friends here yet?'

'No,' I whispered.

'No. So you didn't need to scratch the fucking floor, did you, Claire, but you had to make a point, didn't you? You just had to make a fucking point.'

'I'm sorry, Joel... I didn't—'

'No, you never fucking do,' he snapped, advancing on me, forcing me backwards until I was pressed against the wall. He slapped me with an open hand. It knocked me off my feet and then he kicked me in the stomach twice. I tried to get up again but I couldn't. I couldn't breathe properly. It happened quickly, almost cleanly, as though he had rehearsed the movements before. The bell rang and I realised that the front door which I had left open for Lou had been locked. He had locked the door. No matter what I had or had not done, that day I was going to get hit. He had been pushing me towards it all day, pushing and prodding, inching me closer, but I was still stupid enough to think that I could stop it happening. I couldn't, because it had nothing to do with me.

Then he picked me up and took me to our bedroom, where he threw me on the bed. He told everyone I had a migraine and he struggled through manfully with a smile on his face, hosting a party for 20 ten-year-old girls.

The next day the mother of one of Julia's friends had called.

'How's the migraine?' asked Gillian.

'Oh, much better today. Thanks so much for asking.'

'I know – my sister gets them and she just has to lie in a dark room until they go away. She even throws up sometimes.'

'Oh, well... I'm much better today, thanks.'

'Joel was great, by the way. He just handled everything so well and Maisie told me he even tried to make his own necklace.

Apparently all the girls were laughing because he found it so difficult to hold the beads. I don't know that Jack would ever host a kid's party for me. He always schedules his golf days when he knows we've planned one. You've bagged a good one there, Claire, hang on to him.'

'Oh, yes.' I laughed weakly. 'He's great.' To everyone else, he was the perfect husband.

'I'm sorry,' I said to Julia in the restaurant, because I had no idea what else to say any more.

'He wrote me an email about that time, you know,' she continued. 'He wrote me an email about every single time he could remember and at the end of each one of them he put, "I'm the one to blame. It was all my fault and unacceptable for you to have to experience."'

'So he's apologised.' I nodded because I knew about the emails. He wrote them to all three kids.

'Do you know how many of those emails I have, Mum?'

I shook my head.

'Thirty-four. I have thirty-four apology emails.'

I left it there. We went to get ice cream and I bought her a pair of ridiculously expensive shoes, hoping the sweetness of the after would erase her bitter memory of the before.

'Julia,' I whisper. Thinking of her makes me want to say her name. It's impossible to fathom that I will never call her name again. I buy myself a strong cup of coffee. I leave out the sugar and the milk and swallow the thick acrid brew eagerly. When I get like this I need a physical contrast, something to stop me from descending into an abyss of pain. I can't exactly curl up in a ball on the footpath of the university.

I walk quickly as I sip my coffee, amazed at how much time has passed, realising I am nearly late to meet Esther. I can't keep letting myself get stuck in the memories. I need to concentrate on finding answers.

※

My sweetest, darling Julia,

Thank you for sneaking me into your dorm today. I just wanted to see where you sleep, where you work and where you dream about me. I hope you dream about me. I dream about you. I dream about our time together, reliving your touch and the way your skin feels. I dream about you wearing nothing but the ruby-red shoes I bought you. I'm so glad you like them, even though you've never worn anything like them before. You'll get used to wearing them and you'll grow to love them as most women do. Don't you love the way they make your legs look? Don't you love the way they make you feel? What a beauty you are, Julia. I want to show you how to enhance that beauty, how to make the whole world your stage. When I close my eyes at night I see you in those shoes, in nothing but those shoes.

And then I dream only of you. I dream about our future together when we are, one day, able to share what we have with the world. That time will come sooner than you think and you will no longer have to feel guilty or destroy my letters or look over your shoulder when we are together. No more tears, my darling, no more feeling guilty. Dream about our future as I do and all the wonderful things that lie ahead for both of us.

Love x

CHAPTER SEVEN

Esther is waiting for me outside Julia's room with the director of the hall, a young man named Simon.

'I'm so sorry for you… for your loss,' he stutters, his face colouring. I'm sure this is not something he's ever had to deal with before.

'Thank you.'

'Mrs…' begins Esther and then she stops. I think she realises that she doesn't know my surname but is aware that it doesn't match Julia's surname of Barker.

'It's Claire, please.'

'I'm so sorry, Claire. If I had known, if we had been aware… she was so lovely and I miss her so much.' Esther has a tissue ready and she wipes her nose and eyes. She is a small girl with mousey brown hair and ears that stick out from her head.

I know she and Julia didn't exactly click. According to Julia, Esther hated parties and spent most of her time in her room studying. 'She was brought up in this strict religious sect. Her whole room is covered in crosses,' Julia told me.

Esther, for her part, complained constantly about Julia making noise when she had friends in her room, accusing them of disturbing her. Julia could conjure a party out of thin air. She had the ability to socialise with anyone, to feel comfortable anywhere. In high school she was a magnet for friends – she was friends with a clique of girls all competing to top the year, and friends with girls who were routinely in detention. She could befriend anyone.

I offer Esther a hug even though I know she is not actively grieving my daughter.

Simon unlocks the door and hands me the key. 'If you need any help…' he mumbles, before walking away.

The room is a mess, just as Julia's room has always been. It's positively chaotic. There are clothes all over the floor and the bed is unmade. Her books are piled everywhere and there are random pages of notes scattered on every surface.

Her untidy room was a constant battle between us. 'Leave her alone,' Adrian said more than once, after Julia had slammed her bedroom door hard, while screaming that she would, 'get to it when it suits me.' The temper that Joel has now mastered, the anger that he now so vigorously controls, made itself evident in Julia when she ran full force into adolescence. She would flare up instantly at me if I said the wrong thing at the wrong time. She always simmered down quickly but her teenage years were punctuated with the sound of slammed doors.

'I'm afraid she's just like Joel and that she'll never learn to control herself.'

'She's just a teenage girl figuring out her place in the world,' Adrian said, always the peacemaker. 'I bet you slammed a lot of doors when you were that age.'

'Not really,' my mother said, when I asked her about it. 'You were more of a sulker. You would brood and glower at everyone for hours like you needed to make sure we all saw how unhappy you were.'

'It's my house, *our* house,' I complained to Adrian. 'She has to have some respect for that fact. I'm not asking for it to be spotless but the boys manage to get their dirty laundry into the hamper, why can't she? I'm sick of having to sift through her clothes, trying to decide what's dirty and what's not.'

'Stop doing her laundry, then.'

'Then she'll just yell at me because she's run out of clothes.'

It used to grate on me. I would give anything to open the door of her room at home now and have to sigh at the chaos. But her bedroom at home is tidy, not like she would have left it, because each time she went back to Melbourne I would tidy up so that it was ready for her when she came home again.

I sink onto the bed, not knowing where to begin, wishing my daughter would open the door of her room right now and ask me what I'm doing here. Looking around, I think about the fact that the police have been here. They were surprised by her room. I allow myself a grim little smile. Apparently it would be an indication of foul play in any other situation but I told them the room would be very messy – it was Julia's way. But I don't know why she didn't tidy up if she knew… if she had planned… I sigh.

Esther stands in the middle of the room, rubbing her hands awkwardly together. 'Should I start picking up the clothes?'

'Oh, no… no thank you, Esther. I didn't ask to see you because I wanted your help. I can manage this. I just want to ask if you'd noticed anything in the last few weeks, anything at all.'

'No, nothing,' she states emphatically. 'I told the police that she was just usual, just Julia, you know.'

'Just Julia?' I repeat.

'Yeah, um…' Esther fumbles for something more to say and I watch her, wanting to understand who 'just Julia' was.

'She was chatting to everyone like she usually does, like she knew everyone's name in the whole dorm practically and she was always running late for class even though I told her to set two alarms – which made her laugh. She was working hard on an essay, I know that because she kept complaining about it – something to do with journalism in the age of social media. She was just…' Esther's words dry up, and I understand she has little idea of who Julia was.

'I know you told the police that she didn't have a boyfriend but I spoke to two of her friends in Sydney and they seem to think that there might have been someone.'

'I never saw her with anyone. I mean, no one special.'

'But even if you never saw her with anyone, could there have been someone? Maybe someone she didn't want to introduce anyone else to? Someone she met outside of university?'

'Not that she ever said. I mean, not really, but she was…'

'Was what?'

'In, like, the last few weeks before she… before she… She was a little different.'

'So not "just Julia",' I state, feeling a rush of anger at Esther. I know it isn't fair but I cannot stop myself.

'Well, most of the time she was just… just the same but sometimes, now that I think about it… sometimes she was different.'

'Different how?' I ask, finding Esther's breathy voice irritating and her inability to tell me what she's thinking infuriating. I know my anger is misplaced. She's just a young woman who lived next door to my daughter. Julia's life and the way she chose to end it have nothing to do with her, and she's simply trying to help me.

'Like she had a secret. Something that was worrying her but she didn't want to discuss. One minute she was all happy and then I would see her in the bathroom and she'd been crying. I even heard her throw up a few times. I asked her what was wrong but she wouldn't tell me and, anyway, the next time I saw her she was really happy again, like over-the-moon happy.'

'When did you hear her throw up?'

'Um, like… sometimes… it must have been in the morning because that's usually when we were together in the bathroom.'

Julia wasn't a child who threw up a lot. I can only remember one case of gastro when she was seven and threw up for days.

Esther watches me process what she's said. I would like to tell her to leave but can't think how to without being rude. I know that Julia may have been throwing up in the morning because she had been drinking the night before but I also know there is another reason why women throw up in the morning. *Pregnant*,

I think, before shaking my head. It doesn't seem possible and yet it would explain her erratic behaviour. But if it was true, who got her pregnant and why hadn't she told me?

'Why didn't you tell the police that?' I ask Esther.

'A lot of the girls cry in the bathroom here. Like, a *lot*. Besides, she was always up and down. Everyone is. I have my bad days too, but I don't…' Esther looks at me. 'I didn't think it was anything. I'm sorry. I should have told the police.'

'Don't worry about it,' I say, seeing that Esther is on the verge of tears again. 'Anything else? Maybe something that you've thought of in the last day or so?'

Esther runs her fingers through her hair, looking up at the ceiling. She wants me to know she's really trying. 'Only once, when I asked her if something was wrong, she said to me, "You'll know soon enough. The whole world will know soon enough."'

'What did that mean?'

'I don't know,' sighs Esther. 'I assumed it was a guy. Isn't it always a guy?'

I nod and look down at the floor. She's right. There is always a guy. So, despite what everyone has been saying, there was a guy, a boyfriend, a man. There *was* someone.

I can remember my own secretive smiles and giggles when I first met Joel, and then again when Adrian and I started dating properly. I also know that I spent my fair share of nights crying over Joel before we got married, when he didn't return a call or something equally ridiculous. Then, when we were married, I cried tears of shame, anger and pain. I even cried over Adrian when I was unsure of his intentions. There's always a guy.

'Do you think she could have been pregnant?' I ask Esther, conscious of a deep feeling of humiliation that I am asking someone she's only known for a couple of years – a girl she didn't even count as a friend – a question that I, as her mother, should know the answer to. How could we have drifted so far from each other?

She came from my body, she carried my blood and yet she had become a stranger. 'It would explain why she was up one minute and down the next.'

Esther shrugs her shoulders and regards me warily. 'Maybe… I mean, the throwing up… but there are at least three girls here that throw up after each meal. I've told them they need to get some help but they don't want to listen.'

I can just imagine how a young woman suffering from an eating disorder would enjoy hearing the truth from Esther.

I realise that I have asked too much of her. She is not the kind of person Julia would ever have confided in, no matter how bad things got.

'Thanks for talking to me. I'll pack up as much of her stuff as I can to take home with me but I may have to come back again.'

'I can get you some boxes,' she says, eager to be helpful, now that the inquisition is over.

'Thanks.'

Esther leaves, closing the door quietly behind her. The truth is there is not that much left in the room that had any meaning to Julia. All her favourite things and her computer were in her car. I was surprised to see so much stuff when Adrian brought it inside. She usually brought her computer home with her when she came, but this time, this last time when I had no idea she was coming, when I didn't know until it was too late, she had more than just her computer and two days' worth of clothes with her. She had BB, and he usually stayed in Melbourne. She had all her jewellery and most of her clothes. If I had known she was driving home instead of flying, I would have known something was wrong – but she didn't tell me. She drove all that way with only BB and her anguish over something or someone for company.

The police think that this is a sign that she never meant to come back but I wonder now why she wouldn't have tidied up this room if that was the case. Surely she meant only to come for a visit, albeit a surprise visit? Perhaps she was going to take a few weeks off from university? Maybe she came home to tell me she was pregnant so that I could help her do whatever she wanted to do? Was that what she meant when she said that the whole world would know soon enough? Was she going to tell Adrian and me about the pregnancy and the relationship she was in, or had been in?

But if that's the case, then why didn't she do that?

What on earth could have happened in her long drive from Melbourne that would have made her decide to take her own life?

Was she pregnant? Was my little girl pregnant?

'I'm not a little girl any more, Claire,' I can hear her saying. 'You need to regard me as another adult woman, just like you are.' I think I laughed at her when she said that. I shouldn't have laughed but the petulant words and her deliberate addressing of me as 'Claire' instead of 'Mum' struck me as the behaviour of a toddler, and I couldn't hold in my reaction.

'You're still my little girl, even if you are twenty,' I had replied, composing myself as she clenched her jaw. I thought all of that stopped when they were finished being teenagers. I thought we had successfully navigated the turmoil of those years and made it through to the other side. We hadn't, we didn't. She sank. She slipped under the water and I let her go.

Pregnancy would be a reason, at least. A terrible one at a time in history where it is possible to take care of such a problem, but at least it would have been a reason of sorts. Many years ago, I am sure that countless young women would have seen death as the only way out of an intolerable situation, but this is not years ago. Surely she knew that there were options for an unwanted pregnancy? I always told her to come to me if she found herself in a situation like this. I told her I would support her through whatever emotionally traumatic decision she needed to make. I told her I would be there for her. 'There is nothing you could do to stop me loving you, Julia, to stop me from trying to help you, no matter what the situation,' I remember telling her when she was sixteen and I was routinely giving lectures on drugs and alcohol and unprotected sex.

'What if I were a criminal?'

'I'd still try to help you.'

'What if I murdered someone?'

'I'd get you a good lawyer.'

'What if I dropped out of school and married a rock star?'

'I'd come to his concerts,' I said, laughing along with her.

I lean down from my position on the bed and pick up a pair of jeans. I sniff and then fold them in half when the only scent I can detect is a floral chemical smell of washing powder. I want to lie down on her bed and rest for an hour or two or three but I have a flight booked for tomorrow morning. Devastatingly, I have not found what I came here to find. It is best I return home to what is left of my family.

There is a light knock at the door and I open it quickly, expecting Esther with boxes, even though she has only been gone a few minutes. But it's not Esther. A tall, thin young man with riotous curls and thick glasses smiles down at me. My heart thrums. Is this the boy in Julia's life?

'Mrs Barker, I'm Brian. I sit… I mean, I sat next to Julia in International Affairs.'

A young woman steps out from behind him. She is much shorter, wearing a purple skirt and matching purple top. Her black hair is a fountain on top of her head, spilling over her shoulders and down her back. 'And I'm Ara. You sent us a text.'

'Oh, yes, of course. I didn't know if you got my message, please come in.'

They shuffle into the room and look around at the mess. I am about to explain when I see Ara look at Brian and they both smile.

'Not the tidiest person,' I say.

'I used to tidy up whenever I came round,' says Ara. 'She used to sit on the bed and talk and I would fold clothes. My mum says I have a terrible need for order.'

I smile, despite the situation. 'I was hoping there was something else you could tell me about what she was like in the last weeks before… before…'

Ara nods her head and wipes her eyes. 'She was the best, she really was. She made me laugh every single day. We were in Digital Communications together and she was so good at mimicking our professor and her funny way of speaking. Once she made me laugh so much my drink came out of my nose.'

I nod, listening eagerly, picturing a grinning Julia surrounded by people who are laughing with her.

'She was such a… just, like, a nice person, you know?' says Brian.

'But in the last couple of weeks…?' I ask.

'Um, I guess up and down, you know. I thought it was because exams are coming up soon.'

'She did seem like something was bothering her but we all go through stuff. I asked her if she was okay and she told me she was "dealing with some stuff" and I left it there. I knew she would talk to me when she was ready,' says Ara. She shakes her head. 'I thought we had lots of time to talk. I thought we would talk when exams were over and assignments handed in. I didn't know.' She is crying hard now, her body convulsing as tears drip off her chin. I move forward to put my arms around her in an attempt to offer some sort of comfort but Brian steps forward and holds her tight. I wait as her sobs subside and she calms down. Brian grabs some tissues off a box on top of Julia's desk. I have to resist the urge to tell him not to touch my daughter's stuff, as if holding on to the tissues might undo this mess.

'Do either of you think she may have had a boyfriend?' I ask, quickly dismissing Brian as a likely candidate. He just doesn't seem like a possibility.

'She had a thing for older guys,' Ara says, and then she blows her nose again. 'She hated how immature everyone at uni is.'

'Hey,' says Brian.

'Not you, but most of the guys you meet.'

'She never said I was immature,' says Brian, and I see longing written across his face.

'You had such a crush on her,' laughs Ara and then as if she has just realised they are talking about someone who is no longer alive she bursts into noisy tears again. I stand awkwardly while Brian comforts her into silence.

'I think she was seeing someone,' he says. 'I told the police but said that I didn't know for sure. She didn't see him a lot but there would be whole weekends they spent together. I mean, that's just what I think because who else would she have been with if she wasn't at school and she wasn't at home? I always thought she had gone back to Sydney but she told me she wasn't going home, just having a weekend out of residence. I didn't know how she could afford that so I assumed she was with some guy in a hotel, or at his place.'

'And you told the police that?'

'Yeah, but the guy I was talking to, the detective or constable, asked me if I had any proof of a relationship but I didn't – I mean, I don't. I had no evidence or anything and she didn't post any pictures on her Instagram or anything. She never talked about him so I guess he decided it didn't matter. I mean, if there had been someone, you would think she would have put up some photos. But I still think there was a guy. It's just a gut feeling.'

I understand from listening to Brian why the constable would have dismissed his theory. But what if it's the truth?

'Where would she have met someone like that?' I ask, and they both shrug.

Julia wasn't just keeping secrets from me. She was even keeping secrets from her friends.

'Thanks for coming,' I say, aware that they have nothing else to tell me. 'If you think of anything, anything that you think I should know… I just want to know for me, not so I can tell anyone else. Would you text me?'

'Sure,' they both mumble together, and then we exchange awkward hugs before they leave.

I am so tired I feel dizzy. Once more I sink back down onto her bed. I lie looking up at the ceiling for a few minutes, wondering what thoughts roamed through her head as she lay in the same place, looking at the same ceiling.

Instead of allowing the lethargy to pull me down, I start moving and in an hour I have cleaned up the room. Esther has dropped off some boxes that I've filled. I have two suitcases packed with what remained of her clothes that I can take with me back to Sydney, even though I know that I will eventually just have to give them away to charity. There are a couple of boxes that I will post back to myself this afternoon filled with some other stuffed toys, the extra duvet and pillow set she had, her handwritten notes from her classes and assorted knick-knacks. I have thrown away her make-up and skincare, pausing every minute or two to wonder if she still wants an eye shadow in bronze or a bright pink blush, only to remember that she no longer needs any of this stuff, crushing my heart in the process. What an impossible thing this is. I don't know if I could ever explain to someone the horror of throwing away your own daughter's make-up, in the knowledge she will never wear it again.

When I helped my mother pack up my grandmother's flat, I was saddened by the photographs and cards she had collected that would simply be disposed of, as though her memories had no meaning. I feel the same sense of despair as I clean Julia's room.

Finally, it is time to go. I call a taxi, arranging to meet it downstairs. I haul everything out into the corridor, drawing sympathetic glances from the girls walking past on their way to and from class. I stare hard at them as they pass, wondering if any of the girls who drop their eyes and turn down their mouths as they see me have posted vile messages on Julia's Facebook page. It's such an odd thing to do, to say something awful about someone who is dead and who had little or no impact on your life. It feels as if by merely commanding some attention by the unfortunate way she left this world Julia has enraged a whole lot of people.

I know that Julia's story is being discussed all over the university. There are extra counsellors on campus in case students need to talk about what happened. **'You Are Not Alone'** read the words on black and white posters below a sketch of a face looking down, with the number for Student Health in a sunny yellow. I have tried not to see these posters but they are plastered on the walls of every building I have passed on the campus. I don't know if they are always up or if they've just gone up in the last few days.

There was also a general letter sent out to all parents and students on the university database. I thought it particularly cruel that they did not remember to remove my name.

Two girls in matching workout outfits walk past me, quickly tilting their heads towards each other and whispering dramatically behind their hands. Could one of them have written the words, *There is a reason she took her own life and the world is probably better off without her.*

I think about Liam's post or what I have assumed is Liam's post, about his simple message of love. Was she coming to Sydney to see him and tell him she was pregnant? Did he already know?

I will call Kayla, his mother, when I get back to Sydney. She's left a voicemail on my phone expressing sorrow and I wonder if she's knows more about what happened, if she knew about their relationship.

None of the girls who I pass offers to help me as I drag the suitcases down the stairs and then return for the boxes, sweating through my shirt by the end. Perhaps they do not wish to intrude. Perhaps they do not want to be infected by my grief.

Before I go I fold everything left on the bed and then take a quick look underneath. I don't see anything at first but then a dark patch catches my eyes and I lie on the floor and stretch my arm right under the bed until my fingers encounter a box tucked between the bed leg and the wall. It's an old shoebox, which I pull out, meaning to throw in the garbage. It's heavy, and inside is what looks like a transcript of a book, printed out neatly, but when I start to go through it I realise it is a box filled with letters, all printed out and mailed to Julia. Fold lines are clear on all of them, where they must have been pleated into envelopes that my daughter tore open.

But there are no envelopes, no indication of who the letters are from. I grab the box and make my way downstairs, my heart pounding, certain that I am holding something that will reveal more about Julia's life in Melbourne. I want to rifle through the box, to inhale each and every letter, but the taxi is waiting for me and I scramble into the car. I hold the box gently on my lap, like a prized possession. It's from a pair of stiletto heels. There is a picture on the side of the box and a colour code indicating they were red. I didn't know Julia owned such a pair of shoes. She hated stilettos, preferring chunky wedge heels instead.

As the taxi driver pulls out of the campus and onto the road I lift the lid of the box and look closely at the first letter. I do not read the words, only the greeting, knowing that I need to be alone to absorb the contents.

'My sweetest, darling Julia' is typed at the top of the letter.

My sweetest, darling Julia.

✹

My sweetest, darling Julia,

How wonderful you looked last time we were together. It seems to me that the longer we are together the more beautiful you become. You were a vision in that dress with those delectable red shoes.

I know that you said you wanted it to be a final dinner and I am so glad that you changed your mind and joined me at the hotel instead.

It was a night I'll never forget, Julia. A night of love and wonder. Please don't worry about anyone but us any more. We are all and we are everything that matters.

Love x

CHAPTER EIGHT

My mouth is dry by the time I am safely alone in my hotel room. I haven't eaten lunch and I know that I should at least get myself a bottle of water and something small, but the letters demand to be read.

It feels like an invasion of Julia's privacy. It *is* an invasion – I know she hated the idea that I was so interested in every thought and feeling she had.

'I don't have to share everything with you, Mum.'

'You don't but you used to.'

'Things change.'

'Oh, how they change,' I mutter as I stare down at the stack of letters. I have purposefully not focused on the words beyond the greeting. It is the greeting from a lover, a romantic, a boy or a man who felt a great deal for her. She was twenty, a young woman who was mature beyond her years, so she could have been dating a boy her age or even a much older man. I have friends whose daughters are dating men that are ten and twenty years older than them. Anything is possible. I realise the letters could even be from a woman, although Julia has never said anything to indicate she was interested in women. Her walls used to be covered in ubiquitous boy band posters when she was thirteen and fourteen, and if I asked I would receive a rundown on how much she loved each one of them, how gorgeous they were and how one day she was going to marry a musician.

I want to scream with frustration at all the things I don't know about my daughter, at all that can now be called into question.

My sparse little room is equipped with a kettle and sachets of coffee. I make myself a strong cup and add three sugars to sweeten the brew. The box of letters sits innocuously on my neatly made bed. I could simply throw it away and leave this part of Julia's life in the past, as I'm certain she would have wanted. But the idea that the letters may have some answers for me means that I know, regardless of the moral right or wrong of the situation, I am going to read them. Was there ever a question? I was prepared for her to grow up but not quite ready for the feeling of seeing her so little and then not quite knowing what to say to her when I did. I assumed that even when we fought she could still feel the same physical pull towards me that I could to her. It wasn't so. I know it wasn't so because I don't feel it with my own mother. I thought my relationship with Julia would be better than mine with my mother, even though we are very close. Haven't I been a better mother? Isn't that what every generation is supposed to do? Improve on the concept of mothering?

I start at the bottom of the pile with what I assume must be the oldest letter. I want to read them all immediately but sense that I have to start here at the beginning, at the beginning of whatever this is. I feel my heart rate speed up. I am unsure of what I'm going to find, frightened of what these letters might hold. I run my fingers over the first letter, expecting it to communicate something to me through touch, but it's standard printer paper and feels too ordinary to hold the biggest secret in my daughter's life.

My sweetest, darling Julia,
    I cannot tell you how much this afternoon meant to me. I could not even begin to detail how it felt to have your lips against mine. It was only a kiss but you and I both know it was so much more. It was us admitting that, after all this time, we both felt the same way. I loved that you laughed after we kissed. It made me laugh,

too. What a wonder it is to discover this truth about each other. What a wonder you are. Don't be frightened, my love. Don't shy away from this. I am ready for you. I am waiting and when you are ready, I will be here.

I tried to convince myself not to do this, not to expose myself in print like this but in the end I was unable to resist. I think of you as I type. I think of you and you're near me again. My words conjure you out of the air and there you are, my sweetest darling. I didn't want to send it to you but I found that I couldn't help myself. Look how you've changed me, Julia. With just one kiss you've turned me into a different man. What a miracle you are.

I know you will want to hold on to this letter, my love. I know you will want to keep these words forever, my darling, but I need you to destroy this letter and any others I write to you. I need to know I can trust you to do this for me. One day I will write you letters that you can share with the whole world if you desire, but for now our love must be a private thing, a delicious secret just for you and me. Read my words and know that I am always thinking about you. It's not possible for anyone else to know about us right now, not yet. But it will be one day, one day soon, I promise.

Please destroy this after reading it.
Love x

Who is this person? How long had they known each other? She has only been in Melbourne for eighteen months although I suppose that eighteen months in the life of a twenty-year-old can feel like a lifetime. Or it could be someone in Sydney she'd known for years. It could be Liam. I know he used to send her poems but the language in the letter seems beyond what I would have thought him capable of producing. The writer of this letter sounds older than twenty. I don't know why but he does.

I put the first letter aside even though I want to read it over in case it holds some clue I have missed. But I am desperate to read them all and I pull the next one out of the pile.

My sweetest, darling Julia,

It was wonderful to hold your hand today as we walked down the street. It was worth the drive just to get out of town, wasn't it? It was worth the wait to be somewhere that we cannot be recognised. I promise you that no one saw us. That boy you thought was your friend from uni was just some stranger on the street. No one was watching us, no one at all. We were two hours away from everything. No one knew us and no one cared. I know you hate the secrecy, my darling, but it has to be that way for now as we explore exactly how we feel about each other. I am so grateful that we have the chance to do this.

I liked the way you kept looking at me as we walked because I knew that you were feeling the joy of it as well. I imagined that we were not just in a little town where we were anonymous but in another country where we didn't even speak the same language. I would like to take you away somewhere so we could truly be alone for days at a time. I would like to guide you through the art galleries in Rome and take you to the top of the Eiffel Tower in Paris. I want to show you all the things I have learned in my life. I want to give you what I know about the world.

I lie awake at night imagining what it will feel like to finally feel your skin against my skin. I know you don't want to rush this between us. I'm not rushing you, I promise, but whenever you're ready, I am ready too.

Remember – destroy this.
Love x

Whoever this person is, he knows how to write a love letter and that makes me think that he isn't a boy, but a man. I can imagine Julia being swept away by an older man. I can see how attractive it would be to have a boyfriend with a job and a car when she was living in a hall of residence and queuing up for the shared bathroom.

It feels very wrong to be reading his words to my daughter, about my daughter, these private whispers of love. But I cannot stop myself.

I pick up the next few letters, glancing over them, noting that they are all written in the same vein.

Certain sentences jump out at me in the midst of his adoring prose. *Stop worrying about who can see us. I promise you no one knows. It's our special secret.* Why did they feel the need to be anonymous in a small town? What difference would it have made if she had seen someone she knew from university? Why were they hiding? And why does he want her to destroy the letters? Exactly what kind of relationship were they having? Questions tumbling through my head, I pick up another one.

My sweetest, darling Julia,

Last night was incredible. I know you were sad afterwards but you shouldn't be. Only true love can make a sexual connection as special as that was. That is what I feel for you – true, pure love. I know we have both agonised over the decision to be together but we shouldn't. Some things are bigger than right and wrong, bigger than a bad marriage or what your mother would think. Some things are bigger than everything, and that's what we have. I watched you sleep afterwards and I want you to know that I have never known such complete happiness. You are not just beautiful, you are magnificent. You are a work of art, a goddess and all I want is to worship your body.

Love x

I drop the stack of letters back into the box. Clearly not a boy but a man, and a married man at that. What else can his words mean? She was evidently worried about what I would say about the situation and a small part of me is warmed by the idea that she was still concerned with what I would have thought. Was she too worried? Is it possible that she believed I would judge her too harshly? I shake my head.

This is a married man, I am sure of it. Not Liam, not Brian, not a boy from university, but a married man.

Even if she was concerned with how I would feel about her dating a married man, it wouldn't have been enough to push her to… I groan… I can't fall down this rabbit hole.

In truth I cannot believe such a choice of Julia. I spent her whole childhood encouraging her to try and perceive the grey areas in certain situations. To her everything was always black or white. 'I *hate* bananas.' 'I will never play with Katie.' 'I can't *do* math.' 'I am never ever talking to Nicholas again.' There was no room for nuance with Julia.

'Leave room to change your mind,' I always told her. 'One day you may want to try a banana or play with Katie.'

'No, I never will.'

I encouraged her to give herself space to vacillate between ideas and opinions because she was so hard on herself if she did back down on a stance she'd taken. I think she ate bananas in secret for at least a month before I caught her and then she was furiously embarrassed to have been caught out. As she grew older she had strict ideas about what was acceptable and unacceptable behaviour. 'Hannah smiled at Josh today and she knows, she *knows* that Michelle likes Josh.'

'It was just a smile, Julia, it doesn't have to mean anything.'

'God, Mum, you have no idea about these things. It's never just a smile. It was the *way* she smiled. Josh belongs to Michelle until she doesn't want him any more. That's the rules of our group.'

'What does Josh think about that?'

'Josh is just a boy, he doesn't think much.'

She made me laugh all the time as a child, as an adolescent and even as a surly teenager. I place my hand over my still beating heart, wondering how I can keep going, knowing that Julia will never make me laugh again except in my memories. 'Oh, Julia,' I say, as I press down on my chest.

She liked things to be fair and right. She would never have dated a married man. It would have gone against everything she stood for. Where would she have even met one? Unless she knew him from Sydney. Eric Peters pops into my head again. The image of the year-book photo. But he lives in Sydney and Brian said that Julia was taking weekends away in Melbourne. The letters seem to indicate that they were together in Melbourne. Sydney's only a short flight away, but still.

I hate that I have no answers to any of these questions. I get up and pace restlessly around the hotel room. Who was this man and if he was capable of cheating on his wife, what else was he capable of?

I dial Adrian's number, even though I know it's Wednesday and he's probably showing a house to a prospective client right now. I really just want to hear his voice and his voicemail will do. I am surprised when he picks up.

'Hey, love, how are you?'

'I'm… you know. I didn't expect you to answer.'

'I'm between showings at the moment. I was actually thinking of calling you before the next one starts. The last one was a complete wash-out. It's only been on the market for two weeks and already the number of people coming through has dropped to almost nothing.' He pauses, probably aware that he has fallen into the old pattern of updating me on his work day without thinking, like nothing has changed. 'How is it going? Are you getting anywhere? Have you found anything out?'

'This was probably a bad idea,' I mumble. I hadn't meant to cry but hearing his voice allows me to let go.

'Oh, Claire, oh, love.'

'I just wanted to see if I could find out anything and I wanted to see her room,' I sob. 'I didn't want anyone else touching her things.' My discovery of the letters sits between us, my own secret now. I can't think how to tell him.

'Take a deep breath, you need to breathe. It's okay, it's going to be okay. Should I come down there? I can get on a flight tonight.'

'No, no.' I struggle to compose myself. 'You need to be there for the boys. I need to know that they're being taken care of.'

'Nicholas is eighteen and Cooper is sixteen and they are perfectly able to take care of themselves. Anyway, Joel is here.'

'Oh, yes, of course. He told me he was coming.'

'You never told me you spoke to him.'

'It never occurred to me to mention it.'

'Yeah, well, I would have appreciated knowing he was coming. He just turned up on the doorstep last night, and the boys went off with him. I don't know where. He brought them back after eleven and all three of them looked like they'd had a rough evening. He said he's going to stay until the police say we can go ahead with the funeral.'

'But that could be weeks. I told him that.'

'So he knows that. He told me he's got some connections because of his work so he may be able to hurry things along. I guess I have to feel for him, Claire. I think it will be good for the boys to have him here as well. This morning I told Cooper that I thought it would be better if he went to school because he wouldn't get out of bed and he told me that I had no right to tell him what to do because Julia wasn't my daughter.'

'Oh, Adrian, I'm so sorry. That's so unfair. She was your daughter, too.'

'No, Claire.' He sighs. 'She wasn't really. I loved her but she was yours and Joel's. I don't want any of this to upset you. I know my place in all this so I'm going to step back a bit and let Joel take the lead. You need to mourn as a family, even if you're a fractured family… but I miss her…' Adrian stops talking and I realise that he's crying.

I have no idea how to help him. He's known Julia since she was twelve years old and he's worked harder than any real father would to get my kids to like, to even love him, especially Julia. She was the most prickly when we started dating, even though she professed to hate her father. At ten and eight Cooper and Nicholas were oblivious to Adrian's presence in the house, assuming he was simply a friend of mine. But not Julia. Julia, of course, was far more perceptive.

'Why is he always here?' she yelled right at Adrian when she opened the door to find him standing on the front porch. It was after Joel had worked things out with the bank and I had assured Julia that we no longer had to leave our home.

After I hadn't heard from Joel for a month, I knew that the only way I would be able to support myself and my children would be to sell the house. I needed Joel's permission to do so but I contacted Adrian's agency to start the process.

Adrian wasn't even supposed to be the agent I met with. I was expecting a woman named Kathy that day but she had to stay home with a sick child and so Adrian came instead. I only told Julia about selling the house. She was angry about having to move but by then she was even angrier with Joel for ignoring us.

When I realised that I would no longer need to sell, I was worried about Adrian's reaction. He had been nothing but kind and I felt guilty for wasting his time. He had taken me through what needed to happen step by step. He sat quietly with his face turned away a little as I cried over my newly renovated kitchen, created to perfectly suit my every need. The beautiful kitchen that I would now have to give up to save myself and my children. He bought me lunch unnecessarily and even managed to make me laugh with stories about strange clients and unsellable houses.

When Joel texted me saying, *Stay in the house. I'll pay off the mortgage. Stay until the children have left*, I wanted to throw the gesture back in his face but I couldn't. And I felt as though I owed Adrian something.

If I had been more aware I would have realised that there was no need for him to come over so often. Even when I was planning to go ahead with the sale, he was over almost every day, making me cups of tea, offering me advice. But I was in turmoil, unable to think beyond my dire circumstances.

'I'm sorry,' I said for the tenth time, after I had explained the whole situation to him on the phone.

'Stop apologising,' Adrian said. 'To tell the truth… do you want to know the truth?'

'Of course,' I replied.

'I'm glad. I know it would have been a big sale but now you're no longer a client I can ask you out.'

'Ask me out?'

'Yes, like on a date. I mean you can say no… I don't want to push or anything. I know you've only just separated but I think… I feel like we have something. It's why I've been coming over so much… I mean a lot of it was work but I… I really like talking to you.'

I had been astonished. Truly astounded. After the years of confidence-draining abuse from Joel, the fact that a man could find me attractive was extraordinary to me. 'Adrian, I have three kids and a full-time job… I'm just not sure about dating yet.' Standing alone in my kitchen I felt my face flush. I was assailed by the memory of the excitement I felt before I met Joel when a boy or young man called to ask me out. With my new status of 'single mother', dating was so far from my mind that it seemed like an alien concept. I was amazed that Adrian didn't see a wreck of a woman when he looked at me – and I stood up and pushed my shoulders back, even though there was no one to see me. Somehow, despite my obvious distress and the sleepless nights written across my face, Adrian had seen a woman he wanted to spend more time with. I allowed myself a small smile. I was not 'useless' and 'stupid' and a 'real ball breaker'. I was not 'always upset' or 'impossible to talk to'. I was a woman, with whom a nice-looking, sweet man, wanted to have dinner.

'I understand and I get it but maybe just a dinner or a lunch with no strings attached… actually, no, don't worry about it,' he said. 'You're probably right. I shouldn't have asked.'

'No, don't be sorry,' I reassured him. 'It's nice to be asked.'

And it was nice to be asked, especially by a man whose kindness had been a small shining light on some of my worst days. Adrian allowed me to reassess some of my toxic ideas about men that had developed over the years of my abuse. In my mind Joel was the enemy and his existence tainted all men for me. For years I had looked at men with suspicion, wondering if behind closed doors they were subjecting their wives and children to uncontrolled anger.

When my brother had found out about the divorce he called me and said, 'I'm really sorry, Claire. Are you sure you can't fix it? He's a good guy underneath it all.'

'He hit me, Cal. Didn't Mum tell you?'

'Oh, no… I'm so sorry, Claire. Why? Why would he do that?'

It wasn't a question asking me to justify Joel's behaviour but rather a plaintive wail to the world as to why his sister had been hurt. But I became enraged with him and hung up. 'They're all the same,' I muttered to myself, leaving my mother to smooth things over between us like we were still children.

All men were alike I decided, ignoring my patient father who was helping me in any way he could. I was happy to never have to get close to another one. I would never trust a man again. I would never allow myself, or my children, to go through the pain again.

In the months leading up to me finally telling Joel to leave I had counselled myself to accept that I would be alone forever.

Only when I was certain that life as a single mother who had to struggle for money and to take care of her children was preferable to the way I had been living, did I tell Joel to go.

I had a vision for myself, far into the future, where I was peacefully alone in an apartment with only a cat for company but with the comforting knowledge that somewhere out of sight my three children were fine and happy. Adrian's request interrupted that vision.

I had waited a few days, thinking through his invitation from every angle, trying to find a concealed truth behind it. 'What does he want?' I asked my mother on the phone. I was eating lunch in the staffroom at the college where I worked. Other teachers walked in and out, raising hands in greeting when they saw me but politely staying away, aware of my fragile emotional state and not wanting to interrupt one of the many fraught conversations I had taken to having during lunch, with my mother and my lawyer and Barbara. I think they were all relieved when I went back to part-time work and they didn't have to face my emotional baggage on a daily basis.

'Lunch or dinner with you, I imagine,' she replied.

'It's too soon.'

'Claire, yesterday you yelled at Nicholas for forgetting to take out the garbage. Do you remember what you said to him?'

'I said he has to take responsibility for some things around the house – which is the truth, Mum.'

'I'm not debating that but you ended your lecture with, "I don't need another man giving me crap right now."'

'I didn't say that,' I protested.

'You did. You were angry and I am sure you didn't mean it but I was going to talk to you about it today. You need to apologise to him. He is only a boy and not every man is Joel, Claire, not even the little men who share his genetics. Don't alienate them because they happen to be boys. Love them into being wonderful men like your father.'

I ended the call with my mother, ashamed about saying something so hideous to my ten-year-old son. I promised myself I would apologise to him the second I got home that night.

I had finished my last mouthful of food, taken a deep breath and called Adrian.

'Maybe… maybe we can have lunch on Sunday?' I said, my voice cracking at the end of my sentence, betraying the butterflies colliding in my stomach.

'Yes, yes, great! I'm so glad you changed your mind. I'll come and get you at twelve. Will the kids come with us?'

'No way,' I laughed. 'I could use a nice lunch without them. I'm sure my mother will babysit for me.'

'Excellent, twelve it is. I look forward to it, Claire.'

'Me, too,' I had replied. I felt a grin spread itself across my face and I realised I was actually excited.

The words I had flung at my young son haunted me for weeks. I reminded myself every day to be conscious of the way I spoke to both my boys, to see them as not simply extensions of their awful father, but as my beautiful boys who only wanted to protect and love me. Spending time with Adrian seemed to make that easier.

I was grappling with Joel returning to our lives, questioning his motives as he made endless overtures to the children, hoping to regain their trust and affection. I was trying to accept that Joel was not the same man I had been married to and that everyone is capable of change on a grand scale, but I was finding that almost impossible as incidents of his abuse woke me in a cold sweat at night, and I waited for him to do something that revealed who he truly was.

Adrian was a wonderful contrast to Joel.

'I'm so sorry, I'm so sorry,' I apologised one night when I cooked dinner for him at his place, presenting him with chewy risotto.

'Relax,' he laughed, stroking my hand. 'It's just dinner, it's not life threatening.'

I wanted to laugh with him because it *was* just one bad dinner, but I knew that sometimes one bad dinner led to a deep purple bruise on my arm for which I had to dig into my box of excuses for a reason to explain it away.

'Please just relax, Claire,' Adrian said again, and I had nodded and finished my glass of wine, reminding myself that Adrian was one of the 'good ones'.

But Julia was angry at Adrian's existence, even though she had vowed about her father that she would, 'never speak to him again'. She knew that there was no real reason for Adrian to be at our door and she was justifiably suspicious of our coffee dates and dinner dates. I should have told her what was going on, but at the time it was so new to me that I was still trying to process it myself.

We deliberately kept things casual at first. He didn't formally ask me out again. Instead he turned up unexpectedly when he knew I had a half day off from work or he came by at dinner time on a Saturday night and asked me if I was hungry, knowing that I was happy to leave the boys with Julia – for an hour at the most.

'I didn't want to scare you off,' he told me later, when we had begun to discuss marriage. 'I thought if we could both pretend for the first few months that we were friends then we wouldn't have to have any difficult conversations.'

But Julia realised, even before we did, that there was something much more between us, and she was angry not to have been told, to have not been asked for her permission, really. 'I don't want another father. I hate Dad and I don't want another man to hurt you!' She shouted and stamped as I tried to explain.

'This man is not like Dad,' I had yelled back. 'He won't hurt me. He won't hurt us.'

'How do you know?'

I didn't know. I questioned myself after every date, after the first time we had sex, after the first family dinner, after the first time he came with us to visit my parents, chatting easily with my father who loved perusing the real estate section of the newspaper, predicting what houses would sell for.

'What do you think, Dad?' I asked my father after the first time he met Adrian.

'I think no man is good enough to deserve you, darling, but I can see how much he admires you and he is very kind to the children. Kindness is what you need now, Claire, and it's what I wish for you.'

For months on end I questioned myself, waiting for Adrian to lose his temper over something small, to throw a fit because the day wasn't going his way, to roar his impatience at the kids, but it never happened. It took him at least a year to win Julia over. He made careful steps towards her. He bought her gifts as he did with Nicholas and Cooper, but he agonised over his choices.

'Just tell me what to get her,' he would say.

'Adrian, you don't have to buy them gifts, you know. They don't need anything. And if you do buy them something, whatever you bring will be appreciated.'

'I know, but with Nick and Cooper I just buy stuff I would have wanted as a kid. I have no idea when it comes to girls.'

He worked harder with her than with the boys. I think he understood that she was the key to his being accepted into the family.

'I'm sorry,' Adrian says now. I hear him taking deep breaths, tearing me away from my memories.

'Don't be sorry,' I say. 'I need you to miss her as much as I do.'

'I do.'

'I wonder if I'll ever feel okay again,' I say.

'Grief feels like that,' he says. 'After my mother died I thought I would never be able to wake up and not think about her first thing in the morning, but over time it lessens. You never forget, but it gets easier.'

I bite down on my lip, preventing hurtful words escaping. Losing a parent is completely different to losing a child but I don't want to dismiss Adrian's feelings. I know that after my father died my grief scraped my skin red raw and I felt like I was exposed to the world and without protection. But as the months passed that faded and I was able to remember the wonderful lessons he taught me and the compassion he'd always shown me. He went too soon but he'd lived a life where he'd had children and grandchildren, found time for retirement and travel. He helped raise me and sent me out into the world so I could live my own life, but always know he was there for me.

But this, this grief is different. My body is changed. I listen to my breath going in and out and it doesn't sound the same, it doesn't feel the same. I don't remember the woman I was before Mia's screams and I don't recognise the woman I see in the mirror now. My life will be forever divided into two distinct parts. My heart aches and my soul aches but I don't know how to explain this to Adrian, who has never had children of his own.

'I don't know if this will ever fade,' I say instead.

'Maybe,' he agrees. 'Did you find anything, anything at all that can tell us how she was feeling?'

I take a deep breath. I want to tell him about the letters but I don't feel I have the right to share them with anyone else. They were her secret and I haven't even read all of them – I shouldn't even be reading them. It may be that whatever relationship she was having ended ages ago. She could have simply held on to the letters, mementos of their time together.

'No but…'

'But?' he asks.

※

My sweetest, darling Julia,

I keep wondering what if? What if you had decided to become an actress and moved to New York like you wanted to? What if you had stayed in Sydney for university and we had never found time to be alone without being watched? What if I had kissed you and you hadn't kissed me back? What if?

Love x

CHAPTER NINE

'I think she was seeing someone. A man.' I blurt it out. Julia was better than I am at keeping secrets.

I hear Adrian take another deep breath and then he is silent. 'Okay… I mean, it wouldn't be all that surprising but what makes you think that?'

'I found some…' I hesitate. I fumble for something to say. 'I found a note from someone.'

'A note, what kind of note?'

'Just a note from a man.' I look around the room, remembering all the things I had thrown out that belonged to Julia. A bottle of expensive perfume was one of the first things I picked up. I sprayed it into the air but the smell was unfamiliar and not something I ever remember smelling on Julia. It was a sexy scent – too grown up, too not my daughter. I threw it away because it held no meaning for me and therefore no tangible connection to her. 'I think it must have come with a gift he gave her,' I improvise.

'Claire, what did the note say? Why are you so concerned about it?'

I'm terrible at evasion. 'Just some stuff about loving her and wanting her.'

'Read it to me.'

'No, it doesn't feel right to do that. I shouldn't have opened it. I'm sure she wouldn't have wanted anyone to see it.'

'Well, now you have so read it to me. Maybe I can help you figure out who it is. Does he sign his name at the bottom? It was probably just some boy from university.'

'No… look, I don't want to talk about it. I shouldn't have mentioned it. It's just that everyone said she had no one in her life and she clearly did. I feel like this might mean something. About why she…'

'Okay, so maybe she did have someone in her life, but you don't know who he is and does it really matter? If she had a boyfriend it was obviously over or the police would have found out about him by now.'

'I guess.'

'You shouldn't really be going through all her things that closely. She wouldn't have liked that.'

I know he is right, but what choice do I have? 'I know, Adrian, but I did and there was no way I wasn't going to. I feel like I have no idea who she was or what she was doing with her life. I need to know and also…'

'And also?'

'Esther says she heard her throw up a few times in the morning. She may have been… she could have been… I mean it's possible that she was pregnant.'

'Oh. I… I don't know what to… she couldn't have been. Maybe she was just hung-over.'

'I don't think so. I think she really was pregnant. Brian and Ara both said she was up and down in the last few weeks and her being pregnant would explain that. Maybe she was unsure of what to do or scared or something and that's why she—'

'Maybe, but… yeah, maybe…' Adrian sounds sad, almost disappointed, as though Julia has somehow failed us by making such a mistake.

'And if she was, it means there was a man and he must have known and maybe he… I don't know. Maybe he was angry with her and…' I don't know how to explain my thoughts. I barely even know what I am thinking.

'The note gives you no clue as to who he is?'

'No. I'll go through her stuff at home. Maybe I'll find something else with his name on it.'

'You know she would have hated that you're doing this.'

'You don't have to keep saying that.' I am suddenly angry, although I cannot tell if it's more at him or myself. 'Don't you think I know that? But I have to find out what happened to her. I have to have some reason for why she did this, and if I have to invade her privacy to do it then so be it.'

'But if you find out something about her that she didn't want you to find out then all you will have achieved is a way of tainting her memory.' I can almost hear Adrian rubbing his face – something he does when he's very tired. He is finding me exhausting, finding this exhausting. 'Even the dead are entitled to their privacy, Claire. Imagine how this would have upset her.'

'Upset her?' I shriek. 'I'm her mother, Adrian, and she was obviously keeping secrets from me and maybe one of those secrets led her to take her life! I deserve to know because I am her *mother*. You're not her mother, Adrian, not even close.'

'I was just… that was a shitty thing to say. Why would you say something like that to me? I feel like I don't know how to talk to you any more.'

'I'm so sorry for you,' I hurl at him bitterly.

'Stop shutting me out, Claire.' There is real hurt in his voice. 'Stop making me the bad guy. I'm trying to support you here. I told you not to go to Melbourne and now you're imagining a boyfriend for her and going through her things? She may not have been my daughter but I knew her well enough to understand that she would have hated you doing this.'

There have been moments in our marriage when I have been aware of how difficult it is for Adrian to be a father figure to children who are not his own. There are lines he cannot cross and decisions he has no right to make. As the boys have grown older I have noticed him anticipating a time when it will just be him and me, and he will be the sole focus of my attention. When we got married we talked about having a child of our own, or at least he talked about it – I shot the idea down. I had no desire to have another child. I trust Adrian not to hurt me but I never wanted to put myself in the frightening position I had been in when Joel left. I still had young children but they were at school and while a baby would have been lovely, I knew that if things went wrong it would be impossible to support my family and take care of a baby on my own. I didn't anticipate things going wrong, I didn't want them to go wrong, but I understood, after Joel, that the possibility always existed.

Now that I am past the age when having a baby would be a simple thing I am aware that I may have made a mistake. He gave up on the idea easily enough, telling me, 'It was just a thought. I'm not really sure I wanted a child, more that I like the idea of someone with our combined genetics.'

He has given up a lot to take on a woman with three children and a complicated ex-husband and I understand that he has the right to look forward to us just being a couple. At least he did have that right. Now the trip to Europe we planned for after Nick's final exams have finished will have to be cancelled. I cannot see myself flying across to the other side of the world or choosing to do anything enjoyable ever again.

The silence between us grows and I feel my heart rate slow. I want to end the call but I know that would be a childish move that would only lead to more silence between us. It doesn't take much to destroy a marriage and the death of a child must be number one on the list of reasons for why two people can no longer stand being together. I don't want that to happen to Adrian and me. I know that I can barely see beyond this now, but I can see enough to know that I don't want to look up in a year and find I have no husband.

'Are you okay?' he finally asks.

'Yes…' I am embarrassed about shouting at him.

'So can we discuss this logically now?'

'What else is there to say, Adrian?'

'Let's say she was seeing someone. His name isn't on the note and he would have come forward if they were still involved in any way. It was probably just a passing thing and what's the point of going into that now? You're making an assumption about her being pregnant and jumping to conclusions. Anyway, what are you going to do? Find this mysterious boy or man and talk to him?' He follows this statement with a hollow laugh, as though the idea were ridiculous.

'I don't know,' I answer, aware of the absurdity of the notion. 'Maybe, yes, no… I really don't know but I would like to find him, to look at him at least.'

'Whatever she had with this boy, and I'm sure he was just some boy from university, is over and probably was over a long time ago. Leave it alone, Claire.'

'I have to—' I begin, before Adrian cuts me off.

'I need to go now. It's nearly time for my next house open. Please just get on a plane and come home. Leave this all in the past where it belongs. Come back and be with your family.'

'Okay,' I agree, as he ends the call.

I am exhausted. I look around my sparse hotel room. I would like to close my eyes for a week. I know that if I had told Adrian about the letters he would have been more concerned, I know he would. Even listening to myself speak about the note I knew that he was going to dismiss me. It does sound like I'm jumping to conclusions, making things up where nothing exists – out of desperation. But there is more. There is so much more.

I look at my phone clutched in my hand, tap his name in my contacts, but I immediately end the call. I can't tell him, not now, not yet.

Adrian has a good point. What *am* I going to do if I find out who the man is? Right now I can barely function. I don't have the energy to turn into a detective and yet… and yet.

I flick through the rest of the letters, not reading them properly but catching words here and there. I'm a little sickened at the thought of my baby girl having sex with a man who speaks to her like this. I don't want to think about her having sex at all. The grown-woman-Julia is always overlaid by the child-Julia in my head, and I don't want to think about her like that. No mother does.

I was sure she wasn't a virgin – she was too pretty, too popular, too confident for that – but I imagined that she had only been with boys her own age. It wasn't something I liked to think about but if it crossed my mind, I saw my daughter as I was at twenty, flirting with boys and fumbling through naïve, clumsy sex together. A married man changes the way I see her. The things she said to me in the weeks before her death take on a new significance, a new depth. Perhaps she was trying to tell me all along.

'Nicholas is such a *boy*,' she fumed, when her brother locked himself in the bathroom for an hour.

'He's only two years younger than you.' I smiled, almost enjoying the sibling grumbles because they were few and far between now that she lived in Melbourne.

'Two years younger but he might as well be ten years old. Men take years and years to grow up. I can't stand being surrounded by all these boys.'

'Some men never really grow up, sweetie, and some eighteen-year-old boys are already grown up. It's more about who they are than their age.'

'Age helps. I prefer men to boys. Men know how to talk to me.'

'Oh, Julia,' I laughed. I thought she was being overly dramatic, considering the only men she knew well were her father and her stepfather.

But I was wrong. There was another man. A man she met at school? A man she met at university? A man she met in a dark, crowded club one night?

I pick up a letter, searching for answers.

My sweetest, darling Julia,

I couldn't concentrate at work today. All I could think about was you. I thought about your perfect breasts, the small curve of your stomach, the arch of your back, and I was lost. I want to be near you, to be inside you. I want to watch you eat and sleep and laugh. I want you, Julia. I want you so much. Please stop questioning this. Live in this moment with me. That is the only thing to do. It has been said over and over again that you only regret the things you don't do. Us being together is something you have to do. It's something we both have to do. I don't think you understand the power you have over me. You cannot know how special you are. I would never want to hurt my wife. I know you would never want that either but us being together will only hurt her if she finds out and even then it will be only a momentary pain. Only the people in a marriage can understand what is wrong with that marriage and I promise you, if you could speak to her about our intimate life, she would tell you the same thing. We are no longer the strong couple we once were. I know it pains you to hear me speak of her and I don't want to either. But you need to understand that I know how far we have drifted from each other. I have tried to make things better between us, believe me I have. I don't want to think about her when I think about you. I want to pretend it is just you and me. Just you and me, my darling.

Love x

Reading the things he writes to her and about her makes my skin crawl. They are too personal, too private. So he is definitely married. She was still a child, a twenty-year-old child, but still my baby. Still five years old and shouting, 'Look, Mum, watch me, watch me do a cartwheel!'

Who could this man be? Her phone has provided no clues. I began scrolling through her text messages the day after she died, having remembered her mentioning that her ID code was the year she got the phone, but so far I have found nothing beyond a young woman talking to her friends. I was pleased to see she texted her brothers at least once a week, less pleased to read them making fun of me and my endless rules. There were a few texts from Joel, asking her how she was and if she needed money and inviting her to visit him. She rarely replied to those and if she did it was usually with just a few words: 'Fine thanks, really busy.'

There was only one name I didn't recognise as a new friend of hers – Natalia. It wasn't someone she'd spoken about before. I take her phone out of my bag and switch it on. I probably shouldn't be carrying it around with me but I cannot bear to leave it alone in her room. As it is with most people these days, it was her most prized possession. I have cancelled her contract and asked her phone company to stop calls coming in. The first day after it happened, as news slowly made its way around to everyone, it rang incessantly with people calling to ask Julia if it was true. The illogicality of such a thing made me laugh even through tears as I told each caller that I was not Julia but her mother and that Julia was, in fact, gone. Having to say it over and over again wore me down to nothing. Confirming your daughter's death on repeat sucks at your soul.

'Just switch it off, for fuck's sake,' Adrian yelled when it rang for the tenth time, but I couldn't, unable to stop myself indulging in the ridiculous notion that any call could be from Julia, looking for her phone.

I find Natalia and then I scroll through texts between Julia and this unknown person. I quickly figure out that Natalia was the owner of the temp agency Julia signed up to. She probably mentioned her name to me at some point. I stand up off the bed. Julia worked for a big company in the city for the last three months. She bought new clothes because she said she had to look more professional as it was a big logistics company. 'Boring work but the pay is okay and my boss is quite nice,' she told me.

I wonder now who her boss was. I use my own phone to dial the number before I think about it again.

'Perfect Temps,' answers a woman with a slight English accent.

'Hello, can I speak to Natalia, please?'

'Speaking, how can I help you?'

'It's Claire Brusso, Julia Barker's mother,' I say.

'Oh… yes, Julia. I was wondering why I hadn't heard from her in the last few days. I know that her contract is over but I did ask her to give me a call because I have a new position for her.'

'Um…' I say.

'I assume she's ill?' the woman says quickly. 'Do wish her better and ask her to give me a call when she's available again.'

'I'm sorry, I didn't think to contact you.'

'Contact me about…?'

I hear her typing as we talk. I have interrupted her busy day with the news of my daughter's death. I take a deep breath, unable to say anything.

I hear the typing stop. 'What's happened to Julia?'

'She… I'm afraid she… she… she committed suicide.'

'Oh… my … oh, my goodness… oh, Mrs…' she says, and I'm aware that she has forgotten my surname.

'Claire, please,' I say. I'm sick of saying that.

'Claire, I am so… just so shocked. If I had known, I would never have… oh…'

'It only happened a few days ago. We're still telling people in Julia's life the news.'

'Mrs Brusso, I'm so deeply, deeply sorry,' she says, recovering her professional tone and remembering my surname. 'Julia was such a lovely girl, so clever and quick and such a joy to work with.'

'Thank you, it's… yes, thank you,' I mumble. 'I wanted to talk to you, to ask you who she was working for before she…'

There is a moment of silence and I hear her tapping her keyboard. 'It was Rider Logistics, in the city. Her contract was completed.'

'Thank you, yes, you said. I'm trying to work out what happened, I want to know why. I thought maybe I could talk to the people she last worked with. Can you tell me who her last boss was?'

'Oh, I understand completely but I don't think her work, I mean, I hope not—'

'Please, Natalia, I feel like I knew nothing about her,' I say, shame burning me as I confess this to a stranger. 'Can you tell me who it was? I'm not going to bother anyone. I just want to get a sense of how she spent her time here in Melbourne.'

The silence on the other end of the phone tells me that Natalia is grappling with my request. There is no reason for it to be a secret and yet it's probably something she's never had to do before. I need this information. I don't mind playing the grieving-mother card to get it. This pain should be worth something. 'I miss her so much,' I say.

'She was working for the owner, Colin Rider. His assistant is on maternity leave for three months and he wanted to keep the position open for her so he made do with some temps. Julia was only working for him two days a week so I don't think he knew her very well.'

'No, I'm sure not,' I reassure her. 'Thanks for the information.'

'Any time, and again, I'm so very sorry.'

'Thank you.' I'm about to hang up, but then I change my mind. 'Before I go, did she seem okay to you? I mean in the last few weeks, was she the same?' In my small hotel room, I feel myself colour.

'She seemed fine, Mrs Brusso, happy even. I think she really enjoyed working at Rider Logistics. I called her after she'd been there a few times and she assured me that it was a really nice place to work. She told me that the whole team had gone out for lunch on her first day and that she felt really welcome. From what I know of Colin, he's very easy to get along with. It can be hard sometimes to simply walk into a business and take over someone else's role. I made sure to always check up on my staff. My clients are important but my staff are even more important. I like them to be happy where they are, even if it's just for a short time. And Julia was happy. She was really happy…' she finishes lamely.

'Yes, it did seem so.' All of a sudden I am tired of this conversation. 'Thank you again for your help.'

'No—' she begins.

'Thank you so much,' I say quickly, 'you've been very kind.'

After hanging up I google Rider Logistics and find the company employee page. Right at the top is Colin Rider. I stare at his picture for a long time, so long that the light outside changes, darkening the room. The knowledge settles over me, dusting my head and shoulders with certainty.

If I were Julia, I would have chosen him. I wouldn't have known why, but I would have been attracted to him. *It's him.* It has to be.

✢

My sweetest, darling Julia,

Yesterday I watched you read, your head bent over the book, one hand caressing mine. I felt my world complete. I could watch you forever, Julia. I only need to be near you, to smell you, to touch you. I don't mind what you do when we are together as long as we are together. How silly it seems to send a letter to say these things but sometimes when I am with you I feel shy. I know that you may find that difficult to understand because I am so much older than you. I know you believe that I know how to deal with every situation and it's true. It's true until it comes to you. You make me feel like a schoolboy, desperate for a girl to look at him and see him for who he is. Sometimes I think that you see me as I am in the world – a husband, a married man – and that's why you are so bothered by our relationship, but if you just saw me, just saw the man, you would realise that you don't have to worry about what we're doing. All you have to do is trust me and everything else will be all right.

Love x

CHAPTER TEN

I should leave this alone. I know I should just leave this alone. But I can't. Is Colin Rider the man who sent Julia these letters? Is he the man who may or may not have got her pregnant? Is he the very married lover she had been smiling about?

The taxi drops me off right outside Rider Logistics in an older part of the city. It's housed in a large concrete and glass building along with a whole lot of other companies, dwarfing the smaller buildings surrounding it. I stare up at the structure that rises from the streetscape of small terraced houses and old brick-façade blocks of flats. All along the street I can see signs that this is just the first of many new constructions here: nearly every building has a sign outside displaying a development proposal. I close my eyes and picture Julia walking through the revolving door at the front, dressed in the red and black tailored dress she showed me a picture of when she last came up to Sydney. 'I was worried it would make me look old but everyone says I look fabulous,' she'd said.

I assume this is the head office for Rider Logistics, with the trucks located elsewhere. It's nearly 5 p.m. but I'm hoping that Colin Rider will still be at work. I'm hoping he will be at work at all today. I could have called ahead but I need to see his face when I mention my daughter's name. I need to watch him react.

I take the lift to the tenth floor, noting the hush of the large building, despite the fact that hundreds of people must work here. The lift is mirrored and I glance at my face, shocking myself into attempting a quick repair job of my make-up. I pat some concealer under my eyes, trying to disguise how much I've been crying, the dark grey circles, and rub a spot of rouge into each cheek. At the seventh floor two people get on and stare at me. Usually this would make me stop what I was doing but I don't care right now.

'Mr Rider is not available,' a young man with a wispy goatee tells me. He is sitting at reception with a set of efficient-looking headphones on his head. His fingers fly across a keyboard once or twice directing calls: 'Rider logistics, how can I help you? Hold, please. Rider Logistics, how can I help you? Hold, please.'

'It's absolutely vital that I speak to him,' I say.

'If you let me know what it's about I can leave a message and get him to contact you.' He smiles, stroking his little goatee.

'You need to tell him that I have to see him.'

'I'm afraid that if you don't have an appointment I have been instructed by Mr Rider that he does not wish to be disturbed.'

'I have to see him now!' I slam the palm of my hand against his counter, relishing the sting from the cool white marble. I learned from Joel that most people do not expect outright aggression and will usually do what you want them to before their minds catch up with their physical reaction of surprise and fear.

The young man sits back, shocked that I have transformed from polite to hostile in less time than it takes to breathe in. I watch him deciding that it's the end of the day and I should not be his problem. He makes a call and turns away from me in his swivel chair, whispering urgently.

'He'll be right out,' he says, regarding me warily. I nod, not wanting to lose the edge.

Colin Rider strides down a corridor off to the left. His dark hair is shot through with grey. He has brown eyes that are almost black, and wide shoulders. Not as wide as Joel's certainly but there is enough of a resemblance for it to be obvious to me. It's almost clichéd when I think about it: the young woman who no longer has a father in her life goes looking for a father figure. Colin Rider is shorter than Joel is, slimmer and less threatening-looking in his suit but I can see why she chose him. I could see why the moment his picture flashed up on my phone. Did she get what she needed from him? Perhaps at first, but it is possible that he had promised to leave his wife and then gone back on that promise, breaking her heart in the process. Aren't adulterers always going to leave their husbands or wives? But they never do, do they? Their lovers are forced to exist forever in an imagined future where promises made in the present moment of satisfaction will come true. If she was pregnant and counting on his support she may well have found the world too much to deal with when he broke his promises to her.

I will make you regret every moment you spent with her, I think. Such a silly thing to think. Perhaps I should be grateful to this man that he made her happy. Perhaps he was the light in a dark day for her. But if he was he should have taken better care of her. He should not have been cheating on his wife with a vulnerable twenty-year-old living away from her family for the first time in her life.

'Hello, I'm Colin Rider, how can I help you?' He extends his hand towards me. He glances at the goateed young man, as if to say, 'This is what you got me out here for?'

'I'm Julia Barker's mother,' I say, slowly enunciating each syllable of her name so he can be sure he's heard it correctly. I don't take my eyes off his face as her name fills the space. I am waiting for him to flinch, to start, to blush, to slide his eyes sideways with guilt.

Instead he steps forward and folds my hand in both of his. 'Oh, Mrs Barker,' he says, his eyes shining with sympathy, 'I am so deeply sorry for your loss. She was such a lovely girl. Natalia only just called me to give me the news. We really enjoyed having her here.'

'She was seeing a married man,' I blurt out, hoping that this will elicit the reaction I'm looking for. A clumsy move to reveal myself so soon, but I have been thrown off centre by his warmth and sincerity.

'Perhaps we should go into my office,' he says, stepping back and indicating I should walk down the corridor he emerged from.

Got you, bastard, I think as I walk towards an office with an open door.

Once I am sitting down in a leather chair on the other side of his desk I clench my fists, questions piling up.

'Can I get you something to drink?' he asks politely.

'No,' I snap.

He sits down and sighs. 'Mrs Barker…'

'It's Mrs Brusso, actually.'

'Sorry, Mrs Brusso, I can assure you that Julia was not seeing anyone here at my firm. I mean, I assume that's why you've come? To see if she was having a relationship with someone here?'

'I think… yes.' I stop short of openly accusing him. He seems so calm, almost relaxed, if upset on my behalf. He's regarding me as though I am a little deranged but understandably so.

'Okay,' he nods. 'There are ten people who work here in head office, four of them are women and six of them are men. Leonard out the front whom you've just met is openly gay. Peter and Jackson are both in their late sixties and close to retirement. Aasim and Lance spend most of their time out of the office on sales calls so I'm not even sure they would have met Julia because she was only here twice a week for three months. That only leaves me, Mrs Brusso.'

He waits quietly, giving me time to make my accusation openly or perhaps waiting for me to back down. I lean back in my chair and fold my arms, tilting my head slightly. *Did you break my little girl's heart?* I think. I squeeze my arms tightly enough to leave bruises. I will not cry in front of this man.

The silence stretches before Colin Rider makes a move.

He leans forward and slowly turns a picture around on his desk to face me. It is a photo of him with what I assume to be his wife and two daughters. His wife has burnished red hair but both of his daughters have dark hair like him. All of the women in his life are very beautiful. His daughters look about eighteen and twenty. In the photo the family are posing on a small sailing boat. While I study the image I hear him rummage around in his desk. I look up. Happy family photos mean nothing except that a moment in time has been captured. If anything, the more perfect the photo, the more likely it is to be a lie. Before our divorce the walls of our home were speckled with happy family photos with Joel front and centre, as if he was the person responsible for those smiles. Ever since then I don't trust photographs. I even found taking wedding pictures with Adrian discomfiting.

He hands me a company brochure he has taken from his drawer. Below his image as CEO of Rider Logistics is a picture of the woman in the photograph with him. His wife, Emma Sandofsky. It says she is the general manager.

'She left earlier today or I would ask her to come in and talk to you. Julia worked for both of us but mostly for her. My wife is at work here with me every day, Mrs Brusso. Even if I had the desire to have an affair, which I don't, it wouldn't be possible to hide from her. Julia is the same age as my daughter, Ashley. It's not something I would even begin to contemplate.'

Colin Rider is not angry with me. Instead he speaks quietly, gently. He feels sorry for me and my stupid assumptions. He could be lying but his words jolt me out of the thoughts I have been having about him. I feel as though I can suddenly see clearly, whereas before I was looking through mist. I have made a mistake. I realise that now.

'I just thought…' I begin.

'I understand,' he nods. 'Can I get you anything to drink? I have some whisky here for the bad days.' He smiles a little. I will myself to disappear.

'I'm sorry,' I say, standing up. 'I apologise for bothering you.'

'I am so sorry about her, Mrs… Brusso. I understand why you might have thought… I mean, I realise that people must need to look for reasons, to—'

'Thank you.' I abruptly cut him off. 'I'm sorry to have bothered you.' I repeat myself, on autopilot. I turn and walk out of the office, embarrassment curling within me, not waiting for him to reply. I hold myself rigid, hoping that a dignified bearing will carry me through the next few minutes. I force myself to walk slowly down the corridor and out to the lift. I wait for it to come, feeling my back cramp. Colin Rider, to his credit, does not follow me.

I mouth the words, 'Thank you, God,' as I leave the building and see a taxi right in front. I cannot get away fast enough.

There is a small off-licence next to my hotel. I think about buying some whisky, thinking of the burn as it hits my throat, but then remember that I hate it. Wine will have to do instead. I drink half the bottle watching television, using a glass from a tray on top of the small cabinet containing a mini bar filled with overpriced chocolates and alcohol. I could have drunk the wine in the fridge I suppose, but I need much more alcohol than the miniature bottles can provide. What I am trying to do mostly is to not think. I force myself to engage with a sitcom about a single father. With each gulp of wine I become more and more involved in his dilemma of being attracted to his daughter's teacher. I drink and drink and listen to the laugh track, so at odds with the emotions raging inside me.

I cannot let my little excursion to Rider Logistics play out in my head. I don't think I will survive the humiliation. I decide I won't tell Adrian about this. I can't – it's too embarrassing. I hope that Natalia doesn't lose a client because she gave me his name. It was all over in a matter of minutes and he could have been lying but he's right, having an affair when your wife has the office next door would be difficult. And I would like to think that while Julia might have been foolish enough to choose a married man, she would not be cruel enough to choose a man whose wife she knew personally.

As the wine starts blurring the world around me, I pick up a letter, longing for answers.

My sweetest, darling Julia,

What a wonderful weekend that was. Don't worry about how difficult it is for me to get away. Let me worry about how to find the time to see you. All you need to do is be there when I am. Know that you are always on my mind, always in my heart. I would love to be able to tell everyone I know about our connection, about our love, to shout it from the rooftops, but you and I both know that we have to wait. Patience is a virtue, my darling. I'm sure you've heard that one before. I wish you a wonderful week ahead and success with that assignment you were so worried about. I know you'll do very well. Your intelligence is only matched by your beauty. I love you.

Love x

Where does this man have to get away from? Who does this man need to get away from so he can be with my daughter in secret? He is obviously different to any other man she'd ever known. He's an adulterer, he's older, he's not the kind of person she should have allowed into her life… But who is he? Who is he? *Who is he?*

*

My sweetest, darling Julia,

Oh, how I miss you when I can't be with you. I can't stop thinking about your tears the last time we were together. I want to assure you that regardless of how difficult our situation is I will always love you and be there for you. Don't shut me out, my darling. You cannot let conventions of society interfere with our relationship. You need to look beyond what we used to be to each other and into a future of what we will become to each other. One day, how we met and what our roles were at that time will simply be a distant memory. One that we will laugh about, I'm sure. You are no longer the school girl you once were, Julia. You are a young woman with the world at your feet, with me at your feet.

Don't worry about what others will say. Worry only about what I say, what you say and what we both think and feel when we're together. That is all that matters.

Love x

CHAPTER ELEVEN

The next morning I catch my plane back to Sydney, clutching a giant cup of coffee and missing a large amount of my self-respect.

Colin Rider was not my daughter's married lover.

Landing in Sydney I switch on my phone to see an unknown text message. I open it in the taxi home and see it is signed by him, which makes me groan aloud. The taxi driver glances nervously at me in his rear-view mirror. I assume Natalia gave Colin Rider my number and I am momentarily furious with her for allowing him to contact me. I didn't want to ever have to think of him again.

Dear Ms Brusso,

I can only imagine how difficult yesterday was for you. I wanted to again convey my sympathy for you and your family on the terrible loss of Julia. Please know that in the short time we knew her we all found her to be an intelligent and lovely young woman.

I hesitate to give you this information but my wife insisted I text you. She feels that, as a mother of daughters herself, she understands your desire to know all that you can about your daughter's life. This may mean nothing at all but I did see Julia with an older man over lunch one day. It wasn't on a day she was working for us, but rather a Sunday. She was in the city for lunch with the man and my wife and I happened to run into her near the restaurant where we were meeting friends. I assumed the man was her father but Julia introduced him to us as her former high-school drama

teacher. I'm sure it was just a friendly visit but I thought I would let you know about it.
 Best wishes, Colin Rider

I knew it, I knew it, I think, feeling fury course through my body. I had been right all along.

I wonder how long Colin Rider thought about sending this message before he did it. Perhaps he is trying to shift my suspicions onto someone else but he cannot possibly have known what I know, what I have been suspecting. I reply with a 'Thank you' as the only possible name repeats itself in my head. *Eric Peters. Eric Peters. Eric Peters.* It's not just obvious, but clichéd and banal as well.

'Oh, Julia,' I sigh, earning myself another look from the taxi driver.

When I arrive home Adrian is at work and the boys are at school or with Joel. I texted them both to say good morning, but neither of them have replied. I am glad of the empty house. I unpack the few things I took with me and lug the suitcases into Julia's room to be opened later. I shove the box right under the bed. In order to grab it I will have to lie down on the floor and awkwardly contort my body, but I don't want the box found accidentally.

I had intended to sleep the afternoon away and then to try and prepare dinner for everyone but instead I page through Julia's final year book again. The first year she was at high school Julia couldn't stop talking about Mr Peters. 'He's so funny, he's such a good actor. He's so nice and makes us all laugh and, oh my God, Mum, drama is officially my favourite subject. I think I want to be an actress. Eric, I mean Mr Peters, told me that I had really managed to make him feel Ophelia's sadness. He said I almost made him cry.' Before high school Julia had never had any idea about her future but meeting Eric Peters had changed that. From her first drama class her only ambition was to be an actress.

But that later changed, much to our surprise.

Until halfway through year twelve, she was planning on applying for the National Drama School and for any course at university where she could study acting. She was even looking into courses in New York. 'It's where Mr Peters studied acting,' she told me.

But then she changed her mind, quite suddenly. It wasn't as though I felt strongly about a career in acting but I wanted her to pursue her passions.

'Do you really want her going through all that?' Adrian asked me, when I tried to talk Julia out of giving up on acting and settling for journalism instead.

'It's not that I really want her to do it but I can't help feeling that she's frightened of failing and I don't want her to regret anything.'

'It may be that she knows it's just not who she is any more. Maybe she is a little scared, but I think we should trust that she's making a choice she's happy with in journalism.'

Julia explained when I pushed her: 'I don't want to have to spend my whole life competing with women who may be less talented than I am but manage to do better than me because they look better or because they're willing to do any number of things to get the part.' The horrible sex-abuse stories were gushing out of Hollywood then and I understood her reluctance to become involved in a business where few women seemed to have gotten away unscathed.

'But you could stick to the stage,' I argued. 'No one can ever make you do something you don't want to do.'

'You say that, Mum, but last week Jenna and I went to her sister's play at university and she spent half the time topless. Jenna said her parents have completely freaked out about it but her sister says she has to be willing to give everything to the craft. I'm not sure you and Adrian would want me to do that. And Dad… I can imagine how he would react.'

'It doesn't matter what we want, Julia.'

'I know, Mum, but just leave it alone, will you? I've made my decision. I talked it over with Eric, I mean Mr Peters, and he agreed that unless I was willing to give up everything, go through years of rejection and live overseas, then I had to think of something else to do. He knows about these things, Mum, you don't. After drama, English is my strongest subject and I love the idea of finding out the truth behind the bullshit that we hear. It's what I want to do.'

I remember that in her last years of school Mr Peters grew his hair long and his face was always defined by white-blond stubble, giving him the look of an artfully styled model for a cologne advert in a magazine.

The sound of Adrian arriving home alerts me to the time. I shut the year book reluctantly. I would like to be alone so I can think but I know I need to at least try and act as though I can cope with the mundane tasks. I look at my phone and see that both boys have texted me that they will be home for dinner tonight. I want to have something ready for them. But instead of leaving the room I remain on Julia's bed. I am tempted to get into the car now and rush over to the school to speak to Eric Peters, but it's nearly 5 p.m. and I don't think he would be there. I could find his home address, I'm sure, but I don't want to accuse him without being certain. I need to wait, I need absolute proof before I do anything. I don't think I can go through what happened with Colin Rider again.

If Julia was involved with Eric Peters there is nothing wrong with that except that he is married. I run through some of my interactions with him, trying to determine if he ever mentioned his wife or if I ever saw her at one of the performances, but I can't picture anyone. If he is married and he got Julia pregnant then what would that have done to her, especially if he has children of his own already? I don't imagine he would have wanted to have to deal with his young pregnant mistress. Her suicide would almost have been convenient.

The thought makes me sick, and when Adrian finds me I am curled up on my daughter's bed as usual, crying as usual, more broken than ever.

I don't prepare dinner, I don't even manage to talk to my sons, to find out how they are doing. I know I'm failing them. It is a terrible thing to watch yourself making mistakes and still carry on making them, helpless to change. The boys need me to be with them. They need me to talk to them about Julia and let them know that it's okay for their lives to go on. But once again I leave everything to Adrian. I cannot do what I know I have to do. I am crippled by my grief.

After dinner Nicholas comes into the room with a cup of tea that he places softly on the bedside table.

'I'm awake,' I tell him.

'Your eyes were closed.'

'I know, but I was just thinking. How are you, Nick? How are you and Cooper?'

Nicholas sinks down onto the bed, his weight causing the mattress to dip. 'You know, Mum.'

'I'm sorry, I'm not… I'm just sorry, Nick. I wish I could be better for you guys right now.'

'Don't worry, Mum,' he says, staring at the year book I've dropped on the floor.

'Is Dad okay?'

'Nah,' he says. 'What is okay when something like this happens, anyway? He's trying to help us. I guess we're trying to help each other.'

Guilt is acid in my throat. A better mother than I would be comforting her children, helping them heal, listening to them cry. I don't know what to say to my son, so I say nothing.

I sit up on the bed and put my arms around Nick, comforting him but also taking comfort from his size and his strength, as I remember six-year-old Nicholas, sitting on my lap, cradling his broken arm after a fall in the playground, his little lip trembling as he tried not to cry. He looks just like his father, with the same jet-black hair and dark brown eyes.

I believe that one of Joel's greatest achievements as a father is to make his sons aware of themselves as physically stronger than others, as capable of causing hurt if they don't control their emotions. I know from conversations with them over the years that Joel has always emphasised that they are never to use their physical strength against anyone. A lesson I wish Joel's father had taught him but one that I'm grateful he has passed down to his sons. Both Cooper and Nicholas have their father's height and love of lifting weights but both move through the world aware of their physical power. I worried as they approached their teenage years that Joel's temper would come flaring out of one of them but it never has.

Cooper, especially, has benefitted from the lessons Joel has learned. He has my blond hair and blue eyes just as Julia does… As Julia *did*. As a child he was prone to temper tantrums that bothered me with their intensity but he returned from his first holiday with Joel equipped with a method for keeping his temper under control, a method that Joel uses.

'If something does make him mad he stands still and waits,' Cooper told me when I asked my eight-year-old, my voice trembling, what happened if Daddy got angry.

'Waits for what?' I asked.

'He's counting breaths,' Cooper said. 'That's what he told me. In his head he is telling himself that he doesn't have to lose control. He just has to breathe in and out ten times and then he can handle whatever.'

'Oh, Cooper,' I said.

'It's fine, Mum,' he replied. 'Sometimes when I get mad now, I do the same thing. It really helps.'

Despite everything, Joel is a good father, a great father, to my boys. I wish Julia could have given her father a chance, I wish she could have enjoyed the father that Nicholas and Cooper enjoy. Both of my sons have struggled a little with having Adrian in their lives, even though they are aware that he has never sought to replace their father. He would have liked to have grown closer to them and I know he is hurt by their distance. Sometimes he oversteps the mark, trying too hard or pushing the boundaries as a stepfather, but they deal with it well. They both deal with everything without resorting to violence.

'You know I love you, Nick,' I say now.

Nick allows a dry laugh to escape. 'Course, Mum.' He picks up the year book I have just been paging through and riffles through the pages.

'I remember that,' he says, and he shows me the picture of Julia listening to Eric Peters speak. 'She loved that guy so much. She thought he was like… a god.'

I swallow. 'Do you think, Nick… do you think they may have been more than just a student and a teacher?'

Nicholas is quiet. He closes the book and then chews on a nail. 'Some of the older guys used to say stuff when she was still at school but it was probably crap. No one knew anything for sure. Anyway, that's not the kind of person Julia was.'

I flinch at his words, hating the idea of Julia's name being sullied by teenage gossip and speculation.

'Maybe you're wrong about that. Maybe we didn't really know what kind of person she was.'

'Don't do that, Mum, don't start thinking about her like that. We know who she was. She would never have taken up with a teacher while she was at school. He would have been fired if anyone found out.'

'So maybe she didn't have a relationship with him while she was at school but could she have been having one with him now? Because I do think that she was seeing someone.' I shouldn't be talking to Nick about this. He's too young to take on the burden of this information. I don't want him to think of his sister in a relationship with a man who was her teacher, a man she shouldn't have been with. Yet the words are out of my mouth before I can stop them.

'Honestly, I have no idea. I don't think Julia has gone more than a week in the last few years without having some guy interested in her. Remember Liam? He was completely obsessed. All my friends were in love with her when she was still at school. But so what?'

'It's not "so what", Nick. It's important. If there was someone and he broke her heart then maybe that explains things.'

'No,' says Nick, shaking his head. 'Everyone gets their heart broken. You don't kill yourself over that, and I think Julia was more likely to be the one breaking hearts.'

I cringe at his words, at the way 'kill yourself' bursts out of his mouth.

'It must have been something else,' he continues, as he studies his fingers. 'Maybe she was really depressed and we just didn't notice. We should have noticed. I should have noticed, but I've just been so caught up in all this exam shit.'

'Oh, Nick, don't say that. Please don't blame yourself.' I sit up and wrap my arms around him again. He holds on tight, briefly, and then he lets go.

'I have an essay due,' he whispers.

He gets up to leave but stands at the door for a moment before turning around to look at me. 'I really don't believe she would have hooked up with a teacher but…'

'But?'

'But there's a guy I go to the gym with who goes to a school where Mr Peters used to teach like years ago,' he says dropping his gaze to his feet.

'Oh,' I say.

'Yeah, and a few months ago we were bitching about teachers and final exams, and then we were kind of talking about teachers we thought were weird. He mentioned a drama teacher who taught at his school when his older brother was there, who had to leave after six months because of something that happened with one of the girls. He said his name was Eric Peters, so I think it's the same guy.' The words come out quickly as though Nick has to get them said and off his mind.

'Why would he have had to leave the school?' I ask, feeling my body grow cold.

'He didn't explain it exactly, he just said… he just said…'

'Said what, Nick?'

'He said, "he liked them really young".'

'Meaning Mr Peters liked young girls?'

'I don't know, I didn't really ask… I was running on the treadmill at the time. He could have gotten the story wrong. It was a really long time ago.'

'Did you see him at school today Nick, did you see Mr Peters?'

'Nah, he's taken the senior drama class to a camp. He'll be back next week.'

He turns and leaves without saying anything else.

Next week, I think, irritation rising in me. I have no idea how I will be able to wait that long. I want to confront him now, to accuse him now, to have him somehow help me understand what my daughter did *now*.

My phone beeps with an incoming text. It's from Joel. *Spoke to Detective Winslow today. She told me they're just waiting for toxicology reports but she may have a few more questions for us. Hopefully we can have the funeral soon.*

What questions could she have? And how can she imagine that I would have any answers for her? I want to laugh and then I want to cry. All Julia has left us with is unanswered questions.

❊

My sweetest, darling Julia,

I watched you in the morning sun today. A golden shaft of sunlight fell across your rosy pink nipples and I felt I couldn't breathe for a moment. I wish you hadn't cried last night. I wish

I could explain to you that the guilt you feel is unnecessary. It is true that the two of us together is wrong but I cannot believe it is possible to feel this way if there is not something right about us as well. I feel that you are a gift I have been given. If I had to stop seeing you, to stop touching you, I would die. I am not being dramatic here. I would literally die and then you would know true pain and sadness.

I love you. I have always loved you. I believe the moment I set eyes on you I knew that one day you would be mine. I let you come to me first. You came to me, remember? I know we were just kidding around on our walk after lunch that wonderful Sunday and perhaps you never meant for that first kiss to happen but it did and you wanted it, Julia. We both wanted it. We cannot stop now. We cannot go back. It's happened and we need to push forward into the lives that we are meant to live. I believe that. I believe it with all my heart.

Love x

CHAPTER TWELVE

The ringing of the doorbell wakes me. The house is quiet and a quick glance at my mobile phone tells me it's after ten. I think about ignoring whoever is standing at my door but decide against that, knowing I can't shut myself off from the world forever. I stumble out of Julia's bed, unwashed and groggy, and open the door. My mother and Emily, my sister, are on the doorstep. I should have just let them keep ringing the doorbell. I don't want to listen to my mother sigh or hear one of my sister's lectures. And I know a lecture is coming. Why else would she have taken a day off work?

'Oh, Claire,' sighs my mother, shaking her head. 'What on earth is going on?'

'I was asleep,' I reply, turning away from them and making my way to the kitchen. I fill up the kettle, hoping that a strong shot of coffee will give me enough energy to cope with this visit.

'Adrian says that you went down to Melbourne on some wild goose chase,' begins Emily.

'I had to get her things.'

'They would have sent them up, or Mum or I could have gone to get them. It was unnecessary for you to put yourself through that.'

'I don't think you get to tell me what is and is not necessary in this situation, Emily.' I am sure that there are sisters in the world who manage to grow out of petty resentments and sibling rivalry but my sister and I have never quite achieved that. When I got divorced she was utterly furious with me for making my parents so upset and for having concealed what was going on with Joel for so long.

According to Leslie, my therapist, a lot of her anger towards me comes from the fact that she didn't know what was going on.

'I think everyone knew,' I said to Leslie, 'but sometimes people only see what they want to see.'

'That's possible,' she agreed, 'but once your sister could no longer hide the truth from herself I think it's natural that she felt angry with herself for not helping you in that situation. She may not know exactly that it's the reason she's so angry at you now but I think it may have something to do with it.'

'Well, I'm not going to feel sorry for her because she's pissed off that she didn't see what was going on and drag me out of my marriage. I have my own shit to deal with.'

'Fair enough,' my serene therapist had replied.

'Oh, Claire,' says my mother as she studies me. 'If your father was here…' She stops speaking, tears overwhelming her. 'I'm glad he can't see this and that he can't see that you're… you're punishing yourself like this. I'm worried for you, so worried, Claire.' She hunches over, her hand covering her mouth and my sister places her arms around her. I feel so separated, so alone and angry. I am so angry.

'So time's up for grieving my child, then,' I spit.

'God, no, Claire!' Emily raises her voice. 'Of course time is not up, of course you're suffering, of course you're not coping. How could anyone be expected to cope with this? But what made you think that going to Melbourne when you should have been home with your family was something you should do?'

'I needed to know if she had a boyfriend,' I whisper.

'But why?' asks my mother, her voice shuddering with the last of her tears.

'Because maybe he hurt her or broke her heart and that's what made her do it.'

'Oh, Claire, oh, sweetheart,' my sister says and she comes to stand next to me at the kettle, wrapping her soft arms around me and simply holding me tight. The move is so unexpected that I can't help sobbing in her arms and soon my mother, my sister and I are wrapped in a bizarre group hug, tears flowing and noses running. I am not alone, I realise, I am surrounded by my family, by those who loved Julia as I did. After a few minutes I let go of Emily and we all part.

My mother blows her nose. 'Go and have a quick shower, Claire. I'll make… I'll make pancakes.'

'I'm supposed to be dieting but what the hell,' says Emily and I laugh, because Emily is always dieting and what better reason than her niece's death would there be to fall off the wagon. I mentally shake my head at myself. These days my thoughts are so dark I cannot quite comprehend them.

I am feeling pleasantly numb as I stand under the shower, letting the hot water run over me until my fingers wrinkle. Sometimes you shed tears and no matter how long you cry for you feel as though you could start again the moment you stop but, today, crying with my mother and sister has felt more cathartic than I thought it would. They are grieving with me and for me. I have to remember that. The loneliness of grief I feel all the time is perhaps about perception. But it's difficult not to feel like this. While I have taken a month off work, all around me my family are getting on with their lives. I cannot blame them. Adrian is his own boss and can't simply leave things to his assistant. Nicholas is in his final month of his final year at school, and Cooper has exams coming up, too. They are struggling through work and school but I am here, mostly by myself, in limbo. The police have yet to release my daughter's body so we cannot bury her. We cannot stand with family and friends and mourn the loss of my baby girl. But they are mourning. I know they are mourning.

We eat pancakes in silence. I chew and swallow but even covered in syrup the pancakes taste bitter as I remember how much Julia used to love her grandmother's pancakes. 'Nana puts chocolate chips in them, Mum.'

'Did you find out anything?' Emily asks. 'Did she have a boyfriend? Because if she did and he's the reason she… hurt herself, I will personally make sure he suffers for it.'

'Thanks, Em, but no… I mean I know she did have someone, but I don't know who it was. I think it may have been someone older.' I can't tell them about the letters. They will want to know more and Emily will want to use her accountant brain to deconstruct them. They cannot read the letters that were written to Julia. It's bad enough that I'm reading them. I feel a shudder run through me as some of the words he uses to describe her body return to me.

'Any news on when we can have the funeral?' asks my mother.

'Not yet. Detective Winslow told Joel that they're just waiting for the final toxicology report. It shouldn't be long now.' I don't mention Detective Winslow's questions.

'Toxicology, what's… oh, drugs. What rubbish, Julia wasn't on drugs. Honestly, you have to wonder at the stupidity of people.'

'If it wasn't drugs, Mum, then what was it?'

I have asked my mother this question over and over again and the only answer she ever has for me is to spread her arms and shake her head.

'It's not something I ever would have expected of her,' says Emily. 'I keep trying to wrap my head around it and I can't. It's just not who she was.'

'No,' I agree, and I feel a moment of envy for my sister who has often lamented her single status. She is forty-one and is pretty certain that she has missed out on having a husband and definitely sure she has missed out on having children, but now I can't help but feel that she is blessed never to have to experience this pain. I would give anything not to be this raw bundle of guilt-ridden emotions.

'Maybe it was a professor at university?' says Emily. 'I'm sure that sort of thing goes on all the time.'

'It may be the case but how do I even find out? It's not like I can go to all her male professors and ask them if they were sleeping with my daughter.'

'No, I suppose not…' Emily pauses then continues in a rush: 'But Claire, does it really matter? I mean, she's gone, and nothing is going to bring her back.'

'I know that,' I snap, angry all over again.

We're all quiet for a few moments. Then, 'Do you want us to help you tidy up or do some washing or something?' asks Emily. I can see her clutching at straws. She and my mother don't know what to say to me any more. I don't blame them. I don't know what to say to myself either.

'No, thanks… I may just try and go through some of her stuff but I think I need to be… alone for that.'

My mother picks up her bag, knowing that there's no point in her staying. 'I'll call you tonight and if you need me to get anything from the shops for you you'll let me know, won't you?'

'I will,' I say. 'Thanks for coming over and you too, Em… Thanks.'

'Any time,' smiles Emily. 'I mean it… even in the middle of the night.'

When they are gone, I return to the letters. I have read them all now. Some of them I have even begun to know off by heart and I will continue to read them again and again until I can prove who this man is.

I think about the word 'prove'. I believe I know who he is. I am no longer looking for a name. Now I am simply searching for confirmation.

My sweetest, darling Julia,

Perhaps you are right, my darling. Perhaps we need to slow this down a little. I don't want you making any impulsive decisions. I have a job and a life. I cannot just let you begin sharing our story until I am ready. I have to confess that I thought you would be able to deal with this better, to approach it more maturely. You have always struck me as a woman with her head screwed on the right way. Your confidence and poise as you moved through the years was something I found especially appealing in you. I'm asking you to take a few deep breaths, Julia, and think this through. I want to be with you more than anything in the whole world but we have to wait a little. Let me sort some things out on my end and then I will tell you when the time is right.

Love x

This letter feels like a turning point to me. I can't imagine that Julia would have let the idea of sleeping with a married man slip smoothly off her back. I'm sure she would have worried over it constantly. I wish she'd spoken to me about it although I'm certain that she wouldn't have liked, or even wanted, my opinion or advice. Maybe that's why she didn't speak to me. But are we, as mothers, expected to offer our children unconditional praise and support for everything or risk losing them? What would have been the right approach to mothering a strong-willed teenage girl? How could I have done better?

My mobile rings. I recognise Detective Winslow's number.

'Hello,' I answer.

She doesn't bother asking me how I am. 'We have found the presence of benzodiazepine in Julia's system,' she says, enunciating the words slowly, as though they are being reluctantly dragged from her thin lips. And…'

'And what?' I ask.

'And she was pregnant. The foetus was seven weeks old.'

'Pregnant? Pregnant… oh… oh… seven weeks?' I lay my hand on my stomach, a quick, sharp pain making me gasp.

'Yes, seven weeks.'

'I can't believe…'

'I know, it's a shock. It must be a shock. It means there was someone in her life.'

'So are you going to try and find him?'

'I have discussed it at length with my colleagues but I don't think so, I'm afraid. It's possible that she and whoever she was seeing were already broken up. I don't think we can spend time or resources trying to find someone no one knew existed. I know that might be tough for you to hear and I'm sorry, but we have to be realistic. It may, however, go to explain her state of mind.'

I think about the letters, about telling Detective Winslow about them, but I can hear that she's ready to be done with this case. She's a detective, not a psychologist, and why Julia chose to take her life is no longer her concern.

'What's benzodiazepine?'

'It's a tranquilliser, like Valium.'

There is Valium in my bathroom. I have never used the drug but Adrian was prescribed some by his GP to help with back pain. He doesn't take it much because he says it makes him feel fuzzy. She would have had to take it from our bathroom when she was here only a couple of weeks ago, when she came for her regular visit. I feel a creeping coldness fill me up. If she took it weeks ago she must have been planning this for a long time. I think back to how she was when she was here last but cannot pinpoint anything to indicate she was that unhappy.

'Do you know if she was a regular user of drugs?' the detective asks, and I realise that it's the second time she's asked the question. I have forgotten I'm on the phone with her.

'No,' I say. 'I don't think she was, but then I didn't know she was pregnant. I didn't know anything at all.'

'I understand. The bump on her head is a little concerning so I wanted to check that you definitely remember Adrian dropping her and her head hitting the porch.'

'Yes, I…' I swallow once, twice. I see Adrian on a chair, pulling desperately at the chain and I watch in horror as the bolt holding it comes loose too quickly for us to catch her body. The back of her head hits the porch. The thump sound is loud in the night, echoing all around me, and I hear gasps from the neighbours that are now crowding outside, staring at the spectacle of my daughter's death. Sirens get closer. I close my eyes and blink away that moment. 'I remember it, we both dropped her. I was trying to take her weight so he could release the chain but she was heavy and he wasn't holding her tightly enough… and…'

'That's fine, that's fine… you don't have to say any more. It's not uncommon for head wounds to bleed after death and according to the coroner, her death occurred only a couple of hours before you found her so more blood around the head wound was possible.'

A couple of hours, I think. *She hung there for one hundred and twenty minutes.* I want to scream at Detective Winslow to take that information back. I didn't want to know that. Sometimes I get up at night and go to the kitchen for a glass of water. It's a random thing and it doesn't happen every night but why couldn't that night have been one of those nights? Why couldn't a dry mouth have forced me out of my deep sleep? I close my eyes and imagine getting up at the right time to stop her. I imagine hearing a sound outside and going to investigate. I imagine getting there in time. It was only two hours. Two hours.

Detective Winslow clears her throat.

'So is that your only question?' I ask, dragging myself away from my wishful scenario.

'Yes, it lines up with what the pathologist has posed as a possibility. I just wanted to… I'm sorry I had to ask you about it again.'

'It's your job.'

'It's the very worst part of it. I think that's all, unless you have any other questions.'

'Can they tell if she was a regular user of drugs? I mean, I don't think she would have taken drugs if she knew she was pregnant.'

'We did test a hair sample which can give us an indication of the last few months and, no, she wasn't – at least, not in the last few months. She may have only used the benzodiazepine to relax so she could…'

'Have the courage to kill herself.'

'This is very difficult,' she says ineffectually.

My breath catches at the thought of my child needing the courage to hurt herself and I lay my hand over my broken heart. 'I should have *known*. It's all I can think. If I had known I would have been able to help her somehow. I would have saved her.'

'It's tempting to think that,' Detective Winslow says, 'but in my experience it's not the case. If someone is determined to end their life there is usually very little you can do to stop it, aside from locking them up.'

'But she wasn't depressed. She didn't seem depressed. Aren't most suicides associated with mental illness? Maybe she was undiagnosed and suffering or hiding it from us? Maybe when she found out she was pregnant it triggered something?'

Detective Winslow gives a small sigh. 'It's possible, but from what everyone has told us, she seemed to be functioning very well. Nothing anyone said struck me as an indication of anything more than average young-adult behaviour – and she may not have even known that she was pregnant. It was still early on.'

'She knew. I'm sure of it.' I remember what Esther told me. Of course she knew. I started throwing up when I was five weeks' pregnant with her. They say morning sickness can be genetic. Of course she knew.

'I wish I had some more clear answers for you.'

'I wish I had never let her go to Melbourne.'

'She was an adult, Claire. There wasn't much you could have done to stop her. I can only tell you again how sorry I am. Things will move quickly now and the coroner will sign the death certificate in the next day or so. You should start looking into some arrangements.'

'Don't tell Joel,' I say, 'about the Valium and the pregnancy.' I feel like I want to keep this information to myself, to protect Julia by being the only one who knows these things about her. I am doing the same thing with the letters.

'I'm afraid we have to. He is her father and he has asked to be kept informed of anything we find.'

I knew that would be her answer and I know I'm going to have to share this news with Adrian as well. Julia's secrets are starting to overwhelm me.

I can imagine what Joel will do with the information. However deeply he has buried his rage I know that he will not be able to stop it reappearing against the unknown man who got his daughter pregnant and may have then abandoned her, leading her to make this choice. He is looking for someone to blame as much as I am.

I imagine he would be as relieved as I would be to have concrete evidence that his daughter's death cannot be simply attributed to our poor parenting.

'Okay,' I say. 'Is there anything else?'

'No, that's all I needed to tell you. I hope you can find some sort of closure after the funeral.'

'I… thank you,' I whisper. I put down the phone.

Joel will know Julia was pregnant and that she had drugs in her system. I wonder if he will blame me more than he blames himself. Past history tells me that he will. He's barely had anything to do with her over the last eight years. I stare at my mobile phone, waiting for the call from him that I'm sure is coming.

But my mobile remains silent and I am weirdly disappointed. I want him to yell at me, to threaten me, even. I want him to accuse me of being a shitty mother. I can't keep beating myself up alone any more. Who better than Joel to step in and lend a hand?

I go to the kitchen, stopping at my bathroom to check Adrian's Valium supply. I find it almost empty. There are only two pills left. I stare at the bottle, a ringing in my ears. In my heart I knew that would be the case but it's still soul destroying to have it confirmed. Leaving the bathroom, the nearly empty bottle of pills feeling heavy in my hand, I find the vodka in the freezer. I can drink a fair amount of it combined with juice. I need liquid courage to tell Adrian all this. I don't know if I will be able to get the words out otherwise.

'Hey, how are you doing?' He answers his mobile every time I call these days.

'Yeah, it's… Detective Winslow called. She said Julia had Valium in her system.'

'Oh…' he says.

'And also… she was… she was… pregnant.'

'Pregnant… what? I mean… pregnant?'

'Only seven weeks, so Detective Winslow says she may not have known.'

'I can't believe it, she was always so sensible.' Adrian sounds as shocked as I was. 'They teach contraception at school, don't they? How could she have messed up like that?'

'Are you asking me or accusing me?'

'Oh, Claire, I'm not doing anything of the sort. I didn't realise they tested for that. I would rather we didn't know about it.' I can hear the disappointment in his voice and I want to yell at him for that. He has no right to be disappointed with my daughter.

'I think she took the Valium from you, unless she got it illegally. I mean, it could have been prescribed for her.' She could have gotten the Valium anywhere, of course. I no longer went with her to doctor's appointments. But I have no idea why any physician would have thought it acceptable to prescribe Valium to a twenty-year-old.

Adrian is silent.

'Did you hear me?'

'Yeah, uh… yeah.'

'I think she must have taken it from you because the bottle is almost empty and I know you said you don't like them.'

'Yeah… look, Claire, I think it's best if I just tell the truth here.'

'What do you mean? What are you talking about?'

'I gave her some of my Valium. She told me she was having trouble sleeping and they do relax you. They're a really low dose and they just put you to sleep for a few hours. I wasn't using them so I gave her some.'

'And you didn't think to tell me this?' I shriek.

'I didn't think it was a big deal,' he yells back and then, realising he is in his office, he whispers fiercely, 'I didn't think it was a big deal.' I hear him moving and I know he is leaving his office to go outside and pace up and down the sidewalk while he talks to me. 'She didn't want you to freak out about the fact that she wasn't sleeping. She knew it would worry you.'

'Why wasn't she sleeping?'

'I don't know… exams or something. I can't really remember. I didn't ask too many questions and that's probably why she came to me because she knew I would just listen. She felt like you didn't just want to listen. All you wanted to do was to solve her problems for her.'

'I'm her mother,' I yell into the phone. 'You had no right to keep it from me.'

'She was a grown woman, Claire, and it really bothered her that you never saw that. I saw that so she came to me. We spoke to each other as adults and she could trust that I wouldn't try to manage her life for her. I know you had to protect her, Claire, to protect all three of them after Joel left. I understand, but I don't know if she did. I'm sure she would have, in time… I…' His sentence trails off as he realises what he's saying. Julia doesn't have the time to understand why I was so protective. She will never be a mother herself.

'I can't… I can't believe you don't understand how wrong it was for you to keep that to yourself. Something was going on in her life and I could have helped her if I'd known. I can't talk to you any more. I simply cannot talk to you.' I end the call and throw my phone dramatically across the room. Then I go back to Julia's room and lie down on her bed.

He's right, I know he's right. I did try to manage her life but it's hard to know when you have to back off from mothering your child. It's hard to know how far to back off. One minute she needed me and the next she didn't. And now she's gone and I can't fix any of it.

*

My sweetest, darling Julia,

I need you to think calmly about the things you are saying to me. We both went into this with our eyes wide open. You are well aware of the other people in my life. I am tired of having to defend our relationship to you. I don't want to discuss the people we're hurting. You need to grow up a little and accept the responsibility for your own decisions. You chose to be with me just as I chose to be with you. You talk of ending things but if that's how you really feel, why do you keep agreeing to meet me? I know you think that it would be better if I just left you alone but how can I do that, Julia? How can a love like ours just be extinguished?

I think we need to stop discussing our situation and instead just be together when we can. Let's regard our time together as precious, too precious to debate the morality of our choice.

I love you more with each passing day. I cannot imagine my life without you and I want our time together to be carefree and special. I'm sure you want the same thing.

Love x

CHAPTER THIRTEEN

The police have informed me that they will release Julia's body by the end of the week. We can have a funeral. I would like to simply hand over the organisation that is required to my sister who thrives on such things, but Joel wants to talk, to discuss what will happen at her funeral. He wants to be involved.

'You hadn't really spoken to her for years,' I said to him on the phone when he called. 'If you want to be involved then I have to be involved.'

'I'm happy to talk to your mother and sister about it,' he said mildly.

'But you know they both refuse to speak to you.'

'I know. Perhaps it's time they got over the past. Isn't this hideous enough?'

'I don't know, Joel. Perhaps Emily feels that having to learn you had been hitting me for years was pretty hideous.'

'That was a long time ago, Claire.' He sighed. 'I can't… keep telling you how sorry I am for who I was. I'm not that man any more. All I want from you is a chance to be involved. She was my daughter and I've missed her growing up and now I'll never get to be a proper father to her.' I heard his voice crack and felt myself flush at my cruelty. Joel is an easy target these days. His past behaviour hangs over him like a shroud, making him apologise and back down before an argument even begins. He seems afraid of himself when he speaks to me. It's what I wanted, all those years ago, but now hearing and seeing him reduced to someone always monitoring his own words and watching his behaviour I cannot help but feel empathy for him. He is no longer the man I was married to. For years and years, he has paid the price for being that man, paid it dearly by losing his relationship with his daughter and now she will never fully forgive him. She ended her own life still believing that her father must be punished for his past behaviour. She wouldn't allow herself to see him as anything but a Neanderthal who used his fists to express himself. She couldn't accept he was a changed person and he knows she died believing him to be a man she didn't want to know. This must be torture for him.

'Come over tomorrow morning,' I heard myself say. 'You can tell me what you want included and I'll let them know.'

'Thank you. You have no idea how much I appreciate that, Claire. I'll see you around ten. Can I bring you anything? Anything at all?'

My daughter back, I think. But I manage to hold it in.

'Joel is coming over tomorrow to discuss the funeral,' I tell Adrian at dinner as I push my food around the plate, forming small hills of mashed potato to chase my peas through. I remember Julia playing with her food the same way when she was four or five. 'Just eat, will you?' I inevitably yelled, exasperated with the dinner rush as I tried to get three-year-old Nicholas to try one new food and stop an already walking Cooper from undoing everything I'd achieved during the day. 'But I'm telling a story,' Julia would whine at me. 'See? The peas are going on an adventure. They have to cross the mountains.'

I know when I look back on those fraught evenings now that it wasn't just the overwhelming domestic drudgery that made me yell. It was the fact that as the evening progressed we were getting closer and closer to Joel returning home, the clock inching towards the moment he would walk through the door and I would need to attempt a lightning-quick assessment of his mood to figure out if he wanted the children near him or if I needed to put them to bed early, if he felt like what I'd made for dinner or if I needed to throw something else together, if he'd had a bad day or a good day.

'Why haven't you cleaned up this mess?' Joel asked me one day, when his work day had been difficult. 'What the fuck is wrong with you? You do nothing else all day.'

'Stop yelling at the kids to clean up, Claire,' he said the following day, when he'd been to some work drinks. 'Why are you so angry with them?'

'Don't worry about the chaos, babe, you had a long day,' he said the day after that, when he'd worked out his aggression at the gym. 'I'll clean up and you have a long, hot bath. Maybe I'll join you later.'

I never knew if affectionate, funny Joel was walking through the door at night or if pissed-off, spoiling-for-a-fight Joel was coming home. Some nights I felt like a humming bird darting from flower to flower, flapping hard and fast as I tried to find the right way to be for that particular Joel. I never got it right, of course. I was never meant to get it right. And inevitably, regardless of what I did, on the bad nights I went to bed nursing a new bruise.

'I thought you didn't want him involved,' Adrian says, lifting his glass of wine and draining it. *That's glass number three*, I think but don't say. He's angry with me. I don't care. I'm angry with him as well. I'm only telling him about Joel because I don't want him to think I'm keeping things from him.

The letters don't count. They are Julia's secret. And now they are mine.

I shrug. 'I don't, but... I don't know... I don't want to regret how I deal with all this. I know the boys will want him involved.' Nicholas and Cooper are sleeping over at Joel's place again. Joel has rented a furnished apartment for the next couple of months so the boys can stay over if they want – and they want to more than they want to be here. It's the right thing for him to have done and

I know they are finding it easier to be around him than around me, but I can't help my moments of resentment at Joel swooping in and taking over. At the same time I am aware that I don't have the capacity to take care of my boys the way they need right now. At least Joel is there for them.

'I'm sure they will,' says Adrian, and I watch him fill his glass again. He is drinking more and more. He comes home from work smelling of alcohol and immediately opens a bottle of wine. I feel like he's waiting for me to say something but I don't have the energy for the conversation we need to have.

I cut up a piece of grilled chicken into small pieces as Adrian drinks almost half the glass in one large gulp.

Adrian has never been able to get beyond viewing Joel as an aggressor – an aggressor that I still have an intense attachment to. He cannot understand our relationship and I don't blame him for that. I can't quite understand it, either. The few times Joel and Adrian have been in the same room I have watched my second husband stand up straighter, pull his shoulders back and puff out his chest. He cannot compete with Joel's physicality, with his size, with the beauty of his body – he takes up more space than any man I know.

'He is not what I want,' I've explained. 'You understand what he did to me, don't you, what he put me through?'

'I do, but sometimes I see you look at each other and…'

'And what?'

He's never been able to explain it and I have never pushed him because I get it, I understand it – I feel it. Joel still, after everything, makes me catch my breath a little when he walks into a room. I've discussed this with Leslie over and over again, hating myself for being unable to simply see him as an abuser and leave it there.

'You can't help your reaction to him,' Leslie told me. 'It may be attraction tinged with fear or it may be a kind of addiction. It's also difficult because he has changed, or says he's changed, and you can see that this might be the case. You're marooned in the middle of remembering how it felt when he attacked you and remembering the times when he was the man you fell in love with.'

'So how do I make it stop?'

Leslie looked up at the ceiling of her office – a gesture she used when she didn't have an answer for me, as if to say, 'Only God knows.' And to this day I don't know the reason I am still so attracted to my ex-husband. I don't think I love Joel any more but when I see him, I want to touch him so much I have to hold my hands down to stop myself from reaching out.

'You could stay home and see him with me,' I say to Adrian, but he shakes his head.

'I have a couple coming in from the Blue Mountains to see a house. I can't change it.'

Adrian knows logically that it's him I'm married to and it's him I love, but perhaps the divided loyalties of the children affect him more than he is willing to admit. I know that he took some pleasure in the fact that Julia would not speak to Joel.

I give up pretending to eat. Standing up, I begin clearing the plates off the table wondering, once again, if I should have forced Julia to see Joel. Perhaps not having her father in her life did even more profound damage than I realise. A married, older man is certainly a cry for some sort of help.

I haven't told Adrian about Eric Peters. I've decided I want to talk to Callie first, in case she saw something between the two of them when they were at school, and because I also want to do some research on him myself. I don't want a repeat of what happened with Colin Rider. I'm not just going to turn up at the man's door and fling accusations at him but if it's him… *if it* is *him*… Anger flares up inside me and I throw the dishes into the sink. They crash together in a heap and one of them shatters into pieces.

'Fuck,' I shout.

'Are you okay?' Adrian comes running into the kitchen.

I stare down at the mess, at the broken plate that can never be fixed, only thrown away. I'm not okay but what good would saying it out loud do? 'I'm, yes… I just broke a plate.'

Adrian puts his arms around me. 'Oh my love. I'll sort this out. Go and have a rest. Put on some stupid movie or something.'

I can't stop myself from moving away from Adrian. I know he's reaching out but I can't let go of the things he said to me on the phone. Adrian's face pales and he looks like he's close to tears. 'I'm so sorry for everything I said, Claire. Please believe how sorry I am.'

I turn away from him and begin picking pieces of the plate out of the sink. 'Don't you think I'm questioning myself enough, Adrian? It doesn't help for you to point out how I failed Julia, because I have a list in my head I'm running through over and over again.' I turn around and catch his gaze, making sure he's heard me and hoping he understands why I'm so upset.

'I know and I… miss her too, Claire. I'm sorry for what I said. This is so… hard on me.'

I look down at my hands. There is a small cut on my finger from a shard of plate. It's so tiny it doesn't even hurt and only a glistening drop of red tells me it's there. I don't know what to say to him, how to reply.

There are times when Adrian says something and I feel as though there is some hidden part of him that I've never seen. He has a tendency to turn a situation around so that he becomes the victim. 'How do you think I feel?' he will ask or, 'Imagine it from my point of view' or 'What about me?' I know that these are all valid questions, but if I ever confront him about his behaviour he will first become the victim. Then once I've explained myself and accepted that he must feel bad he will finally apologise.

Tonight I don't have the energy to consider Adrian's feelings. 'Yes,' I say. 'It must be very hard.'

I leave him in the kitchen with the mess.

In Julia's bedroom, I drop a kiss onto BB's head. 'Give Julia sweet dreams,' I say, my voice thick with tears, as I have said every night since it happened. I lie down on her bed, waiting for the longed-for oblivion of sleep, but an hour later I am still awake, my heart racing and my mouth dry.

I switch on her bedside lamp and pick out another random letter from Julia's lover. I still can't help thinking that I will find something that points to why she did what she did. Perhaps he broke up with her when she told him about the baby, or maybe his wife found out, but so far I can't find anything in them to indicate that. I hope that by reading them over and over I will pick up some clues I've missed. I try to read between the lines, to decipher the words he hasn't written, to hear the things he hears her saying, to find the truth of who he was, to find the child that I have lost.

My sweetest, darling Julia,

How lovely to see the wonder on your face today when you opened the present I gave you. Of course they are real diamonds, my love – small but real. Once you and I are together all the time, you will have diamonds for your throat and for your arms and for your fingers. I will cover you in diamonds, my darling, but I need time to do that. For now I ask you to wear the earrings all the time, my love. Wear them and when you look in the mirror and see them, think of me and what we do together. The time for us to reveal ourselves to the world is getting closer. Enjoy what we have now. Think of me often as I think of you.

Love x

I know the earrings he's writing about. Six months ago, when she came up from Melbourne, she was wearing them. I didn't notice them but Cooper complimented her on them. 'Nice earrings,' he said, studying the small diamond studs in her ears. He had been trawling through jewellery sites online, looking for a birthday gift for his girlfriend that wouldn't drain his savings. 'Are they real?'

Julia had giggled. 'Wouldn't you like to know,' she said.

I only registered the moment because then I stepped closer to her and studied them. 'I would love something like that.'

'I thought you hated diamonds,' said Adrian. I had insisted that my engagement ring from him be a sapphire – my engagement ring from Joel was a large diamond surrounded by a smattering of diamond chips. I enjoyed the attention it drew when he first gave it to me but one night, after the abuse had begun, he crushed two of my fingers together as he pulled my arm behind my back and the ring cut into my flesh. I stopped wearing it after that.

'Well, those are nice,' I said, and Adrian nodded and tapped his nose as if to indicate that a gift of diamonds would be in my future.

I wanted to ask Julia who had given her the earrings and I even opened my mouth to pose the question but then I stopped myself. I was trying to give her the chance to come to me if she had someone new in her life she wanted to share. Against my better instinct I was giving her space and time.

And now there is nothing between us but space and time.

I should have questioned the earrings that I assumed were from some boy at university. But boys at university surely don't give diamond earrings as presents. I feel so stupid, so *stupid* for not really thinking about it beyond the idea that I wouldn't mind a pair for myself.

I allow myself a grim smile, before I close my eyes again, willing sleep to claim me. How was it possible that diamond earrings were something I ever had the desire to think about?

When sleep eventually comes, I dream I am in a small room. It's empty when the dream begins but as I look around, objects begin to appear. First a bed and then a desk and a small cupboard and in the dream I realise I am in Julia's dorm room. The walls are a shiny white and I reach out to touch one of them, only to have it move out of my reach. I take a step towards it, only to have it move further away again. I start to run, hoping to catch the wall before it slips out of my reach although I have no idea why I need to touch it. Finally I make it and in the dream I can feel my triumph at having reached the wall but then I see the words written on it in thick, black marker: *My sweetest, darling Julia.* I look up and suddenly the whole wall is covered in *My sweetest, darling Julia* over and over again. Everything in the room disappears and then I am alone in the small room, empty now, surrounded by walls smothered in *My sweetest, darling Julia*. I wake up, heart pounding, throat dry and body shaking and I only manage to doze again at dawn. I start awake again when I hear the buzz of the lawnmower next door.

'No sweet dreams for me then,' I say to BB, who cannot give me any answers either.

✽

My sweetest, darling Julia,

Oh my darling, I am sure you don't mean to hurt me when you speak of boys at university. I know you don't mean it when you talk about dating someone closer to your age. You're only talking to me about other boys and men to make me jealous, to make sure that I am always thinking of you because you know I hate the idea of other men looking at you. You don't have to worry, Julia. I am always thinking about you.

When we discussed what you would have to do to pursue your dream as an actress, I confess that I told you how difficult a path it would be because the thought of you being stared at by other men made me sick. You were too young for me to tell you that then but I am glad that I can tell you now. I knew you would have to get used to being on display for the whole world and that felt so wrong to me. I suppose because, even when you didn't know yourself, I always knew we would be together one day.

I knew we would be together when you were old enough. I knew it the same way I know that tomorrow there will be a dawn.

I didn't want you up on stage or in a movie being ogled by the whole world. You are for my eyes only. How much more can I do and what more can I say to assure you of my devotion?

You don't need to be with anyone else, Julia. You don't need attention from anyone else. All you need is me and you have me. You have me.

Love x

CHAPTER FOURTEEN

When Joel arrives to discuss Julia's funeral, I am still wrapped in a towel. I stood in the shower for ages, trying to wash the dream out of my head, trying to erase the letters from my mind. The more times I read them, the more things fall into place, things I couldn't understand at the time they happened. Her decision to give up acting came from *him* because he wanted her to stay here so he could have a relationship with her. Her moving to Melbourne must have put a crimp in his plans but it didn't stop him. He simply followed her there, probably disguising his true intentions as a friendly visit. She may have thought he only had her best interests at heart but all he was ever thinking about was himself. I can feel it in my gut.

'I'm sorry, I slept late,' I say to Joel.

He is dressed in his weekend uniform of blue jeans and a black T-shirt. He gives me a weary smile. 'I know you, Claire, don't worry.'

I bristle at his condescension but realise quickly that he means nothing by the remark. It's the first time I've seen him since it happened and I feel the familiar thrum of my heart at the sight of him. He looks tired and his hair is now more grey than black. I wonder if that has happened since our daughter died.

'Make yourself a coffee or something,' I say. 'I'll just throw some clothes on.'

I settle on a pair of jeans and a faded black T-shirt. 'You've been wearing that T-shirt forever, Mum. You need some new weekend clothes, let's go shopping,' I hear sixteen-year-old Julia say.

In the kitchen Joel has the kettle boiling and he is opening and closing cupboards looking for the coffee. 'On the counter behind the toaster, where I always keep it,' I say.

'I never understood why,' he says, filling two mugs and handing me one after he has added a teaspoon of sugar for me. 'You still take it that way?'

'I do, thanks. We can sit in the living room.'

Joel follows me and sits on the couch with me, leaving one seat in between us. You never imagine on the day you don a flowing white bridal gown and gaze adoringly at the man you are going to marry that there will come a time when there is only space between you.

'How are you?'

'I'm… just horrible,' I reply, leaning forward to grab a tissue from the box on the coffee table. I don't know if I will ever be able to be in a room without a box of tissues again. I didn't want to cry in front of Joel. I don't like to cry in front of anyone, really, although it seems to be all I do right now. I can tell that Adrian is finding me wearying. I am starting to feel he's used up his resources of comfort. And I don't blame him. He is having trouble dealing with his own grief. I haven't spent the night in our bedroom since it happened because I can't seem to leave Julia's bed. I feel her there, in her bed, in her room, amongst her things. I don't sleep properly any more and I find myself wandering the house at odd hours. More than once I have heard the muffled noises of Adrian trying to hide his distress coming from the bedroom. I have wanted to go in and put my arms around him but found myself paralysed by my own grief. I have no capacity to help anyone else. I think perhaps he is grieving not just for Julia, but for our lives that were to come once the boys had finished school. I will never again be the woman he married seven years ago, and I know that right now he can only see a future where he is tied to a wife who is so broken that a single good day will never be possible.

'I know.' Joel nods, staring into his cup of coffee. A tear makes its way down his face.

'Oh, babe,' I say, falling unconsciously back into my name for him. I grab another tissue and dab at his chin before he salts his coffee. It is more than I have done for Adrian and I don't know why this is.

'I'm sorry,' he says, putting the cup down and leaning back. 'I can't believe she's gone. I keep remembering and every time I remember it feels worse. I thought I would have more time. I have so many regrets I don't even know how to count them up. I fucked up so badly and I deserved what I got but we were getting somewhere, we really were. I keep thinking that Julia would not have done this. She would not have taken her own life.'

'I know, it's not who she was but maybe… maybe we didn't actually know who she was.' I can't tell Joel about the letters or the married lover. I have no idea what he would do if I mentioned Eric Peters to him and I certainly don't want him using his connections in the police force to go digging up everything Julia wanted hidden. I need to do this myself. But I know that when I finally confirm it's Eric Peters, I will tell Joel. Once I know the truth and I am certain, not just that it's him but that he knew she was pregnant and did nothing to help her, then I will tell her father and let him deal with the piece of shit who hurt my daughter.

Joel stands up. He moves restlessly around the living room, picking up pictures and small knick-knacks and putting them down again. 'I don't have any recent pictures of her. I can't even go on her Facebook because she wasn't my friend on the site. Cooper and Nicholas don't have anything either, but you must have some stuff. Can you give me a few?'

Such a simple request, but I feel a bolt of rage flash through me. I stand up and stalk towards him. 'What good are pictures, Joel? You've barely been in her life for the last eight years so what good are pictures?'

It has always been like this between us. I love him, I hate him, I love him, I hate him. My feelings shift back and forth so rapidly sometimes they make me giddy.

'That wasn't my fault,' he hurls back at me. 'I tried, you know how I tried. She wasn't interested. I apologised time and again but she never wanted me in her life.'

'Yeah, well, who could blame her for that?'

'Oh, fuck you, Claire,' he says and he moves towards me. I flinch. 'I'm not going to fucking hit you! You know that!' he roars.

'I don't know that,' I yell back. 'How would I know that? You could have a girlfriend at home that you beat the shit out of every other day for all any of us know.'

Joel takes a deep breath, calming himself. 'You don't have to believe I've changed. *I* know it's true. It's been true for years. And you must know on some level that something is different or you wouldn't have let the boys spend time with me when they were younger. I tried to get her to forgive me, Claire. I tried. I have written her an email once a week for the last eight years and sometimes she responds and sometimes she doesn't. I have invited her to stay with me over and over again. She was angry, I understand that, but it felt like I was getting somewhere in the last few months. We even had a conversation that lasted longer than a few minutes.' He sighs, rubs his eyes. 'You know what I think? I think you didn't want her to reconnect with me. I think you made sure it never happened.'

'So it's my fault?' I shriek. 'Just like when you hit me and hurt me, it's all *my* fault?' I am pushing him, goading him, allowing myself to lose control instead of fearing his loss of control.

'God, Claire, does every conversation have to end here? I know what I did. I know who I hurt. I know, I know and you don't have to keep reminding me. I live with it every single day of my life. How many years do I have to be punished for it? I would have spent less time in prison.'

'You're an arsehole, Joel,' I shout. 'What an arsehole thing to say! Maybe you *should* have gone to prison. Maybe that's where you belonged.' I am panting with the effort of screaming but something inside me seems to have broken. I know I should tell him to go but I want to watch my words hit him in the face. I want to watch him hurt. Perhaps because he is the only other person who is hurting as badly as I am. I held her first, after she slid out of my body and they placed her on my chest. I held her first but he held her second, still covered in blood and vernix. He held her second.

I have never yelled at anyone like this. When we were married I knew never to raise my voice at him. Part of me cannot believe that I am standing here screaming at him and he's doing nothing but yelling back. It is freeing and unsettling at the same time.

I had no intention of telling Joel about Julia's relationship but I wade in without thinking: 'If you'd been a better father, in fact if you'd been any kind of father at all, she wouldn't have been having a secret relationship with an older man. She wouldn't have been looking for a father figure in the man she was fucking.'

'What?' says Joel, his face fading to white.

'How do you think she got pregnant, Joel? You got that little piece of information from Detective Winslow, didn't you? So how do you think that happened?'

'I don't… I thought a boy… I was going to ask you… I thought a boy at university.'

'An older man,' I hiss, 'that's who your daughter turned to because she didn't have a man in her life she could trust. Adrian wasn't enough because she felt hurt and rejected by her real father.'

'I never…'

'Never what, Joel?' I step towards him, hot with fury, and I slap his arm. 'You never *what*, Joel? You never thought that all the shit you did when we were married would affect our kids for the rest of their lives?' I slap him again, this time on the chest.

'You never thought that you couldn't just walk away from us?' I slap him again and again. 'You never anything, Joel – you threw your fucking fists around and broke four people and then you wanted to be forgiven.' I hit him again and again. I slap and hit and form a fist and punch him on the chest. I hit him over and over as he walks backwards around my living room. I can see what I'm doing but I cannot stop this, any more than I could stop a speeding freight train.

As I keep hitting I realise that what I want, what I really want, is for him to hit me back. I want him to send me flying across the room because then at least I would feel something different. Then at least there would be physical pain and I could point to a bruise or a broken bone and say, 'See, there is the evidence of my pain. There it is in yellow and purple, written on my body so you can understand how shattered my heart is.' I want something to show what I'm feeling because in my jeans and T-shirt there is no evidence of this horrible, grating, soul-destroying grief.

But he doesn't hit back. I keep going, pushing him around the living room, hitting and slapping until he is in a corner and still I'm not done. I can feel my arms getting heavy. I am sweating and panting but I keep going. Joel sinks onto the floor, puts his arms over his head. 'Please, Claire, please stop,' he moans and I can hear that he is weeping. 'Please, please,' he repeats but he doesn't hit back. I kick out at him and catch him on the shin. He flinches but doesn't move. I need to make him hit back. He needs to hurt me. 'Please stop,' he says again, trying to protect his whole body. 'Please, babe, please stop.'

It is this word that breaks through, this word that he called me affectionately, that he called me in public, that he called me when he was inside me. 'Babe' is the word that penetrates my madness. I stop, dropping my heavy arms to my side. There is a ringing in my ears and I look drunkenly around the room. The air feels thick. I have no idea what just happened. I sink onto the floor in front of him.

'I'm… oh, Joel, I'm so sorry, I'm so sorry. I don't know… I don't.' My body heaves as I try to get the words out. I am exhausted. I am horrified. I am not sure who I am, even. 'I'm so sorry, Joel, please, Joel… please say something, I'm so sorry.' Joel has his head buried in his arms. His body is heaving like mine, he is sobbing like I am. I touch his arm and he drops his hands and leans forward. He folds me into his arms and for a moment we howl together for our lost child.

We use our T-shirts to wipe our faces when we are done. I take a deep breath and I look at Joel, at Julia's father. I lock eyes with him and I touch his face and he is still. I put my lips against his and he kisses me back and then we are crying and struggling out of our clothes, without thinking about who could come in or who we are or why we are here, we are fucking on the floor of the living room.

It is everything I remember and nothing I remember. The feeling of his weight on top of me is familiar but the gentle way he strokes my skin is not. The pleasure of him inside me is a delicious memory but the way he looks at me, as though he is afraid I will disappear, is not. It is Joel but it is also not Joel.

In the years since we were married I have wondered if I will ever be able to trust him when he says he is a changed man and I have always thought that a time will come when the man he was when we were married will make a resurgence and destroy my children anew, thereby destroying me. I have believed, for all these years, that the real Joel is simply being concealed and at any moment the Joel who hurt me will be back. Afterwards as we lie, tangled together on my living room floor, I understand that this will never be the case. This is a different man I have just spent the afternoon with. I could have met him yesterday.

I feel spent, drained and light. The weighted sadness that I live with now has momentarily lifted. But a moment later, rushing through me, is a tsunami of guilt. What have I done? I squash it down, pleading with my own conscience, *Please just give me a few more minutes. Please.*

I curl up against him, tracing a new tattoo of a bear staring out from between two trees on his shoulder. 'Why a bear?' I ask.

Joel rubs his chin and stares up at the ceiling and I can sense that he wants to share the meaning whilst at the same time wanting to keep it for himself.

'You don't have to tell me.'

'No… no, it's okay. I got it after I spent time in the hospital. I was walking around the city and I had just come from the interview with Stuart and he'd given me the job. He'd said, "Jesus, mate, you're the size of a bear," when he first met me. That's what made me think about it. So I was walking around, just trying to feel grateful that the next day I would be able to start working and I was thinking of what I could say to you to explain myself, of what I could do to make up for the fact that I had basically disappeared for two months, and I walked past a tattoo place. They had a whole lot of bears in the window, but only one of them had its jaws open and teeth showing. I chose this one because he looked really peaceful. I got it to remind me to never show my teeth again and that there is another way I can be. It's stupid, I know, but at the time it felt right.'

'It's not stupid, Joel. It's lovely.'

'You have no idea…' he says, his voice breaking a little.

'No idea about what?'

'No idea how much I have missed touching you.'

'Me, too,' I say, my voice cracking. 'Me, too.'

*

My sweetest, darling Julia,

I'm sorry we fought today. I know you are only worried about all the people who will be hurt when they find out about us – and that is why I want to wait, to keep us a wonderful secret. I have opened another bank account and I will start putting money into it. Give me time, my darling, and we will have enough to leave everyone behind. I know you don't want to leave your family but you have to know that what we have is greater than them. I know that is hard to hear, but it is greater than us as well, and if I were a religious man I would say that us being together is by the grace of God. He can only mean for a love like this to happen once in a lifetime. We have waited so long to be together. It won't matter if we have to keep the truth quiet for a bit longer. Let us rather just be together whenever we can and enjoy the sweetness of those moments. You made me laugh when you tried the wine I ordered for you and you gave me a rundown on its history. I love that you are looking into the things that interest me. I love that you are learning from me and opening yourself up to the world. I have so much more to teach you, my darling. So much more to show you. All of that will come in time.

I am not ready to share this love with the world yet and I know that my feelings are important to you. Trust me, my sweetest darling, because I know what's right for you and for us. Just trust me.

Love x

CHAPTER FIFTEEN

The guilt of what I have done gnaws at me constantly the following day. I walked him out but we couldn't look at each other. Not, I felt, because we were ashamed, although shame was settling inside me. Rather we were afraid that we wouldn't be able to resist doing it all over again. Those brief moments of feeling something other than anger and grief and heartbreak could easily become addictive. I've resisted sleeping pills, preferring instead to lie awake in my daughter's room trying to work out where I went wrong, but I don't think I could so easily resist Joel.

I should not have allowed myself that reprieve. I don't deserve it – but they are closely linked they say, sex and death, all wrapped up together in life.

Julia's funeral is in three days. Her funeral is in three days and yesterday I had sex with her father in my living room, cheating on my husband of seven years. Now I am struggling to look directly at Adrian, as though he would see my misdeeds written across my face. In the darkest hours I feel that Julia's death was a punishment for what I have done with Joel, as though karma has acted pre-emptively.

I can't stop thinking about when Joel and I first met, when all of this was in the future. I wonder if we had known what was to come. What choices would we have made? What choices would I have made?

I met Joel outside a club in the city. He was the bouncer and I was a little too drunk to be let inside.

'Sorry, club policy,' he'd said, as he barred me from walking in. The friends I had with me all agreed that we should just go home but Joel told them to go in without me. 'I'll take care of her out here. I go on a break in half an hour and I'll get her a coffee. Maybe then she can come inside.'

'Yes, go,' I told them, flattered by his personal attention. I concentrated on the way his muscles moved under his tailored shirt as he gestured to my friends to keep moving.

'I'll be fine,' I reassured them. I watched my hand move without me really thinking about it towards Joel's arm. I grabbed onto his wrist and he covered my hand with his. His wrists were twice the size of mine, his hand completely enveloping mine. His hair was inky black in the lights from the club. I breathed in deeply, taking in the light musky smell of his aftershave.

'I don't think you're fine,' he said.

'I had too many shots,' I hiccupped. 'Oops,' I laughed, and covered my mouth. I was afraid I was going to throw up right in front of the most beautiful man I'd ever seen. 'I'm dizzy,' I moaned.

'Here, wait here,' he said, and he propped me against a wall. He came back with a chair and sat me down like a parent would a child. For half an hour I dozed, despite the street noise, the flashing lights illuminating the club's name and a scuffle between two people right in front of my chair.

'You were really out of it,' he told me, when it was time for him to take his break. He led me to an all-night coffee shop where the lighting was too bright as it buzzed overhead.

'I need some sunglasses.'

'You need some coffee and a good night's sleep.'

'Do you take care of all the drunk women you meet outside the club?'

'Just the ones I'm going to marry,' he said. It was a line and I knew it was a line but he seemed so certain, so strong and so clear about the way forward. And he was gorgeous and sexy and after a few months I knew he had a dark sense of humour to match my own and a way of making me feel safe, taking charge in every situation.

The irony of that has not escaped me.

My family, my life, my real self, feel very distant to me now. Cooper and Nicholas rarely come home after school, instead taking themselves off to the apartment Joel has rented. Last night they slunk in late, well fed, with their homework completed. I have no idea why they chose last night to come home. Perhaps Joel sent them to comfort me or to remind me of him and what we did and what that act has produced in the past. Perhaps it is something as simple as them needing more clothes.

'You need to be home now,' I told Nicholas. 'I didn't buy you a car so you could be out all the time. I need you boys here.'

'Dad needs us as well, Mum.'

'But I need you more.'

'Can I be honest with you?' My eighteen-year-old son asked, flexing his muscles, something he does when he's nervous, something his father does as well.

'What?' I sighed.

'It's easier at Dad's. You're… I don't know… And I'm not blaming you but it feels like we all need a little space. Adrian is not our dad. He doesn't want to cook or do laundry or discuss homework or what happened at school. I mean, he has been trying but it feels like it's… forced. He's not our dad. Coop and I need Dad, and you need time.'

'Did your father tell you to say this to me?'

'God, Mum, you have to let the shit about Dad go already! It's been eight years. He's not that guy any more and right now it's easier to be with him. He makes dinner and he discusses school and sometimes we all talk about Julia and I don't feel bad because it's okay to do that. I hate mentioning her here. Adrian gets a weird look on his face like he doesn't want all this family drama and you just freak out and lock yourself in her room.'

I wanted to argue with him, to plead my case for still being a good mother, but I couldn't. I barely get dressed. I exist on fruit and toast and I spend hours and hours in her room. Sometimes I read the letters that sicken me, sometimes I google her name so I can see her Facebook and her Instagram and mentions of her in past school advertising brochures as their star drama student. The internet doesn't know Julia is gone. How strange that is. Your digital trail exists forever, as though in some other dimension you are still living your life. There are a couple of articles on her suicide but they don't mention her name. They identify her as a twenty-year-old woman who tragically took her own life on Hallowe'en night. I think she only made the papers because of her ghoulish choice of timing. 'Hallowe'en is the best thing ever to have come out of America,' she once told me. She enjoyed the theatre of it, the dressing up and the parties that came along with it. That night will never be the same for me. I don't know if I'll ever be able to stand the pumpkins, the trick-or-treaters, the costumes floating around.

The letters tell me that both Eric and Julia were struggling with what they were doing. I think of the writer as Eric Peters now. I hear his voice when I read them. Everything points me in that direction. Colin Rider seeing them in Melbourne, the things Nick has told me, the way she looked at him in that photograph in the year book, the things he says to her in the letters. It has to be him. I feel like Julia was struggling more than he was, but then that was my Julia. Her fierce sense of fairness would have been challenged. It's not fair to sleep with a married man, to help him deceive his wife, to keep him from his children. Julia would have been deeply troubled by that. Is that what forced her to make this choice, this dreadful choice that I am finding so very, very unfair?

My sweetest, darling Julia,

I felt your anger last night and you have a right to it. I suppose when we are together I prefer to block out the world, to just be with you so that we can enjoy the precious time we have, so, no – I don't want to constantly go over our situation. Marriage is a complicated thing, Julia. Two people get together for one set of reasons but over the years find every one of those eroded away. Some people manage to develop a new set of ideas for who they are as a couple and go on, but some don't. She doesn't understand the way I feel and I know that, but to tell her would devastate her and then to tell her about you would kill her. I still feel love for her. How could I not? I don't want to hurt her any more than you do but it's my marriage and you have to give me time to decide when the right moment will be. Even though you were angry and sad last night I still loved being with you. I still loved holding you and touching you and I know that whatever happens in the future I will always feel that way. You are my soul mate, Julia. My whole reason for being born was to one day meet you. I am completely convinced of that and while there will be people who are hurt when we finally reveal all, I know that they will survive and move on with their lives. There have been more complicated situations than ours, Julia. Other relationships have had more difficult beginnings and are now thriving. This connection between us is deeper than anything I have ever felt before and I know it is the same for you. Shut out the world with me, darling Julia. Shut out the world and let us treasure our moments together until the time comes for us to reveal ourselves.

I hope you are still destroying these letters after you read them. I trust you to do that for me, for us. It must feel impossible to you to keep this to yourself and it feels impossible to me too, but it won't be for much longer, my sweetest darling. I am doing everything I can to make sure we have enough money to be together and away from work and family. Think about that when you question this, think about how hard I am working so that you can have the life you deserve when you're with me.

Love x

I have never met a man who writes or speaks like this.

Feeling my eyes burn from peering at the words I get up off the bed in Julia's room and go to the kitchen for coffee. I am surprised to find that it's ten in the morning. I don't remember hearing Adrian leave. It cannot be possible for two people to drift this far from each other and yet we have. At first, I thought it was because death can do this – crack a chasm between a couple – but now I know it's my fault. It's my fault but I cannot think how to speak to him any more. He loved her, I know he loved her, but he doesn't feel this visceral brokenness that Joel and I do. Children tie you together, link you for all your lives. Regardless of how much you hate each other, your children reawaken a time when things were different. Nicholas looks so much like Joel did when we first met and Julia looks like I did. If you gaze on your children with love then you can't help but feel some residual love for the person who helped create them.

If Adrian and I got divorced now, if Julia's death drives us so far apart that we cannot come together again, then he will walk out of my life and disappear and I need never see him again, despite my love for him. It's a strange and heartbreaking thought but I know it's the truth.

He was married briefly when he was in his twenties to a woman named Anna. When it became more serious between us he told me about her.

'It was only for a year but we were both too young and had no idea how to be together as a married couple. I cheated on her with someone from work. I'm not proud of it and I've never done something like that again, but it's what happened.'

'Do you have any pictures of her or of your wedding day?' I asked.

'No, I threw everything away after we separated. I didn't need a reminder of my failings. I have no idea where she even lives now.'

I was surprised by that and a little concerned. I still had childish love letters from my first boyfriends buried somewhere at the back of my wardrobe. I didn't understand his ability to simply wipe someone from his life. I asked him about her again, searching for reasons for him to have gotten rid of everything to do with her.

'I just did,' was his reply, and I understood he didn't want to discuss it any more.

I imagine things would have been very different for Adrian if he and Anna had had a child together. My relationship with Joel is filled with complication. Love and hate, adoration and fear, sit alongside the unconditional love we have for our children. We are bound tightly together, regardless of how far apart we live.

I hold on to my mug of coffee, drawing comfort from its warmth, even though outside the temperature is climbing. 'We are in the middle of a spring heatwave,' the perky meteorologist said last night on television. Weather like this usually drives me into the garden, where I pull out weeds and trim blooming roses, but I can't imagine finding pleasure in the activity now. I wonder about Eric Peters' wife. Did she suspect what was going on? Did she find a copy of one of the letters on his computer and confront him? A secret relationship exposed often fails to stand the scrutiny of the light. Is that what happened? Did Eric look into his wife's eyes and finally understand the reality of leaving his family for his young mistress? Did he tell his wife that he loved her and that Julia was a mistake? I close my eyes and see him pleading for another chance. I don't know if I would allow an adulterous husband back into my bed but for years I accepted Joel's apologies, hoping that each fading bruise was the last bruise. I was terrified to be on my own, certain that Joel was right about me not being able to survive without him. Perhaps Eric's wife was scared to be alone, too. I sigh. I am hardly in a position to judge Eric's behaviour, anyway. Yesterday I broke my wedding vows and committed adultery.

I put my coffee down, finding it suddenly too hot, and lay my head on the cold, dark granite of my kitchen counter. I imagine Eric telling Julia that he's going back to his wife, that he doesn't love her any more. I see Julia's shock and the tears that come as he watches her, his warm brown eyes flat and cold.

A broken heart can feel impossible to live with and not everyone recovers from it. Is that what pushed her over the edge?

I am exhausted before the day has even begun, but I want more proof that Eric Peters was my daughter's lover. And I need to know what he said to her or did to her to make her decide that the only way forward was to end her life. I need to speak to Callie. I dial her number and feel myself tense, almost hoping for a voicemail so that I don't have to ask the question.

'Hello?' she answers, unable to recognise my number but also unable to simply let it ring for fear that it might be something interesting.

'Callie, its Claire, Julia's mum.'

'Oh, hey, hello… how are you?'

'I'm… I wanted to ask you something.'

'Yes?' She is cautious, suspicious of what I might say, of the possibility, perhaps, that I have found a way to blame her for Julia's death.

I wonder if people who commit suicide consider this before they take their lives. I realise that their pain must be so immense as to block out everything else but does it occur to them, perhaps in some final moment, that those around them who love them will not be able to accept their choice and will instead search for a reason or a person to blame? And that inevitably – whether they are a family member or a friend – that person will allow the blame to fall on their own shoulders. If only I had been a better mother or father or friend or husband or wife or lover. If only I had noticed or paid more attention. If only I'd called her that day and asked if she was okay. Perhaps it is hubris to assume that we play such a big part but perhaps it is what we are meant to think.

I have been reading about suicide a lot, about how those who make the choice feel that there is no other way forward. A young boy who had tried and failed to end his life writes a blog about how grateful he is to have been saved. His first post talked about the day he tried to kill himself by swallowing two bottles of sleeping pills.

> I just needed the noise to stop. I needed it to be quiet for a bit so I could think properly. I knew that if I could just have some real quiet then I would be able to figure out how to live my life when I was in so much pain. It was stupid because I wanted to die but I didn't want to die at the same time. I felt like if I could just die a bit then everything would be better. I wanted people to be sorry for every shitty thing they'd ever done to me. As I was falling asleep I thought about her, about my ex-girlfriend, and about how I should have called her and said goodbye so she would know how sorry I was for everything I had done to her and so she would feel bad for leaving me. I wanted to call her but by that time I was feeling too tired to even lift my hand. I didn't think about my mum and dad or about how sad they would be. I had already tried thinking about them and it didn't help. I just needed it to be quiet. Now when I think about that day I break out into a sweat. I think that if my mum hadn't come home just at that time I would be dead and I would never have known that it's possible to move on and move past the pain. I'm so glad I know it now and I want to let anyone else feeling that badly know that it's possible. Hang in there. Call a friend, call a relative. It's possible to move past the pain.

His blog makes me cry and then it makes me angry because I want Julia to be the one writing those words. I want Julia to have been saved in the nick of time. I want to be the mother who averted disaster and I'm not. All I have is this bizarre, heart-crushing search for someone else to blame. I have to take what I can get.

'Um… what did you want to ask?' says Callie.

'Did… did Mr Peters, you know Mr Peters the drama teacher, and Julia have some sort of relationship?'

There is almost a full minute of silence. I begin to think she may have hung up on me. 'Callie?'

'Yeah, no, I'm still here. I don't know… Why? I mean, what made you think that?'

'I can't explain it, Callie, and I really don't want to but I'm trying to figure all this out. Do you know something? Was there something going on between them?'

'Okay, Mrs Barker,' she says, and I don't bother correcting her. 'I really don't want to say something and, like, get other people in trouble or whatever. It was mostly just rumours anyway.' The same thing Nicholas said. 'Just rumours' – but rumours are the smoke that indicate that somewhere a fire is burning. What were they saying about the two of them? Who was talking about them? Was it just the students, or the staff as well? Why didn't anyone say anything to me?

'So there was something going on?'

Callie sighs loudly. 'I don't know. I mean, they were together a lot because she was in every play and she was the best. She was so good and he was helping her with auditions for outside stuff, too, so they were together like a lot. But it was mostly in the last year of school and even though people said stuff, we never knew for sure. I think all the girls had kind of a crush on him. I mean, he's gorgeous.'

'So you don't know for sure. Did you ever see them together outside school?'

'No,' Callie says, and I can picture her vehemently shaking her head.

'So then why were there rumours? What were people saying?'

'Um, I can't really… like, I don't actually remember anything specific, people just used to laugh when they saw them together and sometimes the boys, like the older boys, would shout something like… well, "Guess who's getting some," when they saw them together.'

'So what did Mr Peters do about that?'

'Nothing that I ever heard of – I mean, everyone says stuff at school. They used to talk about this one guy and the French teacher as well, but she had just gotten married and so there was no way she was doing anything. Mr Peters just used to ignore stupid stuff people said and so did Julia. I never talked to her about it or anything, but then we didn't really spend that much time together in high school. We kind of had our own groups, you know.'

'Okay, okay. Thanks, it's probably nothing,' I lie. 'I'm sure there was nothing. Please don't say anything to anyone. I'm probably just being silly.'

'That's okay, Mrs Barker. I'll see you at the funeral, okay?'

'Yes, okay. Okay, thanks, Callie.'

Hanging up, I google Eric Peters again as I have done before. His Facebook page is set to private. The profile picture is of a man – I assume it's him – standing on a paddleboard in the sunset. He is photographed from the back. I scroll down a little through all the changes he has made to his profile picture and find one from a year ago. It's of a woman and two little boys. She is standing by a beach. Her body and those of the two little boys are turned towards the ocean but they have all swung their heads around to smile at the person taking the photograph. The boys look very little, maybe two and four. The woman and the boys share the same clean, blond look Eric Peters has, as though they have all been styled as a family for a photoshoot. The woman is pretty, very pretty.

'You absolute arsehole,' I say aloud.

He has a wife and two young children.

Why wasn't she enough for him? What more could he have wanted? Even as I think the question I am aware that beauty isn't enough, that intelligence isn't enough, that having a kind heart isn't enough, because for some men nothing is ever enough. It's the thrill of the chase, of the forbidden. It's the new and shiny girlfriend who believes everything you tell her without question, who allows you to see yourself as the hero of your own life. I imagine this must be doubly true of an older man and a younger woman. Perhaps Eric Peters preferred the company of my daughter over his wife because she was, in some respects, still his student, still looking to him for advice and guidance.

How powerful she must have made him feel.

I think for a moment about sending him a friend request and then realise how demented this would seem to him. I will have to go to the internet for any more information.

I take my computer back to Julia's room and climb into bed. I haven't eaten breakfast but I couldn't swallow if I tried. I have to think for a moment before I realise it's Tuesday, and I am briefly grateful to Joel for being here and taking care of the boys. Images of the two of us flicker and shame me. I shiver. It felt so right when he was inside me. I am a hideous human being. I am busy judging Eric Peters for cheating on his wife and questioning why the beautiful woman in the picture wasn't enough for him, but why isn't Adrian enough for me? He's stood by me for the last eight years, supporting me as I raised another man's children, loving me as I recovered from the damage done by Joel and being there for me without question. What more could I want? And yet I have cheated on him, betrayed him, just as Eric Peters did with his wife. I am, perhaps, no better than him.

Stop, I yell at myself. 'Enough,' I say. I am not the same as Eric Peters. Yesterday with Joel was about our connection and the loss of our child. It was wrong, but I'm not the same as Eric Peters. I didn't pick a vulnerable young woman and swear her to secrecy even as I manipulated her into staying with me with promises of a future together. It's not the same thing. I have to believe it's not the same thing or I'll go mad. I need my sanity so can I uncover the complete truth and then so I can make sure that the man who hurt my daughter is revealed to the world for what he's done.

I type 'Eric Peters' into my search bar and breathe deeply, calming myself, as the results appear.

Two hours later I am still reading small articles and mentions of Eric Peters. It transpires that he was born in Australia and then lived in the US for ten years before returning to take up teaching. In New York he was in a lot of off-Broadway plays but never more than that. I wonder at what point he decided to give up on his acting career and become a teacher. It may have had something to do with him getting married. His wife may have told him that it was time to give up his dream so they could start a family. Maybe that's how he influenced Julia to give up on her own dream of becoming an actress, by regaling her with tales of all his failures, instead of telling her the truth – which was that he didn't want her far away from him.

Perhaps being with Julia made him feel young again, as though all that had passed him by was possible again. My poor child was probably some sad cliché in the middle of this man's mid-life crisis. I can't find any pictures of his wife or family which I find strange, but not overly unusual. If I google my own name I am in pictures with the staff at the English language school, or in pictures with a group of women I sometimes do charity runs with. I have made precious little impact on the world but I have always taken comfort in my abilities as a mother and as a survivor of abuse. Of course I have been fooling myself. My child killed herself and I just had sex with my abusive ex-husband. I cover my face with my hands. I wish there was an off button for the recriminations that play constantly in my head; I wish there was a way to stop the thoughts for even an hour. I know Adrian is using alcohol to get by at the moment and I have tried that, but the resulting headache and guilt in the dead hours that follow just don't seem worth it.

There is nothing for me to find on the internet about this man. I shut down my computer and consider the yawning day of nothing that lies before me. I know both my mother and sister want me to call, would love me to call, but I find I have nothing to say and I know that anything they say will be of little comfort to me. I haven't heard from Joel today. I imagine he is as mortified by what happened yesterday as I am. After we had dressed and I showed him to the door he apologised again. 'It's not your fault,' I said. 'We were both involved and I attacked you and I'm sorry.'

'I'll see you at the funeral.'

'Joel,' I said, as he turned to leave. I have always wondered why he hasn't found another woman after all these years and I couldn't stop myself from asking: 'Is there someone else in your life, someone this could hurt?' I have never heard the boys talk about another woman in his life but he may just be careful to keep her a secret. But I wanted to know then, as I was already mentally chastising myself with the thought that I may have inadvertently hurt another woman.

'No, Claire. There have been women I've… been with, but there hasn't been anyone since you. You were it for me, I think. I live with that fact every day, every single day.'

I was too stunned by his revelation to say anything. It would have been kind of me to let him know that my attraction to him hasn't faded either, but I think I had demonstrated that already, and the words wouldn't form on my lips. In the end I just nodded, resisting the urge to grab him again, and closed the door and looked down at my feet.

He didn't hit me back.

He could have and he would have years ago, but he hadn't. If any situation was going to bring out the worst in Joel it was this and yet he hadn't raised a hand. It's difficult to believe in redemption, especially when you are the person who has been hurt, but Joel is not the man he was. He's done the work and made the decision to change. The only person still holding on to the past is me.

Perhaps I would have been a better mother to Julia if I had encouraged, really encouraged her, to believe her father had reformed.

I have always told myself that I tried to get her to forgive him but I have to admit to sometimes feeling a small, mean triumph at her continual rejection of him. I should have tried harder and I should have wanted their reconciliation with my whole heart.

Certainly having her biological father in her life may have prevented her searching for a father figure. I have to accept some of that blame. Indeed I will simply add it to the list of reasons why I failed my child. It grows longer by the day, by the hour, by the minute.

I can't stop myself from opening my computer again and returning to Eric Peters articles. There are images of him in groups with other actors or other teachers. He is very good-looking but perhaps a little too 'boy next door' to have made an impact on the acting world. I find a YouTube video of him in a production where he plays Hamlet. He is much younger and I watch him for a bit, realising that while he is a good actor there is nothing spectacular about him.

Unlike Julia. Julia was mesmerising on stage. When she was little she was always the most enthusiastic performer in the class. While other children stared off into the distance or got distracted by their costumes or waved to their parents, she behaved as though she was the only one on stage. As she got older this developed into a real presence. The first time I realised she was more than just a good performer was when she played Juliet. She was only fourteen and hadn't expected to be cast as anything other than a background character in *Romeo and Juliet*. Her greatest hope was for a line or two but she ended up getting the lead. She virtually bounced into the car after school when the list of parts went up. 'The most wonderful thing has happened,' she said, and I laughed at the expression but shared her joy at getting the part. I worried that the more senior students would make things difficult for her because the older drama students usually got the main roles, but they didn't. Instead they embraced her as part of their circle.

I had assumed that she was cast because she was young and had the innocence that gave the character of Juliet depth, but I was wrong. I had sat in the audience at the dress rehearsal and clenched my fists so I would not be tempted to wave, but in the end, I wasn't. From the moment she appeared on stage she was Juliet. Mesmerised, I forgot I was watching my own child. I brought Adrian back with me on opening night and the boys on the second night. Julia said that the other students found it funny that I came back night after night.

'Do you want me to stop coming?' I asked, desperate not to do the wrong thing.

'No, Mum, they think it's nice, funny but nice. I love that you're there. Every night I try to play her a little differently because I know you're watching it again.'

She was a natural, and even though I worried about her pursuing an acting career I couldn't deny her talent.

That was the first time I met Eric Peters. I picked Julia up from the cast party when the play had finished its week-long run and he was there. Julia grabbed his hand and dragged him over to meet me. I remember, for a second, being uncomfortable with her familiarity with him but I reasoned that all the weeks and months of working together to get ready for the play probably changed the dynamics of the student–teacher relationship.

'Mum, this is Eric, I mean Mr Peters. He's the drama teacher. This is my mum, Claire,' Julia announced proudly, her cheeks flushed with the heat of the room and a large amount of celebratory junk food.

'I'm so pleased to meet you.' He smiled, holding out his hand, which I shook.

'Julia has really enjoyed being part of this production,' I said.

'And we have enjoyed having her. She is a uniquely talented young woman and I hope she will be in every play we put on from now on.' He looked directly at me, meeting my gaze, and I felt I had his full attention. I bit down on my lip, suppressing a giggle at his beauty.

'Of course I will, silly,' laughed Julia, making us break contact.

Eric Peters and I exchanged a look, an indulgent parental look. I felt embarrassed at my reaction to him.

'I think it's time for bed for you, young lady,' I said, and Julia nodded and yawned.

I thought he saw her as a child but is it possible that he saw her as something else, even then?

The final article I click on is simply a few lines from a school I know is located a few suburbs away. 'Students farewell Eric Peters' is the headline along with a picture of a much younger Eric. 'After a short tenure in our drama department Eric Peters is leaving for greener pastures,' reads the line underneath.

'That's what my daughter was,' I think. 'Greener pastures.'

I close my computer down, unable to prevent a shudder running through me. I know that illicit relationships between students and teachers happen. I've read about them and seen the fall-out in the court cases on television so I'm aware they exist, but it never occurred to me that Julia would make such a choice. Unless of course the choice wasn't really hers to make. If she and Eric Peters were in a relationship, he could have been grooming her for years.

I feel bile rise in my throat. How long had they been sleeping together? Since she was sixteen or fifteen, or even fourteen?

The letters say that he has wanted her for a long time. He must have waited. He must have watched. He must have been very patient. He must be a sick, twisted man who cannot be allowed to get away with this.

✼

My sweetest, darling Julia,

I need you to think carefully about the things you're saying to me. We have so little time together and you are choosing to make every moment difficult. I know you feel guilty. I feel guilty as well but you have to realise that we are more than just you and me in this world. I am certain that we could go back in time and find ourselves as lovers in a past life. That's how important, how destined, we are. We are above the morality of the situation, above what may or may not hurt others. My marriage is my concern. I know what is between my wife and me and you have not ruined that. You were simply there and all I needed to do was see you. I watched you grow, Julia, I watched you develop into a young woman and I know who you are. I will not let the fear of what the people in our lives will think spoil our time together. I will not let society tell me who to love. In the same way you must not let your anguish about our situation spoil it. Neither of us can know the future and all we have is right here and now. Love me, darling Julia, as I love you.

Love x

CHAPTER SIXTEEN

The last letter from Eric Peters reveals how difficult Julia was finding the affair. He could have decided to let her go and yet he chose to flatter her and feed her bullshit about how they were meant to be together. If I were his wife I would want to know exactly what was in these letters. I know there must be more of them. Something must have happened in between him sending this last letter and Julia coming up here. My phone call with Callie today didn't give me anything concrete, just more rumours and unknowns. I riffle through the letters again, hoping to find one that I've missed, but there's nothing. Frustration makes me edgy. I feel like going out for a run but it's nearly midnight. Eric Peters returned from camp today and he will be back at school tomorrow. I checked the school website where a picture of him surrounded by his senior drama students – all girls – was on the home page.

The boys were home for dinner again tonight. I'm now sure Joel asked them to come. I sat at the dinner table with Adrian and Nicholas and Cooper and pushed my food around my plate as Adrian stumbled through questions about school with them. I kept glancing at Julia's chair, hoping that if I looked up quickly enough she would be there.

The day after tomorrow we will bury my darling child. Visions of the funeral haunt me. I remember my father's funeral where I stood at the graveside with my brother and sister, holding tightly onto my mother whose legs seemed too weak to carry her. We barely listened to what the priest said and all I could think was,

When will this be over? I dropped a red rose from my garden onto his coffin and the sound it made, the light clunk on wood, tore through me, reducing me to a sobbing mess when I was trying to help my mother by staying strong. It cemented the truth of his death in my mind, something I had managed to avoid doing, preferring to believe him just out of reach, just out of sight. When I got home, I remember ripping off the plain black dress I had bought and burying it in the rubbish bin.

How on earth will I survive the funeral? How do you get up in the morning and dress yourself in clothes appropriate in which to bury your child? I was relieved to find a black dress at the back of my cupboard that I don't even remember buying. I was grateful to find it, terrified of the idea of having to go out and buy a dress. I couldn't have faced such a public task.

I know there will be a lot of people there. The cards and emails keep coming from friends of hers, old and new. Those who shared the primary school years and the high school years will be there, as well as new friends from university. She didn't have time to drift out of people's lives as she got on with her own. Her life was just beginning and what could have been for her will forever be an unanswered question. As I bid my daughter farewell, I will be surrounded by her contemporaries who will, no doubt, always remember her as the young woman who took her own life. They will go on to make their mark on the world and create lives and families. But time has stopped for Julia. How will I leave her there? It is inconceivable, a surreal nightmare from which I will never be allowed to wake up.

My mother and sister came over late this afternoon to show me the program for the funeral. It's filled with pictures of Julia right from when she was a baby.

'Where did you get all these?' I asked Emily.

'Mum had them.'

'Of course I did,' said my mother. 'She was my first grandchild… she was—' and then she couldn't continue any more. I know I sighed loudly as she started crying. I am guilty of refusing to see anyone else's grief. I am consumed, literally being eaten alive by my own. When I tried it on, the dress I have found to wear to the funeral hung on me. I was a skeleton inside some draped black fabric. I have stopped looking in the mirror.

I will have to speak at the funeral. I don't want to, I don't even know if I can, but I must.

'I can speak for both of us,' Adrian told me.

'No, you must speak, but I must as well. I was… I am her mother.'

'Will you come to bed tonight?' he pleaded.

'I… I'll try,' I told him but here I am, in Julia's room, hugging the secret of the letters to me, allowing their contents to torture me. I should have told Adrian and Joel. I will tell them, but only after the funeral. I want them to see her as the little girl they both parented for a while longer.

Reading through the last letter again I cannot imagine that this was what sent Julia into the spiral that led to her decision. There is no mention of her being pregnant in the letters.

I close my eyes, willing the black hole of heavy sleep to claim me but, as they have every night, images from that first night, the last night, the night to end all nights, appear. Only Adrian and I were home. Mia's screaming woke me. At first I thought it was someone being attacked and then I realised it was Hallowe'en and it was probably a prank. But the clock on my bedside table told me Hallowe'en was over and the screaming sounded like it was coming from inside our home. Those thoughts only took seconds and as I sat up Adrian said, 'Wait, you don't know what's going on out there.'

'You heard it too?'

'I haven't really slept. Too much noise. People have been screaming on and off all night. I should have taken a sleeping pill as well.'

'We have to go out and see what it is.'

'Leave it, Claire, it doesn't have to be our problem. I told you – it's been going on all night.'

'Someone could be getting hurt,' I said. 'It sounds like a young girl.' I stood up from the bed and grabbed my robe, belting it tightly around my waist. As I moved through the house to the front door I could feel Adrian behind me. The screaming got louder and louder and I realised it was coming from just outside our front door. I switched on the outside light and opened the door to find Callie trying to lift Julia's body and Mia on her knees.

Adrian was the first to realise what we were looking at. 'Jesus,' he screamed. 'Jesus, Julia! Claire, help me, oh my God, help me, Claire.'

He took over from Callie, trying to lift Julia up so the chain wouldn't pull on her neck, and then he dragged over and jumped up on a flimsy garden chair, trying frantically to pull the chain off the beam. I took her weight.

'Call an ambulance,' screamed Adrian, and Mia finally closed her mouth. Callie stopped her strange keening and I heard Adrian grunting with the effort of pulling the chain. I was holding Julia, my head on her knees. 'Please,' I heard myself moan.

'Call an ambulance,' Adrian said again.

'Call a fucking ambulance,' shouted Mia. I turned my head and saw her grab Callie's phone and I heard her yelling about someone being dead.

Adrian kept pulling at the chain. 'Pull it harder,' I screamed. 'Get her free.'

'Just hold her,' Adrian shouted as he tried to lift her body with one hand and pull at the chain with the other.

Adrian didn't seem to be achieving anything but somehow the bolt holding the chain gave way and Julia fell forward onto Adrian, who collapsed under the sudden weight. He twisted her around and she fell onto the porch, her head hitting the timber with a sickening thud.

'You'll hurt her,' I screamed, and then I grabbed her face. 'Julia, Julia, wake up. What are you doing, Julia?'

Adrian straightened her body and I pulled at the chain, loosening it from around her neck. He leaned forward and began compressing her chest, and I blew into her mouth. Her lungs inflated with my breath and her body jerked with his pressing but it was obviously too late. When I heard the siren scream into our street I sat back but Adrian collapsed over her body, 'Oh, Julia,' he wailed. I looked at him and thought about patting his head. I wanted to comfort him, to let him know that this was not real, it was not real at all. 'Julia, Julia,' he wailed.

The paramedics let me ride in the ambulance with her. Once she was hooked up to everything they had and being cared for by the paramedic it seemed possible that she would be okay. The ambulance flew through the empty streets, siren blaring, and I began to hope. But when they wheeled her into the hospital I caught a look between the paramedic – a young woman with her black hair wound tightly in a bun – and the emergency-room doctor and I knew, I knew that she was gone. Pain exploded inside me, obliterating everything else.

I had told Adrian to stay behind, to wait for my sons, but he wouldn't let me go alone.

Instead he texted the boys. *There's been an accident. Come to North Shore Hospital.*

They stumbled into the hospital at five in the morning. I heard Nicholas shouting about his mother. 'Claire Brusso, she's here, my stepfather told me she's here. Where is she? Where is she?' He never suspected it would have anything to do with Julia. Julia was supposed to be in Melbourne. I hadn't been expecting her, either. Instead I had circled Friday 16 November on the calendar for her next visit so I knew to stock up on the foods she liked.

And now that's the day we will bury her.

The emergency-room doctor, a lovely young man with soft brown eyes, came into the room we were waiting in and explained to all of us that she was gone, that they had done everything they could, that it was over. It was only then, I think, that I finally understood that my daughter was dead. Until then I had been operating in a weird sort of vacuum where all my senses were dulled. The world was blurry, noises were muffled, and even when the doctor asked me for her name he had to ask me twice. I felt surrounded by dense air. I felt nothing could get through. But then something did get through. And finally everything got through and I was assaulted by the smell in the room, by the alcohol fumes, the odour of sweat coming off the boys, by the sounds they were making, by Adrian's sniffing, by the doctor's gentle sigh. Everyone in that room came sharply into focus as I finally understood what had happened. And then I believe it was me who was screaming until they gave me something because of course they gave me something. How on earth could they have allowed me to sit there in a busy hospital and scream until I passed out, which is what I wanted to do?

I wanted to scream until I was dead.

I open my eyes, giving up on the idea of sleep. I page through the letters again, looking for something, anything, to jump out at me and explain why she did it. 'There must be more,' I whisper in the quiet room, and as I make the statement I realise that it's the truth. There must be other letters. She would have told Eric about the pregnancy. How he reacted would have influenced her.

I search through Julia's cupboards as quietly as I can but I have already been through everything. I look under the bed, but there's nothing.

I stand next to her chest of drawers stroking BB's head, trying to think of another place to look.

I find myself weeping again. I imagine her stroking the worn toy, as I do now, as she drove back from Melbourne, talking to it, telling it of her distress. If she brought BB with her she never intended to go back. I decide I will give him to my sister to pass to the funeral home so that she can have her first friend with her.

The bear is very ratty. It was a miracle we never lost him. He would have been a nightmare to try and replace. He has lost one of his eyes and he looks lonely and sad. I pick him up and then I hug him to me. 'You'll be with her soon, BB,' I whisper. Something inside him crackles. Something makes a noise. I squeeze him a few times and then locate an opening at the bottom. The stuffing inside feels strange against my hand but I keep moving my fingers until I find what I now know is there.

I realise before I even unfold the thick square what it is. Six letters in all. Six terrible, evil letters from the man who was supposed to love her, who thought she was his soul mate. Six letters that tipped my vulnerable little girl over the edge. Hands trembling, I open them up and I am assaulted by his words.

※

My sweetest, darling Julia,

I am sorry about today. I shouldn't have reacted like that but I was in complete shock. I believed that you were taking precautions and although I am aware, as you told me, that sometimes these things don't work, I have to say that such a thing has never happened to me. I know you didn't want to speak to me after I yelled at you so I thought it important to write everything down, the way I have always done, so that you would understand. Perhaps your contraception did fail but could it be possible, my darling, that you didn't keep it up in the hopes of becoming pregnant? Do you believe that this will lead to us finally revealing ourselves to the world? Because nothing could be further from the truth. Of course one day, one day years from now, I want us to conceive a child of love together. How could I not want a daughter or son who looked like you? But this is not the time. I am still trying to get enough money together to get us some breathing space so that for a few months we can just be together. You are at university and your part-time job can't help us. I don't want you to feel guilty about this, my love, I just want you to see reason. We have been a secret for just over a year now and it has been the most wonderful year of my life. I know you share my happiness, Julia, and therefore you will understand when I tell you that this is the surest way to ruin everything. Your mother will not support you if you go ahead with this. She will hate you when the truth is revealed. Is that what you want, my darling? To be hated by those who are supposed to love you the most? What we have done and who we are to each other needs to be revealed when we are ready to leave everything behind and give everyone time to cool off and deal with the situation. A baby makes that impossible. It makes a life for the two of us together impossible. Please try to see that.

Love x

CHAPTER SEVENTEEN

I cover my mouth with my hand, not wanting to wake anyone. I want to scream and scream. She knew she was pregnant and he knew as well. How could he have told her I would hate her? How could she have ever believed it would be possible for me to hate her? I am wearing a jumper against the chill in the air but I am suddenly burning up. I pull it off roughly and throw it on the floor. My skin itches and my heart races. I read on as my anger grows.

> *My sweetest, darling Julia,*
> *Please tell me you've made the right decision. You need to answer your phone, my love, so we can speak about this logically. It's so hard being in separate cities. I want to be with you as well but we cannot run before we can walk. Don't drag this out any more. It's starting to affect my sleep and my work. I cannot handle this level of stress, Julia. Please just text me and tell me that you've booked yourself in for a termination. I will give you the money. You don't have to worry about that. I will come down and see you. I will even come with you to the clinic.*
> *Please do the right thing.*
> *Destroy this.*
> *Love x*

'Love x' he says, as he encourages her to terminate their child. 'Love x', as though that makes up for what he's telling her. 'Love x', as he turns the tables on her and blames her for a situation he has kept her in. I flash back on the first Facebook post I read on her page after it happened. 'Forever in my heart. Love x'. So this is then who X is. It was never Liam and the pink rosebud was merely a coincidence. I feel bad for ever thinking such a sweet, if somewhat different, boy is capable of breaking my daughter's heart like this. We used to laugh about how big a crush he had on her but he would have been a better choice for her, a much better choice.

What a stupid man Eric Peters is to think he wouldn't be found out. I have found him out. His awful letters will never be destroyed, not until I can destroy him. I resist the urge to tear and crumple up his terrible words and instead read the next letter. How furious with her he was, with her refusing to do as she was told. She was no longer his sweetest darling. She was asserting herself and he obviously didn't like that.

Julia,

Please, please think about what you are saying. I thought you agreed to meet with me so we could have a logical conversation. Do you realise how difficult it is for me to have to fly down to Melbourne every time we simply want to speak? Why can't you call me on the phone I gave you? Why are you being so difficult? You are too young to have a baby. I am married to another woman. We cannot be together right now, we simply cannot. I know you don't believe in abortion but if you don't get one you are in this alone, Julia. It's not even a baby yet. It's just a bundle of cells. It's nothing.

I will not help you at all if you do not terminate as I have asked you to. You'll have to lie to your mother and tell her it was some boy from university. And your father? Imagine what he'll think, Julia. I would be very afraid if I were you, after everything you've told me about him. And what of your brothers? Will you still be their adored big sister when you are an unmarried mother? Your family will be awful about this, you know they will. You will be dependent on them forever. You'll have to live at home and you won't get to finish your degree or travel or anything. A baby fucks everything up. Children fuck everything up. Why can't you listen to me? Why can't you see reason? You're not stupid. Or are you? Because right now you're behaving like you are.

Destroy this when you've read it.
I hope it makes you think a little.

The phone I gave you, I think. He is not referring to her phone. I have her phone and I have been through it. She must have had another one, just for the two of them. I have no idea where to start searching. He knows so much about her, about her life and her family, and I can see him using the things she has obviously told him about her father against her. I imagine them sitting together during breaks at rehearsal all through her high-school years. I see her pouring her heart out to her teacher, seeking understanding and comfort. He may have listened, nodding his beautiful head as she spoke, pretending to be concerned and to care, but when their situation became ugly and awkward and so very real he revealed a different side of himself. He has taken something she told him in confidence, something that affected her at her core, and thrown it back at her, and because she had never managed to develop her relationship with Joel, she perhaps believed that he would become violent upon learning that she was pregnant. He wouldn't have – and I would never have turned against her, not for that. He has used his age and his status in her life to make her question the two people who love her the most. How nasty, how wicked. What kind of a man is this?

I pick up the next letter that bristles with his rage. As I read the words I am afraid for my daughter, afraid for what this man might do to her – and then I clutch at my chest where my heart breaks anew. He didn't need to *do* anything. She solved the problem for him by taking her own life.

Julia,

Listen to me now, heed these words. If you do not terminate this pregnancy I will make your life a living hell and if you do as you have threatened to do and tell everyone the truth you won't live to see what happens. Don't fucking push me, Julia, just don't.

He doesn't end with 'love', he doesn't end with a kiss. He has switched off all emotions except fury at a young woman in an impossible situation. I close my eyes and see my hands around his neck. I feel a surge of energy as I squeeze the life out of him. I can't believe that there is anything more terrible he can say to her and yet in the next letter he surpasses himself.

Julia,

I'm sick of you hanging up on me. Stop behaving like such a child and stay on the line so I can finish what I have to say. I'm warning you, you had better contact me and tell me that you've sorted this out. I gave you that phone so we could speak like adults and now you are acting like you don't understand the concept of being a grown-up. You wanted this as much as I did and you agreed to my rules. I would never have gone ahead with this relationship otherwise. Don't test me, Julia. I am a man with a lot to lose and I am not ready to lose it yet. Don't threaten me, either, because you have no idea what I'm capable of.

What more could he be capable of? I think. Did he not realise the damage he was inflicting? I feel like I can't breathe properly. Why didn't she come to me? Why didn't she show me the letters? I would have protected her. Joel would have… I can only imagine what Joel would have done to this man if he had known about him, and the things he said to his daughter.

Julia,

Listen to me – you open your mouth even once and I will end your useless, fucking life. The reason I send you so many messages is because you refuse to answer the FUCKING PHONE.

I've had enough of this shit. I'll tell you what I'm going to do. I'm going to tell first. I'm going to go to your family and tell. I'll get them all in a room together and I'll let them know that their little angel Julia is actually a vicious, conniving slut who seduced me and who is trying to ruin my life.

That's what I'm going to do. I'm going to put it on Facebook. I'm going to call everyone you know and I'm going to ruin your life. Don't think I don't know how to do it. I can act the part. You know that about me. I can make sure that the whole world sees me as a broken man who was the victim of a disgusting whore who was out to ruin him and his life. I'll do it, Julia. You have a day left to terminate the hideous thing growing inside you and if you don't, if you don't, you may as well kill yourself because there will be no spot on this planet where you will not be subjected to scorn and degradation. The whole world will hate you, and rightly so. Do you understand that? No one will love you. You will have nothing left and no one to turn to. Your mother will feel nothing but disgust for you and your father will stop sending you all those lovely cheques he sends you. You've led such a sheltered life, you have no idea what it will be like to have to raise a child without support. And I will make sure you have no support. I will make sure you have nothing. Don't think I won't. Right now I'm sitting here writing this and I can't believe I ever wanted you or loved you. You never deserved to have a man like me in your life, not when you were some wide-eyed kid, and certainly not now. Don't contact me again unless it is to tell me that you've gotten rid of it and that you're never going to mention what happened between us again.

You better fucking destroy this.

I read this final, horrifying letter over and over. No more words of love, no more promises. The ugliness he was concealing all along is there on the page for my daughter to see. I can imagine her confusion, her feeling of being helpless now that this man had turned against her. She must have been so lost and felt so alone. He told her to do it. I lean forward and put my head on her pillow. He told her to kill herself and she did. The pillow grows damp with my heartbreak. He told her to do it and she did, my poor little girl, she did.

'Oh my darling,' I whisper, 'why didn't you come to me?' He fed her lies about me, about our family, and in her desperate, panicked state she believed him.

I get up off the bed and pace around the room. I feel jittery and tense. I need to do something, to do anything, but it's the middle of the night and if I run screaming from this house as I want to do, I am sure the police will be called and I will not be able to make anyone understand my pain. 'Vile bastard,' I utter over and over as I pace. I open Julia's drawers again, touch everything on her shelves, move books and old toys that have already been moved as I search for the phone he writes about. Round and round her room I go until I have exhausted myself and I collapse back on her bed.

There are no dates on the letters but there don't have to be. I know that this last one must have been sent to her only days before she decided she had no choice. I picture her in her little room at university, tossing and turning, unable to close her eyes because of the guilt and shame at what she was doing. The pregnancy would have been too horrifying for her to handle. But she *could* have come to me. No matter how strained our relationship could get at times she always knew she could turn to me, always.

I remember her at sixteen, in the middle of an argument with me about how much time she was spending online, suddenly bursting into tears: 'Eli doesn't like me any more. He told Michelle.' Eli was her first serious boyfriend. 'That idiot,' I replied, argument forgotten. I shifted into another mode. She cried, I shushed, we went to get ice cream and saw a movie despite her being behind on her schoolwork – the reason for the argument in the first place. Nothing mattered if she needed me. Nothing. Why didn't she just talk to me? And if not to me – why not to Adrian? I flush with anger at him again for giving her the Valium without questioning her further. He should have told me. I would have made her tell me the real reason.

Eric Peters is wrong about Julia's family. The disgusting words he has written about us are lies. She should have known that. For about the thousandth time I think about telling Adrian or Joel. I would like to take Julia's father or stepfather with me and show this man how many people he has hurt but I cannot bear the explanations that will have to be given to the both of them. I wish I could simply let this go. She made a choice, an awful, terrible choice, and nothing will bring her back, but she was pushed into it. She was deserted by a man she loved when she was desperate. She was bullied into taking her own life and Eric Peters cannot get away with that.

I cannot let him get away with it.

Now I need to see this man on my own and confront him. I want to see his face when I mention Julia. I want to watch him grow pale and stammer excuses. I want him to know that he was wrong about her family. We would have supported her, but we will do everything we can to bury him.

I wince at the words I have just thought and then I realise that this is exactly what I want to do to Eric Peters. I want to bury him. I want him dead.

CHAPTER EIGHTEEN

I know that I should be writing my eulogy for Julia. I know that I should be remembering all the things I loved about her, all the moments of her life that have become part of me. I should be at home, taking the calls that I don't think will ever stop from relatives and friends all over the world who have now been given the date for the funeral.

Instead I am on my way to the high school my sons attend and that Julia attended. I am looking for Eric Peters. I am carrying all the letters with me, meaning to fling them at his feet after I confront him. I also have – ridiculously, I am aware – a small hunting knife that Joel left behind when he moved out. I found it in the garage when I was cleaning up after he left all those years ago and recognising the brutal blade – half serrated, half smooth, with a polished wooden handle – as one of his favourites, I hid it. Many months later he asked me about it and I denied any knowledge of it. I am ashamed of such pettiness but the thought of him wondering where it was gave me great pleasure.

When Adrian left for work this morning he brought a cup of tea into Julia's room for me. When he touched me gently on the shoulder I woke startled, instantly hoping that I'd hidden the letters away when I could no longer keep my eyes open. I shifted a little on the bed and heard the paper beneath me, under her duvet and then held myself rigid in case he had heard as well.

'I'm sorry, darling, I didn't mean to startle you. I wanted to make sure you were awake. You have a lot to get ready for tomorrow.'

'My mother and sister are dealing with everything. I just have my eulogy to write. Have you written something?'

'I can't, Claire. I'm so sorry but I just can't. It's enough that you and Joel speak, and the boys. It's enough, and tomorrow this will all be over.'

He turned then and walked out of the room.

'It will never be over,' I muttered, stopping him at the door.

I thought he would turn around again and try to find something comforting to say but instead he walked out.

He wants this to be over, needs it to be over. I can feel his discomfort at being the outsider in this tragedy. He has worked so hard to keep us on an even keel, all the while aware that he is being viewed as her stepfather and not her real father.

I have been trying to think of what I should say in her eulogy, going over her childhood, remembering the things that made me laugh and cry. She never slept as a baby, preferring those forty-minute cat naps some children do. I felt like a zombie for at least the first six months of her life. On very difficult nights, Joel would come into her room at two or three or four in the morning and find me swaying desperately with Julia in my arms. 'Go to sleep,' he would say, 'I'll take over.'

'But you have work in the morning, Joel, this is my job.'

'It's *our* job, Claire. Go to sleep.'

It's such a vivid memory I have of Julia and one that I used to tease her with when she began sleeping whole mornings away as a teenager.

If I use that memory in her eulogy, Joel will nod and smile and my mother and sister and all those who handed out advice to a sleep-deprived new mother will remember that time, but Adrian will have no idea what I'm talking about because he wasn't there. He feels left out and I understand that. He doesn't want to speak because he is aware that those listening will look at him and think, 'That's her stepfather.' The words reduce his relationship with her to less than a parent and I know he's not enjoying that feeling. I know he is in pain.

I wish I could find the right words to assure him that he was as much Julia's father, if not more, as Joel was, but all my energy is being used for what I am going to do today.

I need to confront Eric Peters before my daughter is placed in the ground.

I have no idea why I have the knife. It's unlikely that I will commit murder on the school grounds. The thought makes me laugh out loud in the car and then I bite down on my lip. I don't enjoy the sound of my own laughter. It's jarring and wrong.

I park outside the school gates and make my way to the office. I don't want to run into Nicholas or Cooper so I move fast and keep my head down.

The administration office is a cacophony of ringing phones. Three people sit up the front, transferring calls. I stand patiently in front of a young woman who signals to me that she will only be a moment.

'Sorry, how can I help?' she asks, as she ends her call.

'Um, I'm a… I'm Julia Barker's mother, I mean Nicholas and Cooper's mother. Nicholas is in…'

'Oh, yes, Mrs Barker… um, Brusso, yes of course. I… we're all so terribly sorry about Julia. She was such a bright, talented girl.' Her cheeks burn red as she speaks.

I am a little surprised that she knows my surname but then I realise that Julia's death has probably been the only topic of conversation for the last two weeks. Of course she knows my correct surname. She shifts in her chair. I make her uncomfortable. The mother of the girl who killed herself is not supposed to turn up at the school office. She is not supposed to be out of her house and interacting with the world, making everyone uncomfortable as her tragedy trails her everywhere.

Imagine if she knew what I was really doing here.

I curl my hands around the strap of my handbag, pushing my nails into my palms. I feel like everyone must be able to see the knife inside.

'Do you need me to get the boys out of class for you, Mrs Brusso?' the woman asks.

'I… no… no, I came here to see Eric, I mean Mr Peters. He was Julia's…'

'Julia's drama teacher. I know, yes of course, can I ask what about? Maybe I can help you?'

'No, no…' I stumble. I hadn't thought about this part of it. I saw myself looking Eric Peters in the eyes but didn't exactly see how that would happen. Parents are not allowed to see teachers at the school without an appointment.

I take a deep breath. I sound a little unhinged. 'I just wanted to speak to him to thank him for the lovely card he sent us. I know he and Julia were very… close.' He sent an email but he may have sent a card as well. The kind of man who would write a love letter would send a card. The cards are piling up on the hall table. One of those could easily be his.

'Of course, of course.' The woman gives me a toothy grin and then quickly frowns, as though she has done something wrong. Her gums are overly large and pink. 'I'll try to find him for you. I know he would want to speak with you. Julia was a great favourite of his.'

I'll bet, I think.

I watch the young woman make a call and then another and then another, all the while consulting her computer with quick, efficient fingers. Finally she looks up at me and shakes her head. 'I'm afraid I can't find him. I've checked the drama studio and his classroom and the hall. His timetable says he's with the year eleven students. They may be outside somewhere. I know he likes to take them outside to work sometimes.'

I bite down on my lip. This was not part of my plan. I hug my bag, filled with the letters and the knife, close to me.

'Are you looking for Eric?' a much older woman asks. I really should know the names of the administrative staff – I'm sure that I actually do, but right now nothing comes to mind.

'Yes.' Another toothy grin.

'He's taken the year eleven students to see a play. He won't be back today. It finishes around three so everyone is going home from the theatre. Perhaps you'd like to leave a message for him?'

'Oh, no,' I say. 'I'll… no, I don't, thank you.'

I leave as quickly as I came, cursing the universe and Eric Peters for not being there.

It was stupid to try the school, anyway. He would be unlikely to confess the truth in such a public space. I need to speak to him at his home. I nod as I have this thought. His home is where I will go. He will not be there now but I know he has fairly young children so it's possible that his wife will be there. I will show her the letters. I will tell her about the affair. I will destroy Eric Peter's life before he even gets home. I taste acid in my throat. I don't feel like myself any more but I don't want to feel like that anyway. Anger is so much more productive than despair. Anger drives you forward; despair simply drags you down.

I pull over to the side of the road and google the phone book. There are hundreds of people with the surname Peters, twelve with the initial E and only one in the same suburb as the school. I call the number, my heart pounding. I swallow several times as the phone rings, worried that I will not be able to speak if his wife answers the phone.

'We're not here right now, leave a message.' Short and sweet but just enough for me to recognise his voice. I realise that he and I have probably spoken much more than I remember. At every performance I would find him and congratulate him, and if I picked up Julia from rehearsal he would always find a moment to come over and speak to me. I didn't pick her up often, I now remember because, as Julia pointed out: 'Mr Peters lives a few streets away from us. He's happy to give me a lift home on the nights we rehearse late.' I feel sick to my stomach. What would have been happening on those car rides home? What did I allow to happen?

I lean my head back against my car seat. Of course, of course. I am such an idiot. All I thought back then was: *Fabulous, I don't have to pick her up every night at ten* – the rehearsals always ran late. Eric Peters was emphatic that his students all got their homework done before they began rehearsals. 'It's so cool that he doesn't want us to fall behind,' Julia said. If they were rehearsing a production I always sent Julia to school with money and enough food to last her through lunch and dinner, but Mr Peters often ordered pizza for the cast. 'He's just the best, Mum.'

I watched it happen, even encouraged it to happen by allowing him to give her lifts home. I trusted where I shouldn't have trusted, assuming that he was safe because he held the title of 'teacher'. I have always been so vigilant with my children, keeping them close and safe until I thought they had the ability to deal with whatever came their way. I have lectured on stranger danger and trusting their instincts and yet when it came to this man, this teacher, I did not even feel a hint of concern. The monsters live among us. I know that the person you are supposed to able to trust the most is, inevitably, the person who can destroy you and still, I have allowed my daughter to trust this man.

It's been two years since she was at school. It feels like forever, especially since Nicholas is in his final year and working towards a place in medical school. I drop my head onto the steering wheel, guilt eating away at me. I haven't been thinking about my boys. I am failing them. Nicholas is working as hard as he can to achieve his dreams, even as he mourns his sister. I am, once again, eternally grateful to Adrian and Joel for taking over for me as I go through this… I don't even know what to call it. It feels like a spiral into madness. I feel mad.

'Once I have done this,' I promise myself, 'once I have told his wife and I know that he is paying for this, I will stop.'

It's after two and I have barely eaten a thing all day. I am thirsty and hungry and emotionally depleted but I cannot stop. Eric Peters lives close to where I have pulled over. I need to get this done now. I want to go to Julia's funeral and be able to tell her that I have managed to hurt the man who hurt her. If nothing else, at least I can do that for her.

CHAPTER NINETEEN

Despite the answering machine indicating that no one is home, I drive over to Eric Peters' home. I vow to myself that I will wait until he or his wife return. With a bit of luck I will catch them both at the same time. I will ask him to send the children away before I confront him. No child needs to hear that their parent is an adulterer. Or worse, someone who has groomed a young girl. *How many others were there?* I wonder. *Is this what he has done his whole career? Is this why he became a teacher?* I shudder at the thought. 'It stops now,' I say aloud, as I pull into a parking space from where I can see their front door.

The longer I wait, the more I hope that his wife and not Eric comes home first. I would like to speak to her alone, to explain exactly who she is married to. *Yes*, I nod to myself. *It should be his wife who knows first.* I am aware on some level that my behaviour is irrational but just like I was when I was lashing out at Joel, I am unable to stop myself.

I picture the two little boys from the Facebook photo. This will devastate them. Their childhood will be forever changed but at least they will still be there to learn and grow. Unlike Julia. I see his wife's smile, captured at a perfect moment in her life. This will break her, but broken people can be fixed. Life changes and moves and even the worst possible situations end. Only death cannot be changed. Only that.

Eric Peters deserves to lose his wife and children, his pretty family and lovely home with its neatly tended garden. I study the house – it even has a white picket fence out the front. White pebbles lead up to a burnished wooden front door and a water fountain, sculpted out of white stone, trickles continuously. I open my window and listen to the sound of the water. It's so innocent, so comforting, so out of place for what is about to happen.

He must lose everything.

I sit outside Eric Peter's house for half an hour before a car pulls up and slides silently into the garage. No one gets out and the automatic door goes down before I can see anything. I wait five minutes and then I get out of the car and make my way up the path. The pebbles crunch and slide under my feet.

I have left the knife in the car in the glove box. What I have to show this woman will cut sharply enough. I breathe in and out slowly. My legs feel shaky as I walk to the front door. I lean hard on the bell, quickly. The urge to turn and run creeps up on me. I don't want to do this. I shouldn't do this. I can't do this. *I have to do it.* I hear footsteps from inside the house. It's too late now.

Instead of the woman I am expecting, a man with a neatly trimmed grey beard opens the door. 'Yes?' he says, eyebrows raised. Everything about him is stylish, neat and compact. His hands are small and he is shorter than I am, with slight shoulders in an immaculately pressed shirt and crisp pants leading down to beautifully polished shoes with pointed toes.

I glance behind him into the house without saying anything. I expected a living room filled with worn furniture, covered in toys, despite the pristine exterior of the house. I expected a woman with two little faces peering out from behind her. I am momentarily stunned by the image I had in my head not appearing before me.

'Can I help you?' the man asks slowly, as though concerned for my health.

'I'm looking for Eric, Eric Peters. He lives here, doesn't he?'

'He does but he's still at school or, wait… on his way home from the play—' The man stops speaking abruptly as though just realising that he is divulging the whereabouts of Eric Peters to a complete stranger.

He stands up straight, attempting and failing to look taller than I am. 'Are you a parent from the school? Because you know it's entirely inappropriate for you to come here or even to have this address.'

My throat feels thick with anguish and my nose begins to run. I scrabble through my bag for a tissue, looking away from the man and I hear him mutter, 'not this shit again.' I look up at him, startled, disbelieving. Is it possible I'm not the first mother to try and confront Eric Peters? I think about what Nick told me about him having to leave his last school.

'I am,' I stutter, trying to find the words, 'I mean I was… I just…' I find myself swiping at tears. It's all so overwhelming, so fucking impossible. I wanted to see Eric. If I had seen him I would have known. He would have looked at me and I would have known. That's all it would have taken. He wouldn't have been able to hide his guilt. Failing that, I wanted to speak to his wife. I wanted to devastate his life but now that I am standing here I just want to be at home in Julia's room, surrounded by her things.

'Hey, come in, come in and sit down,' says the man, going from suspicion and anger to concern and worry. 'I'm Raymond. Can I get you something to drink, something…? I don't know.' He seems flustered. Adrian gets flustered when I cry. Joel, when we were married, just got angrier; now, he looks like he's failed a test of some sort. He looks at me like he should be able to find a way to make me stop crying over our daughter. I wish Joel were here. He would know how to handle this. He would have been able to tear Eric Peters apart with his bare hands.

I follow Raymond inside the pristine home, and I perch gingerly on a white sofa. Who has a white sofa? Why is there so much white? The room is surrounded by beautifully carved wooden bookcases, all neatly filled with books and artistic knick-knacks that look as though they were acquired on travels overseas.

'I'm so sorry,' I say, when Raymond returns from the kitchen with a heavy tumbler filled with iced water. I take a large gulp, enjoying the cold sensation slipping down my throat.

'I'm Claire Brusso,' I explain. 'I'm Julia Barker's mother. I wanted to speak to Eric—'

'Oh, Mrs Brusso… oh, I'm so sorry, I'm so sorry for your loss. Eric told me about her. He's really taken it hard. They had such a special relationship. I only met her once but she seemed like a really lovely girl.'

'Just how special a relationship did they have?' I spit. The ice-cold water has helped me focus on what I came here to do. 'I would really like you to tell me how special. Did you know my daughter was pregnant? Do you know that people are saying Eric is the father?' The words tumble out of me, tripping over each other.

Raymond's face pales. He swallows twice quickly, then he stands up straight again. His face takes on a neutral look, shutting down. 'Which people are those, Mrs Brusso?'

I shake my head. No one has said any such thing but I have assumed and I know I'm right. Wasn't the whole school discussing them when she was there?

'Mrs Brusso, I need you to think calmly about what you've just said and I also need you to look around you at our home – at Eric's and my home. The only reason I'm home at three on a Tuesday is because I came home to get some plans I left here. We live here together, Mrs Brusso. Do you understand what I'm saying?'

I look around the beautiful living room as realisation dawns. 'You're gay? He's *gay*?'

'We're gay,' he agrees.

'But I saw a picture of his wife! I saw it on his Facebook page. It was his wife and his two sons.'

'His wife? I have no idea how…' begins Raymond, and then he smiles. 'Oh, on Facebook. That's Jennifer, his sister and his nephews. He changed the profile picture for a few weeks because the boys asked him to. It's his sister, Mrs Brusso, his sister and his nephews.'

I shake my head, unwilling to believe this is true. Raymond sighs. He stands up and goes to a cabinet that runs along one wall of the room and opens a glass door, takes out a picture. 'Look, there we are. This is from last year, when Eric and I got married.'

I take the picture from him, noting that I'm shaking. In the picture, Eric and Raymond hold hands. They are dressed in matching black tuxedos with bright blue bowties and in front of them stand the two little boys, dressed the same way. A little off to the side is the pretty woman I assumed was Eric's wife. She is beaming at the children.

'Why didn't I know that? Why didn't Julia tell me?' I sound shrill.

'Eric prefers to keep his private life out of the school community. I rarely meet his students. It's a large school. Some parents can be quite… well, you know. He had a problem with a young girl at his last school. His care and attention was misinterpreted and things got quite difficult. None of it was Eric's fault, for obvious reasons.'

'But he should have told me or Julia should have told me. I had a right to know!' I am babbling, angry, humiliated.

If Eric Peters is not the man, then who is it? *Who is it?* I am back to square one, fury bubbling in me.

'Mrs Brusso, you had no right to know anything about Eric, beyond that he is a wonderful teacher who took an interest in your daughter's talent. Now I understand that you're upset and I am, as I said, deeply sorry for your loss but I think it may be best if you leave before you say something that you will one day regret. Perhaps I could call someone to come and get you?'

'No,' I snap. 'I'm fine, I'll be fine.' I stand up and slam the glass of water onto the carved coffee table and then blush with shame at the way Raymond winces. Once again I make my exit holding my body rigid and my head high. I have made another mistake, even though it seems impossible. I was wrong about Eric Peters.

In my car I close my eyes and lean my head back. I hear the garage door open again and the roar of Raymond's car as he drives away. I know he's on the phone to Eric right now, telling him about the insane woman who thought he was having an affair with her daughter. I don't need him coming home and finding me here. I start the car quickly and drive away from Eric Peter's house. I vaguely hope that he and Raymond will keep quiet about what I have just done. If they choose to be indiscreet it's possible that news of my behaviour could spread around the whole school. Nicholas and Cooper will be peered at and judged for their crazy mother.

'You're such an idiot,' I say aloud. 'Such an absolute idiot.' I feel a blush of shame heat me. I can't quite believe what I have done and, even worse, what I intended to do.

Back in the traffic I realise that I can't keep doing this. I don't have the energy left to search for this man. Not any more.

'I'm sorry, darling,' I say aloud. 'I tried, I really tried.' The human body never really runs out of tears. Sometimes you think it's possible that it will but it doesn't and, on cue, I find some more to shed.

I can barely see but I keep driving as I cry and wail and beg my daughter to forgive me for not being able to find the man who hurt her.

I have to let this go now. Tomorrow I will bury her and then I have to concentrate on saying goodbye to her.

'I have to let this go,' I say over and over again.

I pull into my garage and press the button to shut the door behind me. In the cool, dim light I feel cocooned and separate from the world. I cry until I am exhausted.

I sit in my car with my eyes closed and think about Julia tasting her first ice-cream and Julia on the swing at the park with sunlight catching the gold in her hair, and Julia reading a story to Nicholas and Cooper, changing her voice for each character. I see Julia at three and at five and at ten, huddled in front of a scary movie at a sleepover with friends, all of them shrieking melodramatically at every frightening moment. I see Julia at thirteen, scrunching her face up as she viewed herself in her first bra and, at fifteen, getting ready for a date, changing outfits and throwing all her clothes on the floor. I see her on stage and leaving for her formal and waving goodbye as she got in her car to go to university. I see her laughing and crying and angry. I see her yelling at me and giggling with her brothers.

I see my child with my eyes closed. I see her with my heart and, without warning, peace takes over my body.

And I know, I understand, that Julia is okay with me giving up. She is happy for me to let it go.

CHAPTER TWENTY

I am not sure if I have met as many people in my life as there are here today to say farewell to my daughter. This morning I forced myself into an early shower, blasting my body with cold water so I was left shivering, needing to feel something different to the heavy sadness weighing me down. I had to do my make-up twice because I seemed to have lost the knack, rouging my cheeks too much and smearing mascara as I rubbed away tears. In the mirror a woman I no longer recognise stared back at me. 'Today you are burying your daughter,' I told her, and watched her shrug her shoulders. I don't think she believes me. And yet here I am, the mother of the dead child, whether I want to believe it or not.

Adrian and I arrived early and sat in the front row. I like this church. I only come at Easter and Christmas but I find it a peaceful place. I cannot sing the hymns without a book but I enjoy listening to the choir. The pews are worn smooth and the colourful stained-glass windows all depict the beauty of nature. I like to look at the window portraying a waterfall. Sometimes the sun will hit the window the right way and the water will appear to be moving. In the past I have sat in this church with my children, stern and chastising when they were young and bored, relaxed and joyful as they got older. I cannot imagine what it will be like to sit here and know that one of my children will be forever missing. I am not sure I will make it back into this place after today.

The priest, Father Julius, grasped my hands when I walked in. 'Claire, I am so glad to finally see you. I have been speaking with your mother and sister but I wanted to tell you that you have my deepest sympathy on your terrible loss. I remember Julia smiling up at me from her seat when she was a little girl. She had such a beautiful smile. What a wonderful, loving soul she was and how deeply you must miss her.'

I don't know Father Julius well and I'm sure he couldn't have picked Julia out from a line of girls her age, but his words comfort me, which is what they are meant to do.

'Would you like me to sit with you and pray for a few moments before people begin arriving?'

'Thank you,' I mumbled, 'but I just need a little time, just Adrian and me.'

I wanted some quiet time alone with Julia but I didn't want to be absolutely alone. I didn't trust myself not to open the lid of her sleek white coffin and shake her, demanding to know why she ended her life. Adrian is sweating and uncomfortable, but he holds my hand tightly as if afraid to let go in case I fall. In the hushed quiet of the church, he lays a hand gently, reverently, on her coffin. 'My heart is breaking for you, Claire,' he says, and I lean into him and let him hold me. I place a kiss where her head is and then we sit, staring at what is inconceivably my daughter.

I have no more answers now than when I began searching for them. I cannot find the man she was sleeping with and even though I know she was pregnant I have no idea why she felt her only way out of the situation was to take her own life. How could she have felt so alone? I feel as though I have failed her as a mother over and over again. The last letters he wrote to her are filled with vile words, bullying, evil words, but I still don't understand why she couldn't have come to me or her brothers or Adrian, or even one of her friends, and asked for help.

I will never know. I don't have the energy to keep looking for the answers.

When Joel and the boys arrive I stand and greet all of them with a hug, holding onto Joel perhaps a little longer than I should in front of Adrian, but I need it. I finally feel safe in Joel's arms. I wish that could have come sooner, I wish Julia could have known it was possible for a man to change, for a person to claim redemption. *I wish, I wish, I wish…* but what is the good of that?

I remain with Joel in front of her coffin for a moment, because I couldn't let him stand there alone, breathing in the smell of the blush pink lilies. I believe I will hate this smell forever after.

'Goodbye, baby girl,' Joel whispers hoarsely. 'I am so sorry I failed you.'

'We failed her,' I say, and he nods. He understands that I don't want him to comfort me by absolving me. Perhaps that will come in time, but not now. Now I need to feel the acidic tinge of guilt when I think about my daughter.

'You need to go and see Leslie again, and talk all of this out,' my mother told me, and I nodded like I agreed with her.

We sit in the front row, my fractured family and I. People begin to arrive, walking up and expressing their sorrow, kissing our cheeks, squeezing shoulders and holding onto handshakes for too long. Out of the corner of my eye I see Eric Peters walk in, accompanied by Raymond. My ears burn and I pray that he doesn't come over and then I look up and meet his eyes for a moment. He nods quickly and for some reason I understand that my behaviour has been forgiven. I see Liam arriving with his mother, his head bowed, tears glistening on his cheeks.

I am not sure how I will survive the next hours. Adrian is on one side of me and Joel on the other. Inexplicably, I feel myself leaning towards Joel more.

By the time the service begins I have found a way to numb myself into stillness. 'Twinkle, twinkle little star,' keeps repeating in my head, drowning out any other thoughts I may choose to have. I see Julia at eighteen months, moving her hands and singing the words, delighted with the applause she got from everyone.

I listen to the priest's words without really hearing them. I know that if I hear them I will dissolve. There will be nothing left of me. My mother reads a Native American poem about loss that she says was Julia's favourite.

> 'I give you this one thought to keep
> I am with you still – I do not sleep.
> I am a thousand winds that blow,
> I am the diamond glints on snow,
> I am the sunlight on ripened grain,
> I am the gentle autumn rain.
> When you awaken in the morning's hush,
> I am the swift, uplifting rush
> of quiet birds in circled flight.
> I am the soft stars that shine at night.
> Do not think of me as gone –
> I am with you still – in each new dawn.'

My mother is unable to finish the poem but Nicholas stands up and holds onto her and together they finish, uttering the beautiful words in unison. She looks so small and frail next to my giant son and I am struck by how much she has aged in the last two weeks. We all have, but I can see my mother's grief in the rounding of her shoulders and the sudden thin delicacy of her wrists. *I will lose her one day soon*, I think.

I can hear everyone in the church. The sniffing and choking sounds are trying to penetrate my armour but I cannot let them. I have to read my eulogy. I have to do this one last thing for her. But when the time comes I am unable to move, unable to speak, unable even to stand up from the unforgiving wooden pew. I have sacrificed my ability to function so that I can have the strength to sit here and ready myself to bury my daughter.

The silence in the church grows and finally I shove the words at Adrian.

'But…' he begins.

'I can't. Please,' I whisper.

He looks at Joel but Joel shakes his head. He too, cannot stand up there in front of everyone. It's ironic that both of Julia's parents were going to speak and now neither of them can. One more failure perhaps, but I am glued to my seat, frozen by my crippling grief.

Adrian finally nods and he stands up to read my words, my last words to my angel child.

Adrian takes the two steps up to the front to stand behind the lectern. He smooths the piece of paper on which my eulogy is written, running his hands over it once, twice, three times. The silence in the church is broken only by someone coughing and the deep sighs of people trying to control their tears. Finally Adrian looks out at everyone, clears his throat and begins.

'I am reading this for Claire,' he begins, 'who will miss this child forever. She really was our sweetest, darling Julia.'

It takes a moment for my head to catch up with the physical reaction my body is having. I am boiling hot, then freezing cold in an instant. Goosebumps run up and down my arms. The words ricochet around inside my head. I risk a glance to the side at Joel and push my nails into the palms of my hands in case I'm dreaming – but I'm not asleep. I'm here in this church, saying goodbye to my daughter, and I know what I heard. I don't hear the rest of my words being read aloud by my husband. All I hear is, 'sweetest, darling Julia.'

Sweetest, darling Julia.
Sweetest, darling Julia.
Sweetest, darling Julia.

Sweetest, darling Julia.

Sweetest, darling Julia.

Innocuous words of love to everyone else in this church, to every single person as they dab their eyes and choke back tears.

But I know different. I know different.

CHAPTER TWENTY-ONE

Sweetest, darling Julia.

Sweetest, darling Julia.

Sweetest, darling Julia.

Oh my God, I know different. I push my hands down onto the pew, grabbing hold of the wood. I am fearful that I will float away. This can't be possible. It cannot be. It cannot be and yet it is. I try to form coherent thoughts but I feel like I've been hit by a truck. There is a great white circle in my mind smothering everything. I am in a vacuum, alone in the silence but for the white noise in my head.

'Are you okay?' Joel whispers. All I can do is shake my head.

Adrian finishes, sniffing and wiping tears away. He is devastated. I did not hear a single word he said, apart from those three words. *Sweetest, darling Julia.*

There is a hymn, more handshakes, cheeks brushed against mine. I nod and nod until I feel my head will fall off. Adrian touches my elbow, guiding me, helping me. My skin crawls.

'The family has asked to be alone at the graveside,' intones the priest as we follow Julia's coffin out of the church and into a waiting hearse. We will have to return here for tea and more sympathy but at least for a short while my family and I will be alone with her.

Adrian will be there as well.

Outside the spring day is the perfect temperature. The sky is a bright blue overhead and I smell the flowers in the church garden and the freshly cut grass. It's too bright for me, there is too much light, too much has been exposed.

I caught a glimpse of Eric Peters as we left the church. His head was bowed and he didn't look at me. What a mess I have made of my search as I suspected first Liam and then flung accusations at Colin Rider and then Eric Peters. I wanted one of them to be the monster who had driven my daughter to suicide but the monster was closer than they were, much closer. He was right next to me – as he is now, while we walk to the waiting hearse that will take us to the graveyard. He was right next to me and I didn't see it.

It would never have occurred to me to look that closely.

All his trips to Melbourne were to see her. He bought the red shoes for her and he bought the diamond earrings she giggled about. As we follow her coffin I cross my arms in front of me, pressing my nails into my wrist. I have to keep reminding myself that this is real, that what is happening is real and that what I know is the truth I have been searching for. The sickening, twisted, terrible truth.

At her graveside Joel and I drop white roses into her coffin. Adrian has chosen something in pink, a rose just beginning to bud, full and soft, just like the rose on the Facebook profile. I watch him drop the flower, sickened by the images that now crowd my brain. My hands twitch. I want to push him in after her. I am such a fool. An absolute fool. How did I miss this? But how could I have suspected such a thing? Such a base, heinous thing?

The white noise has ceased in the sunshine and I make an effort to slow down my thoughts, examining each one as it occurs to me. The last letters he wrote to her must have only been written in the last few weeks. I try to determine if Adrian's behaviour was any different as he worried about Julia telling the world about him and as he chipped away at her in an attempt to get her to terminate her pregnancy.

At first nothing comes to mind but then there is a flash, a memory of a night a week before she died.

We were at the dinner table. Adrian was sitting at the head and Nicholas opposite him. Cooper was next to his brother and I was next to Adrian, a seating arrangement that had developed since Julia left for university. Adrian and Nicholas were arguing about him forgetting to take out the garbage bin that morning.

'Now the bloody thing will overflow before next week, Nick. You have one chore and you couldn't manage that?'

'Adrian,' I admonished, 'you don't need to talk to him like that. He forgot and he's sorry. Why are you so irritable lately?'

That's what I asked him. I had noticed a change in his behaviour. He was more aggressive towards the boys than he had ever been, and more hyped up for an argument over anything with me. I put his mood down to something going on at work.

I had noticed. I did see it. But I didn't see the truth. How could I have seen this truth?

'Oh, please, Claire, as if you would ever say anything against any of your precious offspring. I sit here every night and they both basically ignore me and then they don't do the few things you and I both decided they had to do. I'm so sick of being a second-class citizen in this house. I pay the most of the bills, you know. I go to work so you can eat and live here.'

'Adrian, what on earth is upsetting you?' I asked, shocked by his vitriol. Whilst he had expressed some of these feelings to me before, he had never said such things in front of the boys. We had agreed when we got married that he wouldn't do any of the real disciplining of Julia and the boys. If he had a problem with them he told me, and I dealt with it.

Nicholas pushed his plate away and stood up from the table. 'I said I was sorry, Adrian. You're turning this into something it's not. I worked late on an essay and just forgot.'

'There always an excuse, Nicholas, isn't there? You aren't going to get away with that when you leave this house. Then no one will care about your reasons for fucking up.'

'That's enough,' I yelled.

'I'm trying to get into med school, Adrian.' Nicholas looked genuinely hurt. 'I'm studying for my final exams. You know I'm working my arse off and, by the way, my dad paid off this house and he sends money to Mum for both Cooper and me. I'm too old to have to listen to any of your shit any more. Let's go, Coop.' He turned to look at me. 'Sorry, Mum.'

'I…' I had no idea what to say. Cooper hadn't said a word but he left his unfinished dinner and followed his brother out of the house.

'What on earth is wrong with you?' I asked Adrian.

He had been sitting up straight with his shoulders back as he argued with Nicholas but as the door slammed he slumped in his chair, 'I'm… just… oh, hell, I don't want to talk about it.' He got up and left the table, and then the house, leaving me to clean up and ponder what exactly had just happened. I know he apologised to Nick the next morning and that things were kind of smoothed over but we never actually discussed what triggered his attack on my son.

I should have had that discussion. I should have pushed and prodded until he confessed.

There are refreshments in the hall next to the church. Adrian said that there should be alcohol, probably because that's what he's been using to cope with his… what can I even call this? With his gross, fundamental betrayal of everyone and everything in his life. I said no to serving alcohol. The idea of anyone lightening the load they will carry at my daughter's funeral with some chemical help was unwelcome to me. I want people to stand around in silence, sipping tea. I want the cakes and sandwiches to taste like glue in their mouths. At least I wanted that then. Now I long for something to blot out what I have learned. How am I going to deal with this? What am I going to do?

I think about pulling Joel to one side and telling him what I think I know but then I question myself. *Were they just an unfortunate choice of words, or* were *they his words for her?*

In every letter he used the term until he was angry with her about her guilt and the pregnancy. Then he stopped. It makes sense now. It makes complete sense. How would she have been able to explain it to me? Where would she have even begun? Did she fear, not just having to terminate a pregnancy formed with a person that she was in love with, but the absolute devastation that the truth would have on her whole family? What a burden to bear. I think that I would have forgiven her. In my heart, I know we would have moved on. She could have come to me. But even as another person wraps me in a silent hug, I have to acknowledge to myself that she would have had to fight for that forgiveness. It was a terrible thing to do. It was a terrible betrayal. I don't accept the bullshit about not being able to control yourself.

As this thought enters my mind, I blush. My afternoon with Joel comes back to me. What was that? Why didn't we both control ourselves? Being human is such a messy business.

I think back now to when we found her, to that stretched in time moment when Adrian slumped over her calling her name. As I rewind, studying the scene now, I can see his hands moving on her jeans. At the time I thought he was just touching her, just checking for life, but now I know different. He was looking for the mobile phone he gave her, maybe even the last letters he wrote her in case she hadn't destroyed them.

Once I read about the phone in the letters I searched her entire bedroom again, lifting and moving everything she owned. I found nothing. When the paramedics arrived Adrian went inside for a minute. He came out with a jacket for me but could he have been hiding the phone he gave her? The secret phone that allowed them to communicate privately? Was the phone in her pocket, weighing her down, as she made the decision to take her own life?

'Did she have anything in her pockets?' Detective Winslow asked us and I had to shrug my shoulders. I hadn't thought to check but Adrian shook his head vehemently. 'No, nothing, I checked. Her phone and computer were in the car.' Yes, he had been looking for something when he touched her. I'm sure of it.

I shake my head. What if I am simply imagining all this, making the scene fit what I think I know, because I am so desperate for answers? It's possible that my need to find the man I believe was responsible for her unhappiness has clouded my judgement and yet… I turn my head and look at Adrian, who is weeping into a tissue as my mother strokes his shoulder. *Are those the tears of a father or a lover?* I think. I want to vomit with disgust.

The minutes and hours pass and finally, finally Adrian and I are in a car alone, driving into the setting sun. The light pierces the car at an odd angle, forcing me to squint even though I'm wearing sunglasses. It is still warm and my window, open just a crack, lets in the smell of gardens blooming with life.

I asked Joel to take the boys and I bore the look he gave me. 'I just need a little time,' I said and he nodded, ostensibly understanding. But I knew he thought I was shutting him out again after I had just let him back in. Literally let him back in. Jesus, I wish I could control the places my mind goes.

Adrian drives smoothly, calmly. He thinks that this is over now. He is pleased to be able to put the day behind him. I wonder if he ever loved her at all. I understand his attraction. She was a beautiful young woman, but why did he have to choose her? Never mind that he was her stepfather and that he'd watch her grow from child to woman, never mind that. If he needed to screw around, couldn't he have done it with someone from his office, with a secretary or a client? Did he ever love me? In the car I shake my head. Did he marry me to get to her? Was it all about grooming her?

'Are you okay?' he asks quietly, interrupting my murderous reverie.

'No,' I reply.

'Sweetheart, I'm so sorry,' he says, 'but at least we got to bury her. It was a beautiful service.' His voice is thick with tears.

'Tell me…' I say, amazing myself with how calm I sound, how controlled I am.

'Tell you what?'

'How long had you been fucking my daughter?'

CHAPTER TWENTY-TWO

Here is what I thought would happen. Here is what I wanted to happen. Here is what I optimistically saw in the tiny spark of hope I had left for my life as I hauled my heavy body through Julia's burial and the terrible wake we had afterwards. After I had uttered my shocking question, Adrian would turn to look at me, disbelief and horror etched across his face. 'Are you mad?' he would ask. 'Are you insane to be asking me such a disgusting question? I was her father. I considered myself her father. You're crazy and you need help, Claire.'

Here is what does happen.

Adrian doesn't say anything.

He stares ahead at the road, his hands growing white on the steering wheel. I hear a squeaking, scraping sound. He is grinding his teeth and of course that is all the confirmation I need. His jaw bulges and his breathing speeds up.

I don't blink, I don't breathe. I stare at his profile like a cat watching a mouse.

This is not how it was supposed to go. A hole opens up inside me. 'How long?' I repeat.

'Since she turned nineteen,' he rasps. He begins to sob. His shoulders hunch and tears stream down his face. His head starts to swivel as though he is looking for a place to pull over.

'Don't stop driving,' I say. 'Keep driving.' I have no idea why he listens to me. He can barely see the road.

'Claire, you have no idea, no idea how much it killed me, killed us,' he whines. 'It wasn't something we wanted or planned. It wasn't meant to happen, not ever. It was bigger than us, beyond us. You have to believe me when I tell you that I couldn't control myself and she couldn't control herself. We were... we were soul mates.'

Soul mates. He says it like we're in the middle of a romance novel. If I wasn't sitting here squeezing my arms tightly enough to bruise because I am certain that my body has shattered into pieces, I might actually laugh.

I barely hear the last few words over his crying: 'How did you... how did you know?'

'I found the letters you wrote to her. I've read the letters. I read all of them,' I say slowly. Yes, my arms are still there. I move my hands to my legs. They are deadly heavy but still there. I am still here listening to this.

'You what?' he gasps, turning to me with bulging eyes. I meet his gaze before he turns quickly to look back at the road. He doesn't deny writing them but then why should he... he has already confessed. She didn't destroy them as he instructed her to do. My Julia, the Julia I raised, didn't like to be told what to do. She had other ideas.

His shoulders relax and his colour returns. 'Why would you have done that? She would have hated that.' As if he knew her better than I did, as if he has any right to tell me about my own child. 'They were private letters, Claire, only meant for her to see.'

Unbelievably he sounds almost smug, proud of himself. Real-estate agent Adrian is back in control, hiding the lies, concealing any weakness. 'She hated that you wouldn't give her any space, you know? Hated how you always needed to know every little thing about her. That's why she and I grew closer as she got older. She turned to me because I treated her like an adult. It wasn't meant to happen but you have to accept that you pushed her away by holding onto her so tightly, and who else was she supposed to turn to but me? It's not like she had anyone else she could trust in her life.'

I believe what I am hearing is his justification for his actions. I am sure that he has repeated these words to himself many times over the last year. He may even think what he's saying is true. But the calculated way he is trying to turn this around on me leads me to understand that while Julia was mired in guilt and self-hatred, struggling to cope with the burden, Adrian was managing the betrayal just fine. I don't know how such a thing is possible or what he would have said to himself in the middle of the night, lying next to me, his wife, to allow himself to sustain the belief that he was justified in sleeping with his stepdaughter.

When he was on top of me, when he was inside me, whispering my name, was he thinking of her?

Bile rises in my throat and I swallow twice, pushing it back down. I haven't shared a bed with him since it happened and on all those nights I felt guilty about separating myself from him, but now all I feel is profound relief.

Who is this man? This person? I am sitting next to a stranger and I grow cold at the thought.

'You had no right,' I mumble. My body wants to shut down. I want to experience nothing but black silence but the car continues to drive, I continue to sit next to him with my eyes wide open. 'It's sick, completely sick. She was a child, my child. You had no right… no right.' The surreal nature of what we are discussing makes me feel stupid, confused, helpless.

'Who else have you told?' he asks. The tears are gone now. His hands on the steering wheel have relaxed. He thinks he can control this now. I imagine his brain as a collection of cogs and wheels revolving around and around as he tries to find the right way to get himself out of this unscathed. As if such a thing were possible.

I look down at my own hands that are now tightly clenched in my lap. Who else may know is his real concern and perhaps it is his only concern. Did he even love her? Was he with her as a way of punishing me? Does he not feel bad for betraying me? For taking advantage of my daughter? For driving her to kill herself? How have I lived with Adrian for so long without seeing who he really is?

'You never found a note, did you? You told me you found a note in Melbourne but there was never a note from anyone. You found the letters in Melbourne.'

'Yes,' I say dully. He must have been bothered about the note, assuming that it was from another man or boy, angry at the possibility that there was someone else in her life.

'I thought so,' he says quietly, failing to conceal a small sickening touch of triumph creeping into his voice. I am beyond horrified by his ego, by his selfish concern for himself. He is shameful, he is a shameful human being.

I stare out at the passing cars. Numbness has descended on me. I didn't want this answer. Despite how hard I looked, I didn't want this. Because it means I have to do something and I am so very, very tired.

I think about Joel who used his fists to hurt me. I thought I had chosen a different man, a better man, but instead I opened my home to the worst kind of human being. I allowed him to be around my children, around my daughter, and even though I know she made her own terrible choice and that she was technically an adult, she really had no choice at all.

Adrian held the power cards. He is charming, manipulative and self-centred to the point of narcissism. Oh, how quickly all his faults become clear when I look at them with hindsight. *How long have I been seeing and not seeing?* I think. I leapt into this relationship so quickly, willing myself to be swept away by a man who was the complete opposite of Joel. If something he said or did niggled at me, even a little, I forced myself to dismiss it. He wasn't Joel and he wasn't hitting me. My standards were so low – too low. I should have waited until I had recovered from being married to Joel.

'Who else have you told?' he repeats, his lightly menacing tone making me shiver.

'No one,' I say.

'Okay then,' he says. 'No one has to know. I'm sure you don't want anyone to know.'

His words and tone are bewildering. I almost hear a threat in his voice but it cannot be possible. Surely not. But then I think, *You have no idea what is and is not possible with this man.*

Adrian talks people into buying houses with hidden flaws. He laughs at those people behind their backs. He smiles at the world with perfect teeth. He swept me off my battered feet with kindness and courtesy, roses and champagne. In eight years he has rarely argued with me, acquiescing quickly and then continuing to do as he pleased. I have noticed these things about him. I have known them but not known them because one failed marriage was enough and perhaps I didn't really want to see. But everything crystallises in this car on the way home from the funeral and I know with certainty that Julia didn't stand a chance against him.

We are two streets away from what used to be our home and I look over at Adrian again. He is wiping his eyes, moving his lips as he gets the rest of his argument in his own favour ready.

'Stupid, stupid, stupid,' I whisper to myself.

'It's enough, Claire,' he says. 'We will move on from this. No one will know. We cannot allow anyone else to know. I need you to understand that this is the way it has to be. It is what it is.'

The metallic taste in my mouth is fear. He is threatening me. I cannot believe he is threatening me.

'I'm almost glad you know now. I realise that in the last letters to her I was a little over the top but it was because I was scared of losing everything. I'm not the kind of man who says those things and you know that, Claire. I never wanted her to… I could never have imagined that she would do such a thing instead of talking to me, but at least now you know that I miss her and I am grieving for her as much as you are. It's been so hard for me to keep this to myself, to keep the way I really felt about her to myself. I made that Facebook profile with the rosebud just so I could see the words written down, even if no one knew it was me because she will be forever in my heart. She will be.'

His words settle inside me.

He wants me to acknowledge his pain. He actually wants me to agree that he is suffering as I am. Suddenly I am no longer numb. I am burning with psychotic fury. He cheated on me with my own child, lied to me, bullied her to death, threatened me and still somehow has the audacity to tell me he loved her as much as I did. He expects us to carry on as normal.

He does not deserve to be allowed to exist in the same world I do. He does not deserve to exist.

I stop thinking anything at all.

I launch myself at Adrian. I throw myself at him, scratching and punching and hitting. 'My daughter, my baby,' I hear myself screaming over and over again. My nails pull away flesh on his cheeks, my fingers pull out a chunk of hair and the car swerves all over the road.

The noise of other cars hooting fills my head and Adrian speeds up as he tries to lift his arms to fend off my attack. Blood trickles down the side of his face, thick and red. He turns to me, his eyes show real fear. He is looking at me as though he has discovered a wild animal inside his car. He's right. I am all animal now, I am the mother lion and I am attacking the man who hurt my cub.

He slams on the brake, veering the car sideways. The wheezing scream of his brakes invade my ears as they jolt the car to a full stop in the middle of the road. I take a deep breath because my lungs have run out of air and turn to look at him, just as another car comes straight for us, hitting us on the driver-side door.

There is no slowing down of those last few moments, no watching of my life passing before my eyes. Instead the car hits us at exactly the same time our car stops. The smell of burning rubber seeps in through my window as smoke from desperate brakes fills the air. I catch a glance of the driver as his car hits us. His mouth is open as he screams, shock and despair written across his face.

I feel, rather than hear, the crunch of metal and the shattering of glass. Then I hear noise everywhere. I think I am screaming and there are other screams and then lights and then I close my eyes. *I need to get out of the car,* I think, *but I need a minute. I just need a minute.*

CHAPTER TWENTY-THREE

I open my eyes in an ambulance. 'You're in an ambulance,' a young woman paramedic says kindly. 'You've had an accident.'

'I know,' I say, and then I close my eyes again. I would like to tell the driver to slow down as he or she races over bumps and potholes. Every jolt is agony. There is a rusty smell of blood mixed with the sharp smell of antiseptic in the air around me. *Whose blood?* I wonder.

The paramedic leans forward and rests her soft hand on mine. 'You're going to be fine,' she reassures me, and I feel a shrieking laugh trying to bubble to the surface. How can I ever be fine again?

I can feel a hard board underneath me and my neck is at a funny angle. When I put my hand up to find out why, I feel plastic. 'Just relax,' she says. 'It's a neck brace, just a precaution. And don't worry, your husband is in the ambulance behind us.'

'Not my husband,' I mutter.

She nods and smiles kindly.

'Not my husband,' I say more forcefully, and then I give in to the need to close my eyes.

CHAPTER TWENTY-FOUR

When I next wake up I am in a hospital bed. Joel is peering down at me. 'I thought you were waking up,' he says with a grin. 'You've been making odd noises.'

I take a deep breath. 'Am I okay?' I croak.

'You're fine, Claire, it's a bloody miracle but you're fine. You're going to feel really sore for a few weeks but there's actually just a few scratches and bruises on you. I can help you sit up if you want, maybe give you a drink. Your throat sounds dry.'

I nod and then Joel pushes a button and raises the bed. I feel his arms around me and he lifts me into a comfortable position. He pats pillows into shape behind me, fussing and touching in a way I have never seen him do before.

When he is happy with how I am situated he pours some water into a plastic cup next to my bed. I drink it through a straw gratefully.

'Now, tell me what happened,' he says.

I know that he doesn't want to hear me say, 'I don't know,' or 'It was an accident.' From the way Joel is looking at me I can see that he suspects there is something more here.

'I don't really know,' I answer, as the word *coward* bounces around inside my head, adding to the pounding already there.

'It was a car accident.' Joel tries to help me. 'Adrian was driving and then people, witnesses, say he began swerving all over the road. Then he must have braked and the car turned sideways and you were hit by another car.'

'Yeah... I remember that now.'

'What went on? I mean, why was he driving like that?'

I lay my head back against the hard hospital pillow. 'I promise I will tell you, Joel, but I can't right now.'

'You're going to need to tell me more than that. The police are waiting to interview you.'

'Can you fend them off for a few days, just until I can get myself up and around?'

Joel looks down at me, concern darkening his eyes. 'What's going on, Claire?'

'Please, Joel, I can't speak to anyone right now. I can barely remember the accident.'

'Okay,' he agrees. 'I'll talk to them and ask them to give you a day or two. They may accept that you need some recovery time – it's not as if anyone died.'

Pity, I think.

'The boys?'

'Both at school. You've been here overnight. I told them to go. They need the distraction. I told them I would stay with you until you opened your eyes and spoke but I'm not leaving now. Your mum just popped out to get some tea and something to eat. She's exhausted. I'll text the boys, let them know you're awake and talking.'

'You should send her home, and you should go too. I would prefer it if you were there for the boys. Do you know when they'll let me go home?'

'They were waiting for you to wake up. They sedated you with drugs for the pain. You opened your eyes a few times last night and asked me the same things you've just asked me, but I guess you don't remember. I asked them to cut back on the meds but they can up your dose if you need it.'

I begin to move a little in the bed, gingerly feeling different parts of my body. There are no sharp pains, just an all-over ache that makes my heart speed up. I would like to go back to sleep, to go back to oblivion, but I feel the need to stay awake, to process everything that's happened, starting with the day my darling child took her own life. 'No, I think I can manage for a bit. I would like to get home as soon as possible.'

'I'll see if I can get the nurse to come and assess you. You may need to be here for another few days.'

Joel walks towards the door. I can turn my neck to see him, and although there is pain, it's not something I can't cope with.

'Claire…'

'Yes?'

'You haven't asked about Adrian.'

'Oh, of course, yes, how is Adrian?' I wanted to hear that he's dead. How I wanted to hear that he's dead. As I hear his name the hours before the accident come rushing back at me. The way he looked, the things he said make my stomach turn.

I really hoped he was dead but Joel has just told me that no one died.

'He's pretty badly injured. He's broken his arm and a leg and fractured ribs. He took the full brunt of the car that hit you guys. He's going to need a lot of help to get back on his feet, but the doctor treating him says that with time he'll be back to normal.'

I snort and shake my head.

Joel looks hard at me, and starts to re-cross the room towards me. 'What is it, Claire? What happened in that car?'

'I will tell you, Joel, just not now. I'm sorry, but I can't tell you yet. Can you see if you can get the nurse for me? I would really like to try getting out of this bed.'

I can see he wants to push the point with me. He wants answers. I cannot begin to think how to tell the story and I'm certainly not going to tell the police the truth. I need to think about what to say to them before I let Joel, Nicholas and Cooper know exactly what happened to Julia. Because I am going to tell them everything. I don't want to hold onto this secret alone. It makes me feel dirty.

Joel is back in a few minutes with a nurse in blue scrubs. He bustles around me, checking my blood pressure and taking my temperature before asking, 'How's your head and your neck?'

'Painful but manageable,' I say. The physical pain is manageable, but it's not the pain I have to figure out how to cope with.

'Do you want to try getting up?'

'Very much – I want to go to the bathroom.'

'I can bring you a bedpan,' he says.

'No, I want to get up. Please could you just help me?'

'Okay, don't get overwrought, Claire,' says Joel. 'Mate, I can lift her easily if you think it's a good idea.'

'Okay,' sighs the nurse, as though I am a disobedient child.

He undoes the bedding and with his help I sit up and twist sideways, moving forward until my feet are on the cold floor. Joel holds out his arm and I use it to stand up. Everything hurts and my feet feel puffy and filled with fluid but I take one step and then another, still holding on to Joel while the nurse watches us.

'She's very determined,' he says, and Joel nods his head. 'She sure is,' he agrees.

I make it to the bathroom. 'I'm fine,' I tell Joel, and close the door behind me.

I am not really fine. I'm light-headed and nauseous. Everything about my body feels wrong but I manage to use the toilet and splash some water on my face. A quick glance in the mirror is distressing. My hair is a greasy knot and there are some scratches on my ghost-white face and on my hands.

Adrian cannot get out of bed. He has a broken leg and it will take a while for him to get back on his feet – but I am on my feet right now. I stare at my puffy face in the mirror. I have the beginnings of a black eye, something I have had many times before, but this time I will not conceal the bruise. I am, in fact, not going to conceal anything any more. As soon as I am home and alone with my family I am going to tell everyone who ever loved Julia what really happened to her. Julia's father and her brothers and her grandmother are going to have to share this terrible truth with me and then… and then I don't know what will happen. I honestly have no idea.

CHAPTER TWENTY-FIVE

I am lying in bed, watching the leaves on the tree outside my bedroom window move lightly in the breeze. When Joel and I bought this house it was half the size it is now, with just two bedrooms and one bathroom. The small weatherboard house sat in the middle of the square, flat block of land with only one large tree shading the west side. There were no garden beds, just an expanse of grass, drying out in the summer sun.

'It's a bit small,' said Joel.

'This is the one,' I had replied, because even then, when I couldn't predict what would happen to my life, I knew that I would always want to look at the huge fig tree in my garden and understand that there were things in the world that existed before me and would exist after me. The giant tree, with its rough grey-brown bark and leaves that remain green all year round, creates endless problems with its spreading roots that pierce through the old clay pipes, backing up the plumbing all over the house, but I love it.

The tree has always looked like it belonged in the garden of a house that belonged to a happy family, regardless of the poor condition of the small house it dwarfed.

The house grew as Joel made more and more money. We always agreed on renovation choices, finding ourselves in sync in this aspect of our lives. Over the years, the worse our marriage became, the more obsessed we both were with creating the perfect home, as though we believed that if we could just get the frame right, then the picture of the people inside it would be beautiful.

Rooms and spaces and a second and third storey have been added on, and the tree sits beautifully in the space as a seamless part of the landscaped garden now, not just a dominant feature. When I thought I would have to sell the house my mother was surprised at how upset I was. 'It's where you've suffered through years of abuse, Claire. I know you've done a beautiful job with the remodel but surely you want to move on and start again somewhere without the terrible memories?'

I'm not sure how I answered her at the time. The real explanation would have taken too long. It was too complicated.

Joel and I always tried to argue in the bedroom rather than in front of the children. I was looking at the tree when I received my first shocking slap across the face. We were having an argument about something I had said to our neighbour, about what Joel called my 'callous' attitude. I had begun the discussion with him by apologising, not realising that what Joel wanted and needed was an escalation. I knew when I married Joel that he had been damaged by the violent man his father was. The first time we went away together for the weekend, when I was only twenty-two and Joel twenty-five, we got stoned on pot brownies and drunk on cheap red wine and stayed up all night talking. It was then he confessed to watching his father hit his mother, to witnessing bruises and broken bones and blood. 'I hate him for what he did to her,' he told me. 'She only left him a year before she got cancer and I don't think she got to have any kind of happy life before she died.'

'And him?' I asked, falling deeper in love with him because of the scars he carried. 'What happened to him?'

'Fuck knows. I think my brother sometimes speaks to him but I stopped talking to him when I was sixteen, the year my mother finally left him. I know he's still alive but I don't care whether he is or not.'

The first time he hit me was on the day he found out his father had died. His brother had called to tell him the news.

He arrived home from work, weighed down by memories. He found me sitting with Alyssa, a friend from across the road. He walked in, hunched and sad. I asked him what was wrong and he told me his father had passed away and I said, 'Good riddance.' I turned to Alyssa and said with a flippancy I don't think I really felt, 'Joel's father was partial to kicking the crap out of his wife.'

'Jesus,' said Alyssa.

'Drink?' I asked her.

For years he had told me that he didn't even think about the man and that if he dropped off the planet it wouldn't make a difference to him. I thought it was just a blip in his day.

I should have known better. I should have sent her home and comforted him, but I assumed that he didn't care. At least I used to think I should have known better, that if I had just managed to deal with the situation appropriately, he wouldn't have made that first terrible move. I know better now, of course. There was nothing I could have said or done differently on that day. His violence was about him, not me.

Alyssa left and I went to deal with dinner. Only after I had put three-year-old Julia and one-year-old Nicholas to bed and cleared up after our meal did he ask me to come into the bedroom. Three hours had passed since my insensitive remark and in those three hours I believe something happened to Joel. Some switch flipped and for a reason I cannot understand he stepped right into his father's shoes, as though possessed by the man's spirit. Something he couldn't see or acknowledge until after I ended our marriage took over, turning him into a man who expressed his pain at the world by hitting his wife. And as the years went on, pointing out to him that he was behaving like his father meant a slap across the face turned into a punch. I only tried that once or twice.

Perhaps he had always been that man. Perhaps he had been keeping himself in check, holding back when he wanted to lash out, leaving the room before our arguments went too far. I used to accuse him of not engaging with me when we had a problem. It's possible that he was trying to prevent himself from crossing a line and stepping into the darkness of his own fury.

That first time he had been quiet all through dinner but I had a three-year-old and a one-year-old and they made enough noise to drown out everyone.

In the bedroom I turned to him, surprised that he felt he needed to close us in to talk to me.

'That was a really shitty thing to say about my father, especially to Alyssa, to someone who we barely know,' he said.

'What do you mean, what did I say?'

Joel sighed and clenched his fists. 'You said he used to kick to crap out of my mother. Do you know how awful that makes my family sound?'

'But you say that – that's what you told me.'

'I told you in confidence. I didn't need you to share it with the fucking neighbour. You're socially clueless.'

I felt awful then. I apologised, but it wasn't enough. He kept going and going. He kept listing all the things I was doing wrong in our marriage until I felt my own ire rise and hissed, 'I've said I'm sorry, haven't I? What more do you want?'

That was the first time. He was completely shocked at what he had done. I watched him study his hand as though it had moved of its own accord. Apologies and promises flowed from him for days. I thought it was a one-time thing, an anomaly.

The second time was over my lackadaisical parenting. It had been a long day for him. He came home to find me still in my pyjamas, with Julia and Nicholas eating cereal for dinner and the house a mess. I was on the phone to Barbara, a desperate sanity break in the midst of a fraught day with two young children. One of those, 'Pick me up, put me down', 'I hate Nick, he hit me' days. I hadn't even thought about making dinner for him.

When he asked me to come into the bedroom with him I thought, *Surely not again*. I was so certain he would never hit me again that I willingly followed him. Once the door was closed he began his list of my failures, driving me to defend myself and yell at him. Then he hit me.

After a while, he stopped asking me to come into the bedroom, but I learned to read the signs and lead him there anyway if I could.

When my mother questioned my need to hold on to the house, I couldn't explain to her that I had lost count of the number of times I was beaten while looking at that tree, that I sometimes woke up on the ground and the first thing I saw was the tree. That every time I looked at it, I understood that I was living a life that mattered little to the wider world but also that there were things bigger, more permanent, more important, than Joel. When I knew I didn't have to sell the house I took a glass of wine out to the garden after the children were asleep and sipped it while I stroked the bark of my tree, feeling its strength, its solidity, course through me.

The first time Adrian and I had sex was in this room. It was a Wednesday afternoon when the children were at school and as he entered me, I turned my head and saw the tree. I had not thought I would find love again. 'You see,' I heard the tree whisper. 'Everything changes. Only I am here forever.'

It's probably ridiculous but it's how I feel. I watch the leaves now, despite having a huge pile of magazines on my bedside table and a Kindle full of books. Everything changes and yet here I still am, watching the leaves on my tree. The last few weeks have left me stunned – physically, mentally and emotionally. I wouldn't believe my story if I heard it from someone else and yet here I am, and it is what has happened and the tree remains unchanged.

Joel has moved into the spare bedroom. He is running the house and taking care of me and the boys. Work has granted him a longer leave of absence but I can hear him on the phone right now, issuing instructions to his second in charge.

I find I don't want him to go back home. Everything changes – even Joel.

The boys are stunned and silent.

'You could have died,' Nicholas said to me as he held me, tighter than was comfortable, when he came to the hospital.

'But I didn't and I'm going to be fine.'

'Yeah but… but…' He let go and stood up, turning away from me to Joel, who wrapped his large son in a hug as he cried. 'She's fine, she's fine,' murmured Joel.

Cooper said nothing. He gave me the news of his day and talked about television and I understood that it was too much for him to process. It is too much for both of them so soon after they have lost their sister. Teenage boys are not supposed to understand the fragility of life, the split-second twists of fate that change everything. If they did they wouldn't do all the ridiculous things they do. Both my sons are painfully aware of it now. They lost their sister and I am only here by the grace of the universe. I wish I could take this away from them, or make it easier to bear.

I wish I could go back in time and be married to the Joel who is here now. I want him to lie next to me at night and tell me that it was all a dream, that he never hurt me so much I had to make him leave, that I never had to look to another man for love and companionship. I would like him to tell me that our daughter is alive somewhere, living her life. I want to have no knowledge of Adrian's existence. That's what I really want.

But that's not going to happen. I have been home for a week now and every day there is a moment when Joel gives me an expectant look, asking with his eyes if this is the day I will explain to him what happened in the car. Every day I shake my head. But I need to tell him. I know I need to.

I cannot think how to begin, how to explain. I lied to the police and I am certain that Adrian will also lie. I don't fear Adrian telling the truth. I'm not sure he can even acknowledge it to himself.

'I can't remember,' I told the constable who perched on the edge of the sofa, trying not to be intimidated by Joel who stood with his arms folded across his chest. 'One moment we were driving and the next another car hit us.'

'I understand that you cannot remember the accident itself, but we are interested in the lead-up to the accident.'

'I don't know, it's all a blank.' I shrugged my shoulders and Joel glanced my way and then back at the constable. He knows when I'm lying. I twitch and shrug.

'Witness accounts have your husband swerving all over the road before spinning and coming to a stop across the middle of the road. Are you sure you can't remember why he was driving like that?'

'Like I said, it's all a blank.'

'Your husband's doctor says that he has some deep scratches on his face and a chunk of hair missing. Do you have any idea how that came to happen? These things are not consistent with his other injuries from the accident.'

'Weird... but I really have no idea,' I said, attempting to look perplexed and shrugging again.

'Perhaps she needs more time to rest and it will come back to her,' said Joel.

'Yes, perhaps,' the constable agreed reluctantly.

We have both been tested for drugs and alcohol and I was surprised to learn that while I was stone-cold sober, Adrian was not. He was, in fact, over the legal limit to drive. Just over the limit, by a small amount.

I don't know when he drank, where he found alcohol or how I didn't notice the smell on him. Maybe I didn't notice it because he had been drinking so often in the two weeks before her funeral that the smell had become part of him. Perhaps that's why he confessed the truth instead of denying everything. I read somewhere that alcohol doesn't change who you are – it just lets you show the world who you are. When asked the question directly he couldn't deny the truth.

I don't know why he didn't ask me or someone else to drive. He is going to be charged with drink-driving. Some justice, I suppose, but not enough. Nowhere near enough. He has broken bones and, according to him, a broken heart, and he will never be allowed back in this house, but that's not enough for me. Nowhere near.

He was in a coma for seven days after the accident. I have not spoken with his doctors but Joel has. They were sure he would wake up, certain that his system just needed to rest and reset itself and indeed that's what happened. Yesterday he woke up and asked for me. Of course he asked for me.

'I'll drive you over there,' said Joel, after he had ended his call from the hospital.

'I'm not ready,' I said.

'He's going to be fine. Physically at least, although there will be charges.'

'I can't go and see him, Joel.'

'Claire, there's no doubt he shouldn't have been drinking but he wasn't that drunk, at least not drunk enough to have been driving the way he was driving. To me it seems like something else was going on in that car. To everyone it seems like there was something else going on in that car, and don't just tell me you can't remember. I know what it means when you shrug your shoulders like that. You're lucky I cleaned your hands before the doctors told the police about the scratches.'

'Why did you clean my hands?'

'I was helping the nurse.'

'Lucky,' I said.

'Please tell me what happened, Claire. Whatever it is I can help you with it. You know I can, but you have to talk to me.'

'Not yet and not now, Joel. Don't make me lie to you too.'

'Why would you need to lie to me?'

I sighed. 'There are things, Joel, things I need to tell you, to explain, but I don't have the words right now. What I need to say is so… so difficult, so impossible that I need time to think it through and you're going to have to give me that time. Please.'

I met Joel's stare, stared him down. I wasn't going to the hospital and I wasn't going to explain what happened in the accident. Not yet.

In the midst of this churning anger I have towards Adrian, I find myself questioning Julia.

'Why would you have done this to me?' I whisper so no one can hear me but myself. 'Why would you have hurt me like this by taking up with this man who was supposed to be your father? Was I that poor a mother to you? Was it about punishing me for something? For staying with your real father? For not staying with your real father?'

The internet is filled with stories of relationships like the one they had. I read them secretly at night when I should be sleeping, recovering. Perhaps it began when she was nineteen but perhaps he had been grooming her for years. However lovingly he treated her when she was a child, however much he loved her when they were together in a way they shouldn't have been, he turned on her when she needed him. The last few letters he wrote to her are awful, despicable, and I know there must have been worse things said directly to her on the phone they used to secretly communicate.

The phone. Where is the phone? What else might the phone tell me?

In my pain following the accident, head fuzzy, I have not thought to look for the phone in Adrian's belongings. If she had it on her when she ended her life, if he took it, it may be somewhere in this house. I shiver in my bed, knowing it is probably somewhere close, only metres away from me, a record of betrayal and deception.

I don't want to see it if it still exists, to read the poison on it, but then I didn't want to read the letters either. Once again, I don't have a choice.

CHAPTER TWENTY-SIX

I struggle up off the bed and begin a desultory search of the bedroom. I don't believe it will be in here, I don't think he would make it that easy, but I look through his bedside table and his closet anyway.

After a few minutes I know the only place I need to look is in his home office. I open the bedroom door, feeling my body protest at being asked to move and creep down the hallway. I can hear Joel in the kitchen and I don't want him to ask me what I'm doing. I close the door of Adrian's office quietly and look around. I have to find it quickly if it is here or I will have to discuss everything with Joel before I'm ready. He will be angry I'm out of bed. I don't search aimlessly because I don't have the time. Instead I look around the room, paying careful attention to everything. His computer stands ready for work. There are stacks of home-decorating magazines and flyers from his last two house sales piled on the desk. The desk was Joel's. It's a beautiful piece in heavy, dark wood with a false bottom in one drawer where Joel used to keep his gun. I shake my head – *of course*. I remember showing it to Adrian when he moved in. 'What am I going to keep in there?' he asked me.

'Love notes from me,' I joked. The cruel irony twists in my gut.

Fingers trembling, I slide the drawer with the false bottom out and unload all the files onto the desk. My breathing is heavy. There is a catch I have to push down on which I duly do and the bottom tips a little, allowing me to slip my fingers underneath and lift the bottom. And there it is. A small black cheap flip phone.

I grab it and quickly make my way back to the bedroom. I feel like I'm running but I am only shuffling along, as much as my current state will allow me. On my bed again, I study the phone. It heats up my hand and I want more than anything to throw it against the wall. I think of the satisfaction I would get from hearing it hit the wall, from watching it split open and spew its parts onto the floor. But I don't have the strength for that. Even if I had the strength, I need to find out what it's hiding.

The battery still has some charge. Inconceivably, considering the secret it holds, it's not password protected. Once it is on, I can see that he called her many, many times in the days leading up to her death. I will never know what he said to her on those calls, but I don't need to. I have the letters and as I check the messages I can see the texts he sent. Hundreds and hundreds that I scroll through as quickly as I can. I start with the oldest ones, ones filled with words of love: *This phone is just for us, my darling. I will turn it on when I am alone and we can talk.*

And then there is her voice, there is my child. Finally I can hear her. I can hear my daughter's voice in the texts she sends back to him. I curl up on my side, feeling her here in my room with me, here right now.

Adrian, this is wrong. It feels wrong. I shouldn't have. We shouldn't have.

But we did and we have and believe me it was right. I'm alone now. Call me.

I don't think we should see each other again.

Please, Julia, think about this. You felt it before you moved to Melbourne and I know you wanted to go so that you wouldn't have to see me every day but it didn't help, did it? We are meant to be.

I wish you wouldn't have come up here to see me. What did you tell Mum?

I told her it was work. She doesn't mind if I'm not there. Call me now.

On and on they go. It may be that I am reading into Julia's replies, seeing what I want to see, but to me it seems that she is constantly asking Adrian to help her end their relationship.

Please don't come this weekend, Adrian. Please give me some space.

Oh, my darling. I'm already here. Just meet me at the coffee shop. I promise we don't have to do anything more than talk.

Please just give me some space this weekend, Adrian. I have work to do and every time I see you I end up messing up. People are starting to ask what I do on these weekends. Someone will find out. I know someone will find out.

Oh, my sweetest darling, no one will ever find out. I'm already at the airport. Just meet me and we can talk and if you want this to be over then I promise it will be.

I can imagine how he would have talked to her. I can see them sitting together as he smoothly convinces her to go with him to his hotel, talking her around. He is able to talk himself out of – or into – anything.

I had been pleased that he went there at least once a month. I used to text her and tell her that he was going to be there if she needed anything.

'No, I'm good, thanks,' was her usual reply.

He told me he was setting up another office with someone, but it was too early to talk about it. I never thought to question him. I didn't mind that he was away for a weekend every month. He always seemed so positive and happy when he came back. Now I know why. I close my eyes, take a deep breath and scroll through the texts until I find the beginning of the end. In the last weeks of her life Julia had stopped replying.

Julia, please call me.
Julia, call me.
Call me.
How can you drop a bombshell like that and hang up the phone?
Call me now.
You need to call me.
If you don't call me I am going to come down there.
You were in this as much as I was. You have no right to blame this all on me. You cannot have a child. You cannot have my child.
I'm so sorry, my sweetest darling. Just call me.
Please call me. We have to talk.
Why aren't you answering your phone?
Did you get my letter? Do you forgive me, darling? Please call me.
Listen, we really need to talk. You sounded hysterical last night. You can't tell anyone about us. That's ridiculous.
You had better answer this phone when I call.
You are not going to tell your mother about us. You are not going to have a baby.
If you don't fucking call me back right now I'm going to come there tomorrow.
YOU ARE NOT HAVING A BABY!
I'm so sorry, my darling. I was just angry. I shouldn't have yelled on the phone but you're scaring me. You're going to do something stupid that will destroy both our lives.
Julia, answer your phone.
Answer the phone, Julia.
Answer the fucking phone!!!!!!!!
You had no right to hang up on me, Julia. This is my life as well. Do you know what this will do to your mother? Do you want to be the reason she suffers more pain? Hasn't she suffered enough?

I can't talk to you about this any more but you need to know that I will make sure that you get the blame. I don't care how much it hurts your family, I will make sure they all blame you. You have no idea what I'm capable of.

Answer your phone.

Call me now.

I wish I had never met you. I wish I had never touched you.

You're a real bitch, you know that? No man will ever love you or touch you after I'm done telling the world who you really are.

You are the one who will be responsible for causing your mother pain. You are the one who wants to destroy your family. You are the awful one, Julia. You are.

I wish I had never met you.
I hate you like I've never hated anyone else.
I wish you were dead.
I hope you die.
I hope you die.
I hope you die.

The noises of the birds outside in my garden disappear. I am surrounded only by his hateful words, by his terrible threats, by the ugliness he sent her. I want to reach into the phone and make them disappear, I want to take them away from Julia. I don't want her to have read such dreadful things from someone who was supposed to love her. Tears drip silently onto my chest.

I can feel his loss of control, his rage through his words. How furious he became when he could no longer manipulate her into doing what he wanted. I see him hunched over the phone, typing in his vile threats. He must have been very afraid. There is nothing worse for a consummate liar than having his lies exposed.

She only replied once in those last few days. She replied on the day she died. Looking at the time Adrian's last texts were sent to Julia, I can see that in the nine or ten hours it took her to drive home he sent her fifteen messages. He knew she was coming. He knew and he didn't tell me. Of course he didn't tell me.

Don't you dare come home.
  Don't even think about coming here.
  Don't get in that car. You have no idea who you're fucking with.
  Pick up your phone, Julia.
  Pick up your phone.
  I will keep calling until you pick up your phone.
  Pick up your phone.
  Listen, bitch, you had better pick up the phone.
  Julia, if you are driving home I swear to God… you will regret it.
  I will make sure you regret this, Julia.
  You have no right to treat me this way.
  You are a monster. Only a monster would want to hurt her mother this way.
  I hope your car crashes.
  I hope you die in an accident.
  I am not going to let you ruin my life.

And finally there is the sad, desperate reply from Julia. My poor child, my poor little girl.

Please, Adrian. Please stop. I'm begging you to stop. I can't talk to you on the phone. I can't answer your messages while I'm driving. I thought that if I didn't reply to you for a few days you would calm down. I have tried to explain to you how I feel. Why won't you listen and understand? We should never have done what we did and if I could I would take it all back. I would give anything to go back in time and stop what has happened. We are terrible people, Adrian. What we have done can never be forgiven. I can't go on like this. I can't sleep. I can't eat. I feel like I'm being dragged slowly down into a black hole. Darkness is consuming me. I know that the only way out is the truth now. I have to tell Mum. She won't be happy but she will understand. She loves me no matter what you say. She loves me and even if she never wants to see me again I need to tell her that I'm sorry. I know I can't get rid of this baby. It's a life inside me. It makes me throw up in the mornings. It is a being clinging to its own existence. I will be there soon. I'll talk to Mum and then we can try and find a way forward. Please, Adrian. I understand if you don't want to be there but this is something I have to do. You have no idea of the hell I've been through. I think about dying for what I've done every single day. I can't go on like this.

I watch my hand shake as I scroll down, reading Adrian's reply. She was in so much pain, so much pain, my beautiful daughter.

Go right ahead and die then, Julia. Hang yourself off the front porch for all I care. Do whatever you want to do because believe me when I tell you that I will do everything I can to stop you ruining my life.

Julia did not reply. But there is one more text from him, one more desperate attempt to stop her from talking to me. In it I recognise Adrian's ability to seamlessly switch from one state to another, dizzyingly defying all logic.

Julia, my sweetest darling, I'm sorry. I'm so sorry. You have to understand how badly this is going to affect my whole life. I understand I can't stop you from coming here or doing this now. I've accepted it but I need you to think about me for a bit, to imagine how difficult this is for me. I know you need to do what you need to do but please can we at least do it my way so we can minimise harm to everyone? Listen to me. We can talk about this and put together a plan. Text me when you are close and I will come outside. If you're going to do this we need to think of a gentle way to break it to your mother. We need to both be calm so that we can think about things logically. I'll bring you a couple of Valium. I've already had some. They won't hurt the baby, they'll just help you calm down. If you take the pills and you are calm we can tell your mother together. I'll talk to her first. I will stand by you and help you through, but you can't be hysterical or she won't listen or even try to understand.

I roll off the bed and make it to the bathroom just in time. I vomit until I am shaking, drenched in sweat. He knew how desperate she was. He could have stopped her but instead he gave her the pills that dulled her judgement. He drugged her, pushing her towards her death. She was here with him as I slept. He could have told me, I could have waited up for her. All those hours she was driving in distress and he said nothing. We ate dinner together and then he said he had to work but instead he sat in his office tormenting her as she drove.

He let her die. He must have threatened her again when she arrived home, frightened her, worn her down.

And then he just walked away and let her do what she did.

I was here. She could have come to me. I was a few steps away. In touching distance. Even if he had reduced her to nothing but despair, she could have walked the few steps to me. Why didn't she?

As I struggle to get my breath back I hear Detective Winslow asking us about the bump on her head.

Adrian pulled at the chain and then dropped her.

Did he drop her on purpose because he was covering up how she got the bump on the back of her head?

'You'll hurt her,' I screamed. That's what I said as I heard the thump of her head on the floor. 'You'll hurt her.' But had he already hurt her, before? This thought obliterates all others in my mind.

Had he already hurt her?

She was coming to talk to me. I can tell from her texts, her mind was made up. She was determined. Nothing would have stopped her. Unless she wasn't able to move. Unless her hurt her.

I am crying and trembling when Joel bursts into the bathroom.

'Claire, what's happened?' he yells. 'What's happened?' But I can only shake my head. He lifts me off the floor and places me back in bed. He wipes my face with a cool cloth and brings me some soda water to sip.

In my mind, I see Adrian talking to her softly, his mask firmly in place, handing her some pills and some water. I see him reasoning with her, explaining his feelings over and over again. She would have wavered a little but been resolute. I'm certain of it.

'I'm going to wake her up and talk to her, Adrian,' I imagine her saying.

And I can hear, so clearly I could have been there instead of asleep, the words he would have used. 'Okay, just let me do it. If you wake her up out of a deep sleep she'll freak out. She thinks you're in Melbourne. Wait here and I'll bring her out to you.'

The scenario plays out in my head. She would have waited on the porch swing that Joel bought after we renovated the house. She would have been tired, drained and afraid as she waited for me. She would have lifted her knees up and stretched her jumper over them like she's done since she was little.

'Stop that, Julia, you'll ruin that jumper.'

'But it makes me feel warm and safe, Mum.'

I never came because he never came to wake me. I wonder if he thought about it, even for a moment, if doing the right thing crossed his mind or if he had a plan all along.

Did he return with something to hit her with? Or did she take the pills and demand to see me, making him angry. Did they fight and did he push her, knocking her out? Is that what happened? Is that when he took the phone from her, scrabbling in her pockets, desperately pulling out the piece of evidence that would prove who he really was?

There are so many possibilities. But if he did hurt her, if he did this, I hope she never knew she'd been hit. I hope she was out cold before he put a chain around her neck. I hope she was unconscious as he hung her up for me to find in the morning. I cannot bear the thought of her struggling, suffering. I don't want to think of her legs kicking as she fights to stay alive. I want there to have been no pain in the final moments of her life. That's all I can hope for right now, that she slipped peacefully away, finally free of her guilt and despair.

I wanted the truth but this is too terrible a truth to accept. 'Twinkle, Twinkle Little Star', echoes in my head and her little dimpled hands open and close. Her life was just beginning and everything was possible. I think of BB lying next to her in her coffin and I see her arms wrap themselves around him. I am in agony but I take deep breaths. I slow my racing heart. I am ready to tell Joel the truth.

'Do I need to call the doctor?' Joel asks when I am calm.

'No,' I answer. 'But you need to see something.'

CHAPTER TWENTY-SEVEN

I slide off the bed, wincing at the pain.

I shuffle to Julia's room where I have to lie on the floor to get the box of letters I have pushed far under the bed. When I shove my whole arm under the bed, I can feel the edges of the box. It takes some manoeuvring for me to grab it, my whole body aching, by which time Joel is crouched down next to me, peering under the bed.

He watches me in silence, cracking his knuckles. 'Claire, you're going to hurt yourself. Whatever you're trying to get I can get for you.'

My fingers graze the edge of the shoebox and I grab at it and haul it out. Joel holds out his arm and I hold his hand and use it to pull myself up off the floor. On her bed we both stare at the shoebox. I can feel his questions fill the air, and concern for me emanates off him like heat.

'Let's do this in our bedroom,' I say. I don't want the letters in here with her any more. 'Our bedroom,' I have said, as though Joel has never left. 'Our bedroom,' when in reality it has been many years since it was ours. My mind plays tricks on me and what I wish for becomes real with words but it's not our bedroom. This bedroom belongs to me and Adrian and the idea of him tainting the air in 'our bedroom' suffocates me.

Joel follows me, not bothering to correct me. It's what he wishes for as well but time moves relentlessly forward no matter what anyone wishes.

I want to pour out the whole story to Joel but he won't understand without the letters. He needs to read them first and then I will explain what I think happened.

'I found these letters when I was in Melbourne,' I explain as I open the box and extract the pages I have read too many times. 'They were from the man she was seeing. They're in order so read them as I give them to you. The top ones are all a little bit the same but it's the bottom few you need to see.'

'Okay,' says Joel warily, holding out his hand. 'Why didn't you tell me about them before?'

'Joel, these are not great reading. I know I should have told you about them earlier but I wanted to find this man myself. I wanted to confront him with what he did. I didn't want you to have to read these or see these because I know that even I shouldn't have seen them. I'm going to take a shower and then you're going to take me to the hospital to visit Adrian. After I see Adrian I will tell you who this man is, okay?'

'Why all the cloak and dagger bullshit, Claire? Why not just tell me now?'

'I have my reasons. After today you can go back to the Gold Coast or stay here in Sydney for the boys or whatever you want. I know this isn't how you want to do things but you'll have to accept it, okay?'

'Okay,' he agrees. I hand him the letters, wiping my hands on my tracksuit pants as he takes them. They make me feel defiled.

I close myself in the bathroom with my mobile phone. I turn on the shower and let the water run and then I call Detective Winslow.

'Winslow speaking,' she answers.

'It's, um… it's me… Claire Brusso.'

'Oh, Claire, yes, hello. How are you? I heard there was an accident, you were in an accident.'

'A car accident, yes. On the way back from the funeral. I don't remember what happened,' I say quickly, avoiding any questions she might have.

'But you're okay?'

'I'm okay and Adrian will be fine.'

'Good, good, that's good.'

I listen to the water run. The bathroom is filling up with steam. 'I wanted to ask… I guess… look… what would happen if I thought that someone had tried to hurt Julia? If I thought it hadn't been suicide?'

'Oh, Claire,' she says and I know what she's thinking. 'Do you have any reason to say that, any reason to suspect someone?'

'I… no, I was just wondering. It's something I was thinking about. I mean, you said she had a bump on the head.'

'Yes, but you explained that, remember?' She is being gentle and her concern is sickly sweet.

'But what if someone told me something that I thought could change things?'

'Claire, if you know anything new, anything at all that you think we should know about, you should tell me. We can reopen the case with new evidence. We can examine her body again. We can start the investigation over but you have to tell me why you're thinking this way.'

I shudder in the warm fug of the bathroom as I see them digging up my child to re-examine her. I see her white coffin coming up out of the ground, rotted flowers on top. I see her being dragged out and put on a cold metal slab in some laboratory. I watch BB being wrenched out of her arms and tossed to the side. I see them undress her, removing the red sundress with small white polka dots I had given them to dress her in because she always called it her 'happy dress'. I see her naked and exposed. And I know I cannot let that happen. I hadn't thought of that. I can't let that happen.

She deserves to rest in peace. To be free of all this poison. 'I have nothing new,' I say. 'I'm sorry. It just feels so…'

'So final?'

'Yes.' I agree because I don't want to be having this conversation any more.

'It will get better, Claire. It will get better with time.'

'I don't know if I have that kind of time,' I say before ending the call and getting into the shower.

I feel stupid for making the call, for thinking that there would be an easy way to make him pay. There is no easy way.

After my shower I get dressed as I watch Joel read the letters. I watch his eyes darken and his face cloud. I see disgust etch itself across his face and then I see anger.

When I am ready to leave I stand in front of him, feeling my heart rate speed up. I don't know how he's going to react. I don't know if he's going to blame me.

Finally he finishes the letters, pushing and patting them back into a neat rectangle. He shakes his head and then he rubs at his face. I grab some tissues for him so he can wipe away his tears. I know he wants to talk about this but I can't think how to begin discussing it with another person until I have seen Adrian. I realise that some small part of me is still hoping that his admission never happened, that the car accident was my fault because I misinterpreted something he said but, of course, I have the phone. I want him to know I have seen the phone. I want to watch him cringe and whimper. I want him to hurt, to suffer, to feel immense pain. I want him to look at Julia's father and try to explain what he has done. And I want to know the real story because he is either a manipulative bully or a murderer. Either way he needs to pay.

I swallow, trying to imagine living with this level of anger, this beating, screaming, toxic anger for the rest of my life.

I lean forward and pull Joel towards me. He rests his head on my stomach and I stroke his hair. 'Our baby,' he murmurs.

'Our baby,' I agree. Then, 'Let's go,' I say and he mutely nods. He stands up and I watch as his whole demeanour changes. He doesn't say anything but for a moment it seems as though there is a different person in the room. The air changes, thickens and cools. I know this about Joel. He is waiting. His anger is so intense that he's waiting until he can deal with what he has just read. I can see it in the rigid way he holds himself, in the set of his jaw and the clenching of his fists. He is waiting and I move quickly, following him to the car. I feel like I should drive but he doesn't give me the option.

The fifteen minutes to the hospital is silent, both of us locked inside our heads. Joel is trying to work out who the man is. I am trying to summon the courage to do what I'm about to do.

Adrian will be charged with drink-driving. He will lose me as his wife. His life may very well be destroyed but it's not enough. It's just not enough.

There have been many times where I have seen stories about parents forgiving those who have done their children harm. I have read the inspirational posts on the internet or cried over the emotional tales on television but even as I have wept for the victim and admired the bravery of those who forgive I have known that I could never be that kind of a person. I am not one of those who can forgive. I just can't. She was my baby, my little girl. She drank milk from my breast, she called for me when she was hurt or upset, she clung to me when she was afraid. There is no forgiveness for Adrian lurking inside me, only rage, only hate and only fury. I would like to be a better person but I'm not.

After we've found a parking space near the entrance Joel turns to me. 'Are you going to tell me who it is?'

'Not right now. I need to see Adrian and then we'll talk. Can you give me five minutes with him first and then come in? You both need to hear this.'

'Claire, I'm really not enjoying this…'

'I'm not amusing myself, Joel. Give me five minutes and then come in.' I get out, finding the struggle to move my body difficult to comprehend. I don't know how long it will take me to feel physically myself again but that doesn't really matter. Because even after I heal my body my heart and soul will always be irreparably shattered.

Look what he's done to you, I think, anger surfacing again. I start to walk away from the car. *Why are you even trying to protect him from Joel?*

I turn back. 'Here,' I say to Joel, passing him the phone I have slipped into my pants pocket. 'Read the texts on this. It's a phone he got her so they could speak without anyone knowing. Once you've read them you'll know who it is. And once you've read them you'll need to take some time to calm yourself down. Promise me that before you come into the hospital, you'll make sure that you're calm.'

'What are you trying to tell me, Claire? Is it someone who works there? I don't get it.'

'Just read them and promise me you'll take some time.'

'Fine… I'll make sure I'm calm, okay. Go and see Adrian. Maybe he can help with this.'

I stiffen at his words. I don't say anything else. The fact that he cannot put this together demonstrates how ridiculous the whole thing is, how absolutely unthinkable it is, how very, very wrong.

Just outside the front door of the hospital there are two large pots, filled with jasmine. I'm sure the smell gets lost once you enter the building but as I step through the doors I remember that jasmine is Julia's favourite flower. 'It means spring is here and then I know that the days will be warm and long and everyone will be happier,' she told me at twelve or thirteen.

Once inside the hospital I can still smell the jasmine, in fact even as I walk towards the information desk the smell gets stronger. I don't understand why and then I do. She is here, with me right now. My baby girl is here.

I make a vow to myself, a vow for myself and for Joel and the boys and of course for Julia: *After today I will let this go. After today I will move forward. After today I will only think of the beautiful girl I have lost with love and the bitter-sweet nostalgia of happy memories.*

'I forgive you, my beautiful girl,' I whisper to myself as I stand in the middle of the busy entrance to the hospital. 'But you get that I can never forgive him, don't you?'

'I'm sorry, can you repeat that?' says the nurse at reception.

I look up at her and the smell of jasmine disappears.

'I need to know which room Adrian Brusso is in.'

CHAPTER TWENTY-EIGHT

The walk to Adrian's room feels like it takes me a hundred years. Even after a short time my muscles are angry about being pushed to move again. But it's more than that. I am trying to find the words I need and failing. I move slowly as I experiment with the right way to begin.

I think back over the last eight years, trying to pinpoint the moment when I should have known that what he has done was a possibility, but there is nothing that stands out for me. As human beings we like to think there will be some warning, some indication that the person we love is destined to break us into a thousand pieces but mostly, only hindsight has the clues we are looking for. Even with hindsight I cannot find a specific moment when I should have guessed who Adrian really was.

The first time we kissed, it was so awkward. I didn't know how to kiss another man so even as my body was moving towards his, my face was pulling back. He laughed and then I laughed and it made the second kiss easier. I see the two of us at the dining room table telling the children that we're getting married. Nicholas shrugged. 'I guess if you're happy.' And Cooper nodded in agreement with his brother. 'You have to promise to be nice to her,' Julia said.

'I absolutely promise, Julia, I promise you all that I will be nice to your mum and I will work every day to make her happy.' Julia had nodded her head unconsciously along with his. She was by then his ally, disarmed by his charm and his attention. Should I have seen that as a bad thing? Was it a sign of what was to come?

I think he meant to take care of me, to always love me and never hurt me. But perhaps that is me being naïve, regardless of what I now know. But he must have meant it, surely? He loved me at one stage, didn't he? That's the trouble with looking back. Everything is called into question.

He needs to pay for what he's done but I don't know if he's done anything illegal. The sins he has committed may just be moral and ethical. Yet they are worse than many, many crimes.

The bump on her head comes back to me.

His sins may be greater than anything I can even contemplate.

It's possible because now I know that anything is possible. In the car before the accident, I felt threatened. I felt threatened and he threatened Julia. He threatened to ruin her life. I cannot ignore the menace in his words, the violence, the anger. What else might he have done?

Julia knew I would have forgiven her anything and that's why she was coming to tell me. I did not fail at mothering her. I know this now. Adrian knew this and yet he has let me go through these days believing myself to have failed, beating myself up. He has allowed me to think this way when he knew the truth. This thought is so cruel I have to stop walking and close my eyes as I take it in. He let me think that some of the blame for her death lay with how I treated her. He watched me cry and hate myself for my mistakes and he said nothing. His need for self-preservation runs deeper than anything else. We were all sacrifices he was willing to make to save himself – me, the boys and Julia. Especially Julia.

I would have preferred the shock and horror of being told of their relationship to losing my daughter a million times over. If they had moved away to another country I would have at least been able to take comfort in the fact that she was still here, raising my grandchild with the man I used to sleep next to. It's a sickening, horrible thought but it's the truth. It would have been heartbreaking, it would have been unbearable, but I would have forgiven her. 'I would give anything to have her back, to have him back,' is a phrase I have read over and over again on the websites that bring grieving parents together. It's the truth. I would have given up my security, my belief in love, in the man I had been married to, the belief in my daughter's love for me, my own sanity. I would have given up everything to have her here. I know that if I told this to anyone they would tell me that I was willing to give up too much. But I'm her mother. I gave up the right to my own happiness when I had her. I would give anything, but I can't, so what do I do now?

I stand outside the door to Adrian's room for a few moments. I am sweating and shaking with the effort of having to walk. Finally I summon the energy and push the door open.

Adrian has shrunk to fit his bed. There are machines and tubes everywhere. His arm and leg are in casts and his face is puffy and bruised. He is staring out of the window as I open the door but turns to see who it is. Then he grows pale and starts to struggle to sit up.

'Relax,' I say, and I hear detachment in my tone. The vitriol towards him that has been coursing through me for days has vanished. In my mind his crimes have made him larger and more powerful than anything else in my life but seeing him I realise it's not the case. He is just a man in a bed, nothing more. A thin, duplicitous man who was too stupid to know what he had. Where did all that love go? Did I ever feel it at all?

I smile at him. I can leave here now and not look back. I will remove him from my life band-aid quick so there is no pain.

'How are you?' I ask, more to say something than because I care.

'I'm so sorry, sweetheart,' he says, his eyes filling with tears. 'More sorry than you can ever imagine. I never meant for any of it to happen. We both regretted it after… after the first time. We both cried because we love you so much and neither of us wanted to do anything to hurt you. That's why I agreed to keep paying for her to stay in Melbourne. She asked me to. She wanted us to be far away from each other so we could never hurt you again.' Out comes his prepared speech. Prepared to disarm, prepared to illicit sympathy, prepared to turn him into the victim. But he is not prepared for the new information I have. He is not prepared for that.

'And yet it continued.'

'We tried to fight it, Claire. You need to know that every encounter was filled with guilt for both of us. You can't choose who you love, you know that.'

'You can choose who you hurt, though.'

'I know, I know I don't deserve to live,' he sobs. His nose is running. I feel intense disgust and hand him a tissue from the box on his bedside table. He's trying a different approach to his initial reaction in the car. He's helpless right now, I suppose.

'I want you to know that I never touched her when she was a child. I'm not like that. I never even saw her like that until she was eighteen and it was Julia who came to me, Claire. I know you don't want to hear that about her but it was her who came to me.'

'So it was her fault?' I ask, just to be sure that I have heard him correctly.

'No, oh God, no… that's not what I meant. I would never have… if she hadn't, but I couldn't help myself and even though it was so fucking wrong, you have to understand that I loved her, Claire. I loved her with everything I had.'

'And me, Adrian? What about me?'

'I love you too, Claire,' he whines. 'I love you now and always will. I know it was wrong. I know it's going to take a lot of work for me but I'm hoping that we can put this behind us and move on. No one has to know, and I promise I will spend the rest of my life making up for it. I will never hurt you or betray you again.'

'Well, I only had the one daughter,' I say mildly. The shock that registers across Adrian's face almost makes me smile.

'I… you don't mean that, Claire. You can't think that of me. I've never done anything like this in my whole life. I fell, I succumbed to the charms of a beautiful young woman. It was a hideous mistake but it will never happen again.'

'You know I've read the letters, right? Do you remember me saying that? I've read them all, Adrian, and I have reread, many times, the ones where you threaten her. If you wrote those revolting words down I can only assume that what you were saying to her was even worse.'

'They were a mistake. I don't know why I wrote them or what was going on in my head. It's like I was… like I was possessed.'

He's trying everything now. He knows me well but not well enough to know that there is nothing he could say to me that would change what I think and feel about him now. How could he not know that?

I walk over to his bed and lean down close to his ear. I'm sure he thinks I mean to kiss his cheek and he inclines his head sideways a little, but instead I whisper, 'I found the phone as well. I read the texts.' I stand up and take two steps back, away from the sour smell coming off of him.

'What phone?' he asks, attempting to sound cagey but merely reinforcing his guilt.

'The phone, Adrian. The one that was in the desk drawer with the false bottom.

He is almost panting now as he tries to take a deep enough breath to calm himself. There is too much truth in those texts for him. He has lost his deniability. If he could, I know he would walk out of this room right now and erase me and my family from his life, just as he did his first wife, a woman he cheated on as well. But he cannot walk. He can barely move.

'I… I… I was afraid, Claire. I was terrified of losing you and the life that we'd built together. I just wanted her to terminate the pregnancy and then I was going to tell you. I was going to confess. I didn't think she would—'

'You didn't think a vulnerable young woman in an illicit relationship would feel she had no way out?' says a voice from behind me.

I spin around. It's Joel. I hadn't known he was standing there.

If Adrian grew pale at the sight of my face, he develops a green tinge at the sight of Joel. Fear writes itself all the way across his features and I watch his skin become shiny with perspiration. He pleads like a trapped animal and I should feel some empathy for him but my reserves for him are completely depleted. 'Joel, please… please, man, you've got to believe me when I say it wasn't all my fault. It was a mistake, a terrible mistake and I know I can't go back. I just want… I love Claire… you know how much I love her. I'll do anything to make this right… all you have to do is tell me what to do and I promise I'll do it… please, Joel, you and Claire have to believe me.'

'I've read the letters, Adrian,' says Joel. 'And now I've read the texts. Jesus, you're an embarrassment of a human being, you sick, twisted fuck.' His tone is even and his face relaxed. I had expected rage and violence, and I start to feel some anger myself at Joel's lack of a reaction.

Adrian stares out of the window again. He struggles a little until he is sitting more upright in the bed. I can almost see him thinking, *Time to cut my losses.*

He sighs deeply as though he has found himself in an intolerable situation through no fault of his own. 'I know our marriage is over, Claire. I understand. I don't know how I can ever say sorry to you both, how I can even ask for your forgiveness. Perhaps you should go. I'll have someone come over and get my things and you'll never hear from me again.'

I wish I could just walk out of this room and never think of Adrian Brusso again. But I need the final part of the story. I need to know if he did more than just encourage her to take her own life.

Adrian's favourite saying is, 'It is what it is.' I have heard those words spill from his lips throughout our marriage at just about every crisis point. I used to think it was a wise way of accepting the struggle that life is, a way of applying the Buddhist principles he claims to have studied in his youth. But now I realise it is a way of absolving yourself of responsibility towards not just the situation, but the people involved as well.

The trouble is that I cannot just let that be it. I need more. This cannot be how it fucking is.

'You slept with my little girl and then you hounded her until she took her own life,' says Joel. He sounds like he's asking a question of Adrian or of himself, or the universe. He sounds like he doesn't understand.

Joel is clenching his fists. So he is not calm, merely attempting to control himself. I can see the tensing of his muscles all the way up his arm. His biceps bulge and I feel a flash of the old fear. I know what those hands can do. I know how strong those arms are. The damage they can cause.

Adrian is silent. I study my ex-husband. This is the man who made Julia with me. The man who watched her come into the world and cradled her gently even on the days he sent me flying across the room. He is not the same man any more. I know that. I can see that. I can see the change. He will not use his hands to hurt me again. I have no idea where that certainty comes from but I understand it at my core. His hands will not hurt me again, but as I look at my husband I know that Joel's hands are still capable of a great deal of harm. And I realise not just how it is, but how it's going to be.

'Did she actually take her own life, Adrian?' I ask, now attempting to keep any pleading tone out of my voice. It is monstrous that this terrible man is the only one who knows the truth. 'You knew she was coming and you could have stopped her if you chose to, but you didn't. Now I am wondering if when she got to the house and you spoke to her, she tried to come and talk to me anyway. Did you stop her, Adrian?'

'How could I have stopped her, Claire? You know what she was like.'

I look at Joel and then I reach up and touch my head where Julia's bump was on her head. Unconsciously Joel touches the same spot on his head as he connects the dots.

'The bump on her head,' says Joel. 'Oh God, you did… you *did*, you hit her.' He lunges towards the bed.

I place myself in front of him, pushing him back with the little strength I have. 'No, Joel,' I growl fiercely, keeping my voice low. 'Not yet. I want to know. I need to know.' He stops and takes my arm, holding me up.

'Tell us the truth, Adrian,' I say. 'You owe us that at least.'

Adrian looks down at the cast on his leg. 'I don't owe you anything, Claire. There is no point in talking about this. I think you and Joel should go.'

'Was she afraid, Adrian?' I ask and I hate how I am pleading with him. 'Did she know what was happening?'

Adrian looks at me. 'She was crazy when she arrived, ranting at me and telling me she was going to wake you up. I tried to get her to calm down by taking some Valium but she really wanted to talk to her darling mum.'

He looks out of the window.

I imagine the scene. I see him standing outside the house when Julia pulls up in the middle of Hallowe'en night. The smell of open fires fills the air because the spring nights are still cold. From houses across the neighbourhood, the bass thump of music can be heard as the parties go on. I see her climb out of her small blue car, her face pale, dark shadows under her eyes. She would have been exhausted, battling her nausea and her hormones. I know he would have comforted her initially, trying to disarm her. I see her look at him with… with relief, because she thinks he understands what she needs to do. She thinks he's accepted it. She has no idea of what's about to happen, no idea of who he really is. We will forever share that illusion, my daughter and I, the illusion of Adrian. I watch him lead her away so they can talk. I see Julia throwing her arms around as she does when she's distressed. I watch her crumple and cry.

'She…' I pause. 'She didn't want to die, did she?'

A tiny little smile appears at the corner of Adrian's mouth and quickly disappears. 'She was desperate, pregnant, sad and guilty,' he says quietly. 'Of course she wanted to die. I gave her the Valium and I left her to have some time to really think about what she wanted to do. I went back to bed and that's the last I know until that girl started screaming. I'm not responsible for what your daughter decided to do.'

'Your daughter,' he says, despite what he has said about wanting to be a father figure to my children over the years.

'My daughter,' I repeat, 'my daughter, you animal.' I wish for fangs in my mouth and claws on my fingers. I would like to rip his throat out.

'I just can't…' I hear from Joel. I turn around and he stumbles backwards, leaning against the wall and sliding down to sit on the floor. His face turns white, despite the golden tan he has all year round.

'What's happening, Joel?'

'It's just… fuck… I need a minute, just give me a minute.' He closes his eyes and takes deep breaths. I wonder if the self-control he is using to stop him from hurling himself at Adrian could actually give him a heart attack. I wring my hands. I should call a doctor but I don't want anyone else in here.

'You should get a doctor for him,' says Adrian.

'No,' shouts Joel, his voice hoarse.

I round on Adrian. 'You don't get to talk, not now, not ever,' I whispers fiercely, spitting as I speak. He uses the tissue in his hand to wipe his cheek where a dot of my spit has landed.

'I'm okay, Claire, I'm okay,' says Joel, and he stands up. His colour returns a little.

'We should go,' I say. 'I should call the police.' I want to walk out of this room and call Detective Winslow. She needs to see the phone and the letters but then I remember what it will mean to involve the police. I can't do that to Julia. She's been through enough and they may never find the truth. The only witnesses were Julia and Adrian. One is incapable of speaking and the other is incapable of speaking the truth.

'I didn't hurt her, Claire,' says Adrian. 'I was angry at her but I would never have hurt her. I will maintain that until my dying day.'

I imagine telling Detective Winslow, showing her everything. The investigation will take months. They will have to drag Julia out of her grave to examine her body again and even then Adrian will maintain his innocence. It won't bring her back because nothing can bring her back.

I've had enough now.

Enough.

Next to me Joel shifts and moves, glowering at Adrian. He is stumped for words, afraid to move in case he does something that leads to him being sent to jail.

I take a deep breath. 'You know, Adrian, the doctors told me it won't be long before you're back to normal, but doctors aren't always right. Things go wrong – anything is possible, and your life could change in an instant. Something could happen with your lungs or your heart and just like that' – I click my fingers – 'you could be dead.'

There is an extra pillow on the chair next to his bed and I pick it up, hugging it to myself. 'I have to go,' I say. I place the pillow gently on the foot of his bed.

I am done. I feel light, like I'm floating, removed from it all. I have let it go. There will be no police and no investigation.

'I understand,' says Adrian. He begins to cry again. They are tears of relief. He believes that Joel and I will walk out of here and never see him again.

'He cheated on me,' I say. I turn my back on Adrian, speaking only to Joel. 'He had sex with our daughter. He got her pregnant and then he made her believe it was her fault. He threatened her and he hounded her until she felt she had no choice, and even then she still wanted to tell me, to talk to me. I think he hurt her and even though I know we can never prove it, I think he did.'

Joel nods. 'I think he did,' he agrees.

Joel locks eyes with me, nods slowly again. I feel our history between us. I feel our love for Julia connecting us.

I do not look at Adrian again. I don't wish to see him ever again. I can feel his terror stinking up the air in this room. He doesn't want to be left alone with Joel. I will not think about his fear. I will remember his fake denials instead. I will remember his betrayal and the quick smile when I asked if he had hurt my child.

I walk out of the hospital room, along the corridor. A nurse comes towards me, heading for Adrian's room.

My legs suddenly feel like liquid and I hold on to a bar on the wall.

What could Joel do to the man who killed his child if he was the old Joel? What if he were given permission to be that Joel again? Have I just given him permission?

'Are you okay?' asks the nurse, gripping my arm in case I fall. 'You look very pale.'

'I was wondering where I could just get a drink of water. I've only recently been discharged and I'm feeling a little light-headed.'

'Of course, come and sit down.' She helps me over to a chair in the corridor, leaves and returns with some water, which I gulp gratefully.

'I should call a doctor. Can you get up and come and lie down in the room at the end of the corridor?'

'Oh, no,' I stand up. 'That was all that I needed. Thanks, you've been very kind.' My strength returns.

'Okay, but...' she begins.

'I'm great,' I say. I move off down the corridor, faster than I can comfortably manage but giddy with the need to get to the lift and out of her sight. I don't know if I needed to distract her or not. Whatever Joel does, he does. I won't ask him about it. We won't speak of it again.

I get into the lift and eventually make it out of the hospital, into the warm spring day.

My muscles protest and my breathing becomes shallow with the effort but I keep walking until I get to Joel's car. I stand in the sunshine and as I look up at the hospital I feel peace descend.

Enough.

Tonight I will be with my boys. I will tell them the truth, I will tell them everything. I don't want to hand them the pain that will come with the knowledge of what was going on after everything that has happened, but they need to know the truth because I will begin again only with the truth. There will be no more secrets in my family.

I know Joel will want to be with us but I will ask him for time and space. I don't know if I can ever be with the man who abused me so badly again, regardless of what my heart tells me, regardless of how much he has changed. I need to learn how to be just Claire, just myself again. I need to support my boys and find out who I am now. I am a woman who was abused, I am a woman who was betrayed, I am a mother who has lost a precious child. I need to meet that woman, that mother, head on. I need to get to know her and learn how to live in her skin. Life is messy and turbulent no matter what you do and the only way to survive it is to be completely sure of who you are. I have let one man and then another dictate to me, but I won't do that any more. I will take the time to learn how to exist alone in this skin.

Tonight I will remember Julia at one and at five and at twelve and at sixteen.

Tonight I will run through all the images I have of my child and remember her voice and her laugh.

But tomorrow we will start again.

I will start again.

This is how it will be. This is what will happen. It is what it is.

A LETTER FROM NICOLE

Hello,

I would like to thank you for taking the time to read *My Daughter's Secret*. If you did enjoy it, and want to keep up to date with all my latest releases, just sign up at the following link. Your email address will never be shared and you can unsubscribe at any time.

www.bookouture.com/nicole-trope

For a long time I was told to, 'write what you know,' but that never really worked for me. Instead I write about what I fear.

I write about families in crisis, about lives changing in the blink of an eye and about people who somehow manage to survive very difficult situations. My greatest hope as a writer is that my novels will give you some time away from your own problems, however big or small they may be.

I find that when I am struggling with my days I can always count on stories to remind me that there are others struggling as well and that we are never really alone in this world.

Although this is a difficult novel to read, I hope that you were involved with Claire and that you felt for her and her family. She's had such a difficult time and even though she is a fictional character I see her moving forward with her life with the strength and clarity she has gained through her experiences.

It would be lovely if you could take the time to leave a review. I read them all and on days when I question whether or not I have another book in me, they lift me up and help me get back to work.

I would also love to hear from you. You can find me on Facebook and Twitter and I'm always happy to connect with readers.

Thanks again for reading.
Nicole x

NicoleTrope

@nicoletrope

This is a difficult story to read and if you are struggling with some of the issues raised in the novel I urge you to call:

Australia / Lifeline: 13 11 14
UK / Samaritans: 116 123
USA / National Suicide Prevention Lifeline: 1 800 273 8255

ACKNOWLEDGEMENTS

I would like to thanks Christina Demosthenous, Kim Nash, Noelle Holten and the whole team at Bookouture for their warm welcome and for the tremendous amount of work they have done to help this book out into the world. I knew from the first email I exchanged with Christina that she was someone I could count on to push me to achieve my best work. Editing with her has felt like a conversation between the two of us and has been a joy. Thanks to Belinda Jones for the copy edit.

I am delighted to have joined Bookouture and I am so pleased to be part of the author's lounge and privy to the insights, ideas and experiences from all the authors there.

I would also like to thank, as always, my mother for being my first reader and for then being the first reader again as this novel evolved along the way.

Thanks also to David, Mikhayla, Isabella and Jacob as usual, because although I need to be alone to create, it's nice to have some people to spend time with when I'm not working, especially people I like quite a lot.

And once again thank you to the readers and the bloggers for their continued support.

Printed in Great Britain
by Amazon